CURSED
FAE

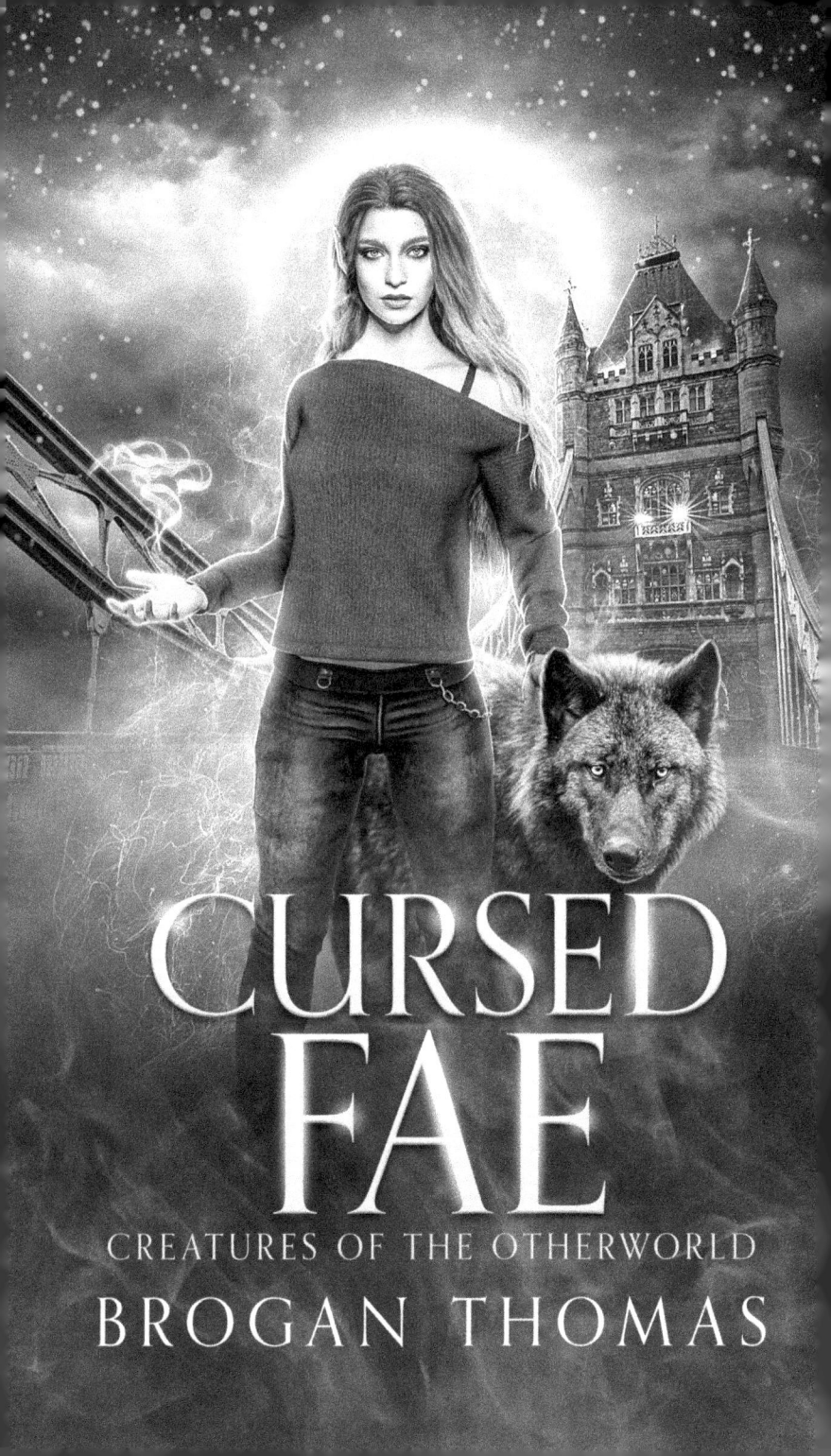

CURSED FAE

CREATURES OF THE OTHERWORLD

BROGAN THOMAS

Cursed Fae - Creatures of the Otherworld
Published by Brogan Thomas
WWW.BROGANTHOMAS.COM

Ebook ASIN: B0CGF3X57W
Paperback ISBN: 9781915946119
Hardcover ISBN: 9781915946126

Edited by Victory Editing and proofread by Sam Everard
Cover design by Melony Paradise of Paradise Cover Design

For my hubby

CHAPTER
ONE

I STUMBLE through the gateway as the ley line violently expels me from its depths and into the unknown. A whimper slips between my lips, and I wait for the angry magic of a protective ward to hit me.

To rip me apart.

I screw my eyes shut, and my shoulders tense at the ominous whoosh behind me. *Oh no.* A magic wind whips out, the loose strands of my green hair batter against my cheeks, and... the portal snaps closed.

I gulp.

After a few more seconds with nothing horrible happening, I open my eyes and straighten. My vision is blurry, and everything around me is a haze of swirling colours. I can't focus, and in my panic, I can't make sense of anything. Over and above my raspy breaths and the frantic beat of my heart, I catch the heavy hum and pungent fumes of a bus engine and sense the weight of the vehicle as its movement reverberates through the ground underneath my feet.

Traffic. People. *Earth.*

I slump against the comforting red brick of a now-familiar alleyway wall as relief hits me and take a deep, shuddering breath through the clawing lump in my throat. It's like trying to breathe through a blocked straw.

Each breath gets easier as the worst of my panic subsides and my vision slowly clears. *I did it. I got out without a fiery death. Go, me.* The brick bites into my forehead, and without my permission, the innate magic inside me reaches out. It tugs, greedily feeding on the wall's strength.

The old bricks give willingly. The wall is strong—being so close to the magic of the ley line—but nowhere near strong enough to repair the damage done to me. It's a drop in the ocean of magic I'll need to fix this mess, and if I take too much, I will damage the sedimentary rocks in the clay. Destroy the wall. That's what trolls are notorious for.

"I can't do that. I will never do that."

I snatch my wayward magic back and push it inside until it's a tiny, weak ball of power in my chest.

My eyes drift unwillingly back to the now-silent gateway.

I'm being chased. I shudder and suck my lower lip under my teeth. The excess salt in my saliva makes the nasty cut in the corner of my mouth sting. My knowledge of portals is rudimentary. I have no idea if they have a redial function. I've used the one near my old clan and only know the two gateway codes. One to here, one to *back there*.

The mess I've found myself in. I can never go back. It's the end of my life as I know it. *Can things begin with an ending? When everything is broken and you've hit rock bottom?* My trembling sigh hurts my chest. "I've done it before. I will do it again."

Look at me, hanging on to my worthless life by a thread. I have just enough energy left to laugh.

Gathering the last of my courage, I push away from the wall. I escaped from Faerie after a *friendly chat* with some elves. When I couldn't answer their questions—you can't answer what you don't know—they became pushy. *Painfully* so.

I got away, used my power to hide, and then took a chance on the random gateway. I had the oh-so-bright idea of dialling a code. Of course in my panic, I frantically smashed in the runes I knew, sloppily entered the code, and only with the grace of fate did I get it right.

It won't take the elves long to find me. They have magic that would make your hair turn white with fright, and they *will* track me. I left so much of my blood in Faerie it's inevitable. And when the spell shows I used their precious portal... I huff out a pain-filled laugh.

Surprise. I do not want to be standing here like a divvy when they come barrelling through.

This time it won't be fists and boots but the pointy end of their iron swords.

You've got this, Pepper. Everything is going to be okay. Hold on, don't lose it now. You will not *let them kill you or sell you to the Lord of Spring.*

Time to get a wiggle on and get out of here. I take a precious moment to deal with my injured wrist. The bone is wonky, and the arm is swelling at an alarming rate.

"That's not good."

White-hot pain rips through my nerves. I carefully tuck the broken wrist more securely, manoeuvring it underneath my tunic, using the tight brown fabric to immobilise the damaged limb against my chest. *It will have to do for now.* With gritted teeth, I move.

I take a heavy step, and my weak right ankle rolls. I half laugh, half cry as it burns with pinching pain. "Mother Nature." I shake my head in disbelief, and my lower lip wobbles. I fix my eyes on the cloudy sky to stop my tears. *Why is my luck always so rotten? Why can't—* I shut the thought down. There's no point in lamenting what could have been. The moaning excuse of *if I'd been born into a different clan, the elves would have never touched me,* blah, blah, blah. That way lies madness.

I take another precious second to rub my watery eyes and still-bleeding nose on my sleeve—blue bloodstains joining the rest of the blotchy mess. With no cleaning magic to help, there will be no saving the rough fabric from the bin, and that's a good thing. I don't want to see this outfit again.

Keep moving, you stupid bug. You're going to get your-self killed. This time my inner voice has a nasty taint. It does the trick. I hobble towards the safety of the bustling street, my fingertips brushing the old wall in thanks for its gift.

The supply bag I *borrowed* from the elves during my escape is almost as big as me. With each lurching step, it digs into my shoulders and whacks against the back of my thighs. Each bounce jostles my poor wrist and ankle. I do my best not to limp. If I limp, I'll throw my hip out. I'm such a prize.

It's morning, and the street is busy with all manner of creatures: humans, shifters, demons, witches, vampires, and an abundance of fae. Earth has an eclectic population.

I drift to the edge of the street, close to the kerb so I can step off the pavement and into the road when needed. I don't need to risk anyone getting too close and bumping into me.

When I was around eight, I followed my second-oldest brother and his uncle—not *my* uncle; long story. They used this mysterious door in the woods near our clan. Before they entered, they were excited, loudly talking about their upcoming adventure. I remember being hungry. *Starving*. I had nothing to lose, and I hoped I could sneak in and get something to eat.

So I followed them.

As they crossed the door's threshold, something inside told me to memorise the pattern of the thirteen runes they'd used to get in. Diligently I did, then followed them.

It was a shock when I was spat out of a portal into a new realm. My brother and his uncle were nowhere to be found. I was stuck—it quickly became clear a different pattern of runes was required to open the magical gateway back to Faerie.

I waited for two days.

During those days, I lingered on the streets of the strange, fascinating new world, eavesdropping on its equally fascinating and strange creatures. For the first time in my young life, I felt safe. Which is crazy 'cause nowhere is safe, not Faerie and certainly not Earth. But the seaside town in North West England appealed to me on a strange level, and as a bonus, nobody noticed or cared about the small, odd green girl.

Two days later when my brother returned, I stumbled back to the clan. They hadn't even noticed I'd left.

All everyone has ever wanted is for me to disappear. Magic has a funny way of making things like that happen. Cultivated by years of wanting, something clicked inside me and I *vanished*.

It was a new power.

I had disappeared.

No scent. No sound. No hint of my magic. I was still there, just cloaked. Yeah, the only downside: I was still there. I could interact with the world, and the world could interact with mc, usually when I wasn't watching out and a creature tripped over me.

From then on, with my new power, I came to Earth regularly for days and weeks at a time. When the local kids would leave for hours, I followed them to school, intrigued, and sat unnoticed in an empty chair or classroom corner, hidden, invisible, watching and learning. I even went home with a few of my *friends.*

I should have been learning to be fae. But I couldn't risk getting caught sneaking around a school in Faerie— where magic is more advanced than it is on Earth. I learned like a human child, and once I had the basics, I floated to and from different classes and different schools, learning all the other skills I liked.

I wobble down Birley Street, a pedestrianised road, and shuffle past the witches' shop. The sign written in bold letters above the door states: TINCTURES N TONICS—SPECIALISTS IN PORTABLE POTIONS. The magic inside buzzes and bites against my skin. Strong. The urge to go inside the shop and ask for help, perhaps trade something in the borrowed bag for a healing potion, nags at me, but I keep moving.

I keep my awkward shuffle going as I trudge towards the sea. No one needs to see me in this state, and I don't want to leave a trail of dead bodies in my wake when the elves come.

Witches. My small smile pulls at my sore lip. Once I was confident with my power, I even spent a year at the witches' fancy academy. There was this one girl, a witch with violet hair, a witch no one liked. Tuesday Larson. *I* liked her and used to sit with her all the time. Not that she ever knew.

I squeak and dodge a swinging arm with a takeaway coffee. *Gah.* Hot liquid almost splashes my leg, and the sudden movement makes my entire body scream in pain. My weak ankle, feeling better from my slow, steady shuffle, gives another angry twinge. Out of breath and fighting dizziness, I stop, prop the bag's weight against a lamppost, and take a deep breath.

An unhealthy sweat beads on my brow, drenching my hairline and trickling a stinging path down my back. I should ditch the bag. It could have rocks in it for all I know. Yet I can't seem to let it go. My temples throb in the rhythm of my heart—I must be dehydrated—and my power flutters, fluctuating oddly like butterfly wings against my skin. I roll my head back against the metal post and catch the eye of a human on the other side of the street.

He is looking right at me.

Oh no. My heart misses a beat. My energy is down to bare fumes, and my invisibility must have flickered.

The man elbows his vampire friend. "Did you see...?" He points right at me.

I pull on the stone beneath my feet, wrapping the concrete's strength around me.

8

There's a crack, and moving outward from my feet, a starburst of hairline fractures appears in the pavement slab. Nervously, my eyes flick about. *I think it was just the human.*

The man rubs his eyes, chuckles, and vigorously shakes his head. "Nah, you know what? That drink from last night is playing with my head. I told ya— Didn't I tell ya it tasted dodgy? I'm seeing ghosts, man. Ghosts." He elbows his friend again.

The vampire grins and playfully shoves him. "You're a lightweight, pal. My cousin can see ghosts. She says she has a bit of necromancer blood." Their voices drift as they continue down the street, playfully pushing and shoving each other.

Thankfully, I am forgotten. *That was way too close.* I gaze down at my feet and wince at the damage I've caused. Feeling bad, I silently apologise to the concrete slab. Then I take a deep breath and push myself forward. *One step at a time, Pepper. This is how you do it—one step at a time.*

I must keep a grip on my invisibility power until I can get off the street.

At the junction where the road meets the promenade, I wait for a gap in the traffic. Crossing the road, I turn left and carefully navigate over the tram tracks, then continue to limp my way down the deserted promenade, following the curved railings of the seawall, away from the bustling town centre and toward the iconic pier.

Central Pier looms ahead, its distant lights flickering.

Each step now sends a jolt of pain through my ankle and travels up my torso to my broken wrist. The winter sun struggles to break through the thick blanket of clouds, casting muted light on salt-weathered buildings. Most are closed for the off-season.

The rhythmic crashing of the waves mixes with the cries of seagulls and the salt-laden breeze. It whips up tiny dust devils made of sand. They swirl, dancing in front of my unsteady feet like they're playfully trying to trip me. I keep going—one step at a time.

I trudge for another pain-filled five minutes and arrive at my destination. Central Pier. The flashing lights and the cheesy music from the pier's amusement arcade are background noises as my stumbling feet land on the old-fashioned subway tunnel. A subway, not one with trains but an underground walkway, is hidden underneath my feet.

Once, it linked the beach and the Central Pier entrance to the attractions on the other side of the street, and in its heyday, it kept people safe from having to cross the busy tram tracks and road. I see it for what it was: a creepy tunnel with toilets.

Around ten years ago, the Creature Council decided the upkeep of the subway was too much. The *accidents* were becoming far too frequent, and they closed it. I'm sure they planned to have the entire thing filled in, but conveniently, the lazy contractor they hired only blocked off the stairs and made it so both entrances disappeared, and that was it. Most people wouldn't know the tunnel existed unless they were like me and had an affinity for stone.

I limp to my usual spot, and with a powerful strum of magic from the concrete, the ground opens and swallows me.

CHAPTER
TWO

OVER THE YEARS, I've fed so much of my power into the tunnels they feel alive to my senses—imprinted with my magic. That's the only reason I can get inside while I'm depleted. The stone magic recognises me and lets me in.

I'm gently lowered, and as my feet touch the ground, a familiar cloying, musty, salty scent fills my nose and hits the back of my throat. It is eerily quiet, and the distant echoes of laughter and music from the pier above create a unique ambience.

Home.

The tunnel is pitch-black. It's so dark here that I can't see my hand before my face. I'm unconcerned. Groaning, I drop the hold I have on invisibility magic, and the sudden lack of its metaphysical weight makes me feel instantly lighter. Like I'm floating.

Oh heck, that's not a good sign.

I've never strained my power so hard before. With a hiss and a tug, my broken wrist comes out from underneath my tunic. Being careful not to jar it—the movement still knocks me sick—I wiggle the heavy bag off my shoulders. It slips down my good arm and thuds to my feet.

"Okay. First, I need to fix the light situation."

This entire section of the tunnel has carefully hidden fae lanterns, but the lights need a spark of power to ignite, and I'm tapped. I'm completely tapped out. If I use more magic right now, the mere attempt will lay me flat out.

With purpose, I hobble into the darkness, and after two wobbly steps, the toes of my boots knock against the wall and my questing fingers find the big battery-powered torch I have tucked behind the concrete pillar for emergencies. I heft it down. The metal is cold and gritty in my palm.

I run my thumb across the barrel, hit the switch, and the solid Maglite turns on. The warm beam of light dances across the tunnel, highlighting the shoulder-height blue tiles with the grotty white walls above with its mouldy blown plaster and the cracked and peeling paint as it curls in rotten powdery strips from the ceiling.

I breathe a tiny sigh of relief; the tunnel is exactly how I left it.

Bracing my broken wrist high against my chest and leaving the mystery bag where it has landed, I shuffle towards the toilets. There's a witch-made healing spell squirrelled away in there, and I seriously need to get cleaned up—I stink.

The entrance to the ladies' toilets doesn't have a door but a sliding security grill. The rusty metal shutter is wedged open, and the gap is just enough for my scrawny self to slip past. I sidestep to avoid the random orange traffic cone. Why a traffic cone has been left down here is anyone's guess.

I'm a tad superstitious—keeping everything the same ensures I don't advertise my presence, not that anyone is rushing to come down here.

But I've altered nothing, and the familiarity settles something inside me. It's safe. It screams of safety. The grill rattles as I squeeze inside. I move past the glass and rotting wood bathroom attendant's office, the old, damaged turnstile—back in the day, to use the toilets was five pence—and past a set of rusty weighing scales with a peeling handwritten sign, its yellow crumbling tape saying Do Not Jump On The Scales.

The bathroom has atrocious bubblegum-pink floor-to-ceiling tiles over a dozen stalls, worn with use and time. Interestingly, in the men's toilets next door, the tiles are pee yellow. The second toilet from the end is mine. The door is solid wood, and I've intentionally left the exterior filthy. The floor in front has a nasty brown stain, but inside, the entire toilet cubical is sparkling clean.

It's the same with the sinks. The one clean sink I use is tucked away from sight, next to a dysfunctional paper towel dispenser. The counter is also wider. Perhaps it was used to double as a baby-changing area.

I shuffle over and place the torch down, angling it up so it doesn't blind me. The light falls, highlighting the side of my face, and what stares back at me in the old mirror isn't pretty.

The light makes my bruised, bleeding skin garish, and I look way worse than I'd imagined. It's a shock. I drop my eyes to avoid my reflection.

I've never been beaten before. No one has ever laid an angry hand on me, and I've never dealt with such physical pain. In Faerie, occasionally I'd been bitten by a rogue plant or animal, fallen over and scraped my knees, but nothing like this.

The elves made me feel…

I take a deep breath, push the thoughts away, and slide the hidden bag from underneath the sink. Inside is a spare set of clothes, a clean cloth, a towel, a washbag, and the almost-empty first aid kit. I plop everything onto the counter and get to work.

As I undo the single button on the tunic, I find a tangle of long, pale blond hairs. A scream bubbles up my throat with the urge to cry and freak out as if I've seen a poisonous spider and have a phobia. I swallow the noise so it's just a whimper.

The elf's hair must have got tangled up when he was hurting me. The skin on my fingers feels itchy, and I ignore the urge to fling the hair away. I want to be sick, but I carefully unwind the hairs from the button's thread.

In my washbag, I have a few reusable small plastic bags. With a grimace that makes my lip throb, I grab one, slide the hair inside, seal it, and then shove it into my washbag out of sight. That's better. I undo the button, lift the bottom of the tunic, and quickly find I'm not only hampered by having one working arm but also by my sweaty, blood-coated skin that wants nothing more than to hold on to the fabric. The tunic sticks to me. It takes energy I haven't got and a lot of grunting and grumbling to prise the bloody thing over my head. I drop the disgusting top to the floor, nudging it aside with my foot to throw away later. I then shuck my pants and boots off.

The sticky warmth of blood makes me glance down. Getting the tunic off has re-opened a nasty gash across my ribs. I whimper as more than a trickle runs across my hip. I ignore it for now, wash my hands, then dampen the cloth—for the hundredth time feeling grateful the water here still runs.

They had turned the main's water off, but the stop valve on the promenade was easy enough to find. I'm still thanking the lazy contractor a few times a week.

Groaning and gritting my teeth, I slowly and methodically clean all the cuts and scrapes across my body. I rinse the cloth, and light blue blood swirls down the drain. I repeat and rinse until I'm clean or as clean as I can get with a stand-up wash.

Hand trembling, I grab the Heal Me potion from the first aid box. I only have the one. The spell should be a vibrant silver, but it's a little dull in the torch light. The liquid glops against the glass as I prise off the lid, then dab and drip the potion sparingly onto the various wounds. It stings and tingles, then itches as multiple layers of my skin respond, stitching themselves back together—accelerated healing at its best.

At least now I shouldn't get an infection.

I glance down at my sore wrist. Ah, now that's another story. Despite all the swelling, I can see the bone has shifted to the right. Even with a top-notch potion, I'd be a fool to think I could fix it.

The only way for it to heal is to have an excellent rune or realign the bones and manipulate them back into position, and I'd need to do that before I could use a potion. I feel sick with the thought there's no way I can do it myself.

No, I need a medical rune or professional help, and if I don't get help, what's the likelihood that I'd lose the use of the arm or the bloody thing falls off? I sigh, and with my other hand rub my face, catching sight of the unsightly mark on the underside of my forearm. I glare down at it.

It's a rune.

The elves tagged me like a dog.

The magic in the rune is set to track me and relay my

status to the realms. It's a slave rune. Acknowledging that fact makes my heart flip, and a whine of fear leaves my sore throat. The only bit of luck is that it hasn't been activated yet. It's not linked to anyone, which I'm glad about. If they'd known I had strong magic, I'd have been in way more trouble. As it is, this rune does nothing but look ugly. I need to get it off my skin.

I stand naked, racking my mind for a solution to all my problems, but my thoughts are dull, as if my brain is underwater. "What am I doing? These are things to deal with when I've rested and I'm not swaying like a zombie on my feet." Goosebumps pepper my skin. I'm ice-cold and shivering. Yeah, no wonder I can't think. I glare at the clean clothes. Now comes the arduous task of getting dressed.

It's slow going.

Once dressed, out of habit, I put everything away, shoving the towel and the cloth into a washbag to be cleaned later. I slide my feet back into my boots that, unlaced, flop as I shuffle across the tiled floor.

I need to be careful I don't trip. My naff ankle is feeling better, and not lacing them will tempt fate. But I'm doomed if I do much of anything else. The black spots dancing across my vision hint that I'm close to passing out.

Squeezing through the grill door, I half clomp and shuffle towards where I discarded the bag. I click off the torch and put the Maglite back. Then, once again, pitch-black darkness surrounds me. Blind, I grab the bag, take a big step to the right, and walk through the wall.

A light-filled curved brick tunnel is on the other side. It is beautifully designed, built in the days when creatures had genuine pride in their work: all brick, no iron or steel rods. The air here is different. It's clean, dry, and warm.

The tunnel continues until a junction meets it roughly at a 45-degree angle and then proceeds to dissect it and continue its journey as it sharply branches to the right. The angle provides some stunning brickwork, with each brick seamlessly joining the two tunnels made especially for its place. The alcove to the left is where the light comes from.

I shuffle, dragging the heavy bag behind me like a champ. If I stopped to think about it, I'd leave the damn bag behind. It's not like it's going anywhere. But I'm in zombie mode now and just going through the motions. Exhaustion pounds in my mind, and I'll be sure to lament my stupidity when I've slept.

I reach the branch in the tunnel, turn left, and step into the light-filled dead end. Home sweet home.

The tunnel's alcove is roughly twelve feet long and eight feet wide. Within the arched brick ceiling, six milky white glass blocks link to the pavement outside, letting the natural light in during the day, and a handy lamppost over them gives all-around light at night. The milky light makes the tunnel cosy.

Businesses line this side of the road, and I can pick up the Wi-Fi for free as it's been years since they changed their passwords—not that I have a datapad or a phone to use thanks to the bloody elves.

Home. This has been my secret space for years, and yes, it's a cliché for a troll to live in a tunnel underneath a road. Tunnel, bridge. Whatever. I've heard all the jokes.

This place fits me just fine, and finding somewhere to live would be a nightmare as I haven't got permission to visit, let alone stay in, this realm.

I prop the bag next to the wall of shelves, toe off my boots, and then flop onto my stainless-steel framed canvas bed. My energy levels have hit an invisible wall, and the fatigue has me shivering. I have enough strength to prop up my broken arm with a pillow, cover myself with a shabby blanket, and I'm out like a light.

CHAPTER
THREE

DRAGGING ME FROM SLEEP, the magic is going off like a klaxon with screaming warnings that bounce around like a rogue ping-pong ball in my brain. As the haze of sleep falls, I groan and groggily try to filter all the various bits of information.

The stone magic might occasionally be touchy, especially since I returned home with my power drained and body battered and bruised. But this goes way beyond the power being narky. From what I can gather, no one has breached the subway or this tunnel, but something serious is happening outside.

A handful of random creatures wouldn't be enough to sound the alarm like this if they were only walking past. *Could it be them?* I prise my eyes open and clean the crusty edges with my fingers. Then I catch the movement. *Whoever they are, they are right above my head.* I hold my breath, and my heart feels sluggish in my chest.

I gulp and force myself to breathe. Tilting my chin, I stare up through the opaque glass in the ceiling at the creature-shaped blobs blocking the lamppost and puppeteering their shadows onto the tunnel's far wall.

The prom gets busy. I lick my lips, sit up, and shuffle to the end of the bed. The canvas creaks, and the steel frame wobbles. *Everything is normal.* But what is not normal is the screaming warnings from the magic still happening in my head.

That's not normal, not at all.

I can deal with this, and everything will be fine. "I'm up. I'm up," I grumble. "Okay, please stop with the racket." I vigorously rub my forehead to get rid of the ache forming behind my eyeballs and drag my sore carcass off the bed. I won't be able to rest if I don't appease the magic and double-check what is happening up there. And if it's the elves... Well, I can't get trapped down here. I've got to go up there anyway so I can run.

For a second, I forget about my arm. The pillow slips, and I bang my broken wrist on the bedframe. *Ouch.* The pain makes me sick and knocks the last of the sleepiness out of me. As if contrite, the magic stops its wailing, and the silence is jarring.

Nursing the wonky, still-swollen limb against my

chest, I force myself to get dressed. Wearing the hoodie and jogging bottoms I slept in, I one-handedly slide into my boots, this time lacing them tightly.

I wish I had a coat. Once I fix my arm, I will see if I can find a new cash-in-hand job. I can't go back to Faerie, so my old job is well and truly gone. It's going to be a challenge to find something; in the past few months, there's been a crackdown on all under-the-table work. The area had a demon problem, and everyone is still a little jumpy, and the hunters—the creature police force— have been checking paperwork on the regular. I can't afford for them to send me back to Faerie. So I'll have to keep my head down and be careful for at least a while.

I shove my loose hair down the back of the hoodie and tug the hood up. Moving towards the main tunnel, my stomach gurgles in protest. I stop. I have no idea how long I've been asleep. *I could have been asleep for hours, perhaps days.* All I know is now it's late at night 'cause of the lack of traffic on the street. Without a working phone to determine the date and time, it could be next week.

I shrug and grab a bottle of water from a shelf, drink, and munch my way through a few handfuls of packaged nuts. All the while nervously eying the shadows above my head. Suddenly, they move out of sight; the tarmac excit- edly informs me they are crossing the road. As I leave, I grab a can of pineapple, pop the lid, and guzzle the juice. Digging a pineapple ring out, I fold it in half and stuff it into my mouth. I could access outside from this tunnel, but my magic is self-taught, and because it's self-taught, I'm paranoid I might make a mistake. I don't want to lead anyone here. I don't want to lose this safe space because of impatience. The risk isn't worth it.

I pass through the wall into the pitch-black subway and shovel the fruit into my mouth. My fingers scrape against the bottom of the now-empty can, and with a disappointed huff, I let go. It clangs to the ground. My power gives the floor a little nudge, and the magic sucks the empty tin through the concrete floor—it will reappear in the rubbish bag next to my bed.

Licking my sticky fingers clean, I fold my invisible power around me, and the concrete silently raises me into the night.

Why am I doing this again?

The moon is behind clouds, so the only light is from the dark grey sporadic lampposts dotted along the road. The surrounding businesses are dark, their heavy shutters are down and closed, and the pier is silent.

Huddled, I take in the group of men around me. It appears I've landed within the melee of a fight. Like a ghostly, hidden observer, I watch. The men prowl. Their breaths fog the night air. It's freezing. Compared to the tunnel, outside the temperature has dropped by around ten degrees. Even in the middle of summer, the wind off the Irish Sea can be cutting. Winter is a shock to the system.

Shifters. Not elves. My tight shoulders loosen. *Thank Mother Nature.* I sigh and rub my face. The movement makes my sleeve roll down, and I catch sight of the slave rune. With a grimace, I tug the sleeve of my hoodie over my hand and make a fist to hold the excess fabric down.

Shifters are a strange bunch of creatures, an immortal race on paper, but regular conflict and birth rate issues keep their numbers in check. I don't know why they are out here this late or what weird *pack thing* they're doing on the promenade. What I do know is they need to go away. They need to bog off and go home so I get some more sleep.

My attention is drawn further away from the posturing main group; ah, I see. It seems they are hunting another shifter.

A tiger. Wow.

My eyebrows hit my hairline. I've never seen a shifted tiger before. *Is he feral?* I tilt my head. *Is that why they're out here? Hunting a feral shifter?*

His predatory grace is evident. The light wind off the sea ruffles his thick brown-and-orange fur. His brown stripes are thicker, making the orange just a highlight running through his coat. Beautiful. Even if there is a man under all that fur.

The massive tiger flattens his rounded ears, drops his head, flashes his teeth—teeth the length of my hand— and hisses a warning. A feline growl comes next from deep in the back of his throat and rumbles into his chest.

It is a primal symphony. The sound makes a shiver of fear run down my spine. I shake my head when the other shifters fan out and menacingly move closer.

With nowhere to go, the tiger backs up against the seawall. Trapped, he continues to growl. Spit and blood foam around his mouth, dribbling down his chin, wetting the striped fur on his chest. The tiger turns to the side to track the incoming shifters, and I notice he has a few nasty gashes on his torso and his left paw is a mangled mess.

I wince, and my messed-up wrist twinges with sympathy.

The tiger is in trouble. There are over a dozen shifters out here. Four have shifted into wolves, and the rest remain in their human forms. A few of them carry weapons. The metal shines when it catches the lamp-post's light. *Silver.*

Oh heck. Silver for shifters is like iron to the fae. It's poison, and from what I've heard, enough silver particles in the bloodstream can kill even a fully grown shifter. It stops them from shifting. Shifters can heal anything if they can shift. Their cells repair every time, but with silver inside them, it's almost a guaranteed death sentence, especially during a fight.

Things don't look good for the tiger.

"Bill, get in there and fuck him up," a shifter with broad shoulders and a prominent Roman nose shouts. Following his comment, a few men laugh and jeer as he nudges a grey wolf with his boot. "Finish this."

With the rude prod, the grey wolf, Bill, prowls closer with a lupine growl. He's flanked by the other three wolves. Massive wolves, their fur a mix of silver and shadowy black, circle the lone injured shifter.

I'm glad to see the tiger is bigger, much bigger, but he is so outnumbered. I shuffle forward. *Pepper, what the hell are you doing? Don't you dare! There is nothing you can do.* I swallow my guilt, grab hold of my leaking common sense, and take a small, indecisive step back.

My good hand balls into a fist. I'm useless. Not helping and standing here watching makes me feel like an ass. Like I'm a horrible person. *Evil happens when good people do nothing.*

But I'm just a troll, a naff one at that. What the heck can I do? I'm only five foot six—average for a human, stunted for a troll—with a broken wrist. I huff a self-deprecating laugh. I can't even keep myself safe. I can't help myself, so how can I help him?

A stupid lone tear born of frustration trickles down my cheek, and I swipe it away with the back of my hand. Coming up here was a mistake. I should have gone back to bed when I saw it wasn't the elves.

And the tiger might be the bad guy. Things aren't always black-and-white; they aren't always what they seem. I should mind my business. I nod. Yes, mind my business.

Coward! my inner voice screams. I rub my chest. *Come on, Pepper, this has nothing to do with you. One beating is enough for anyone. Go back inside.* I need to leave this well alone.

The night becomes a chaotic dance of laughter, fur,

and feral snarls as the four wolves creep closer and closer. Two wolves break to the left, and two break to the right.

I step forward and then back, forward and back. Like I'm doing a jig. I want to help, but I can't. I want so much to scream at them to leave the tiger alone. *I can't.* I swallow. It's an unwritten rule that shifters deal with shifters. Also, in animal form, shifters are poisonous to women.

One bite, and I'm dead. I'm not powerful enough to protect myself from that. From them.

I take another small step back and stand on the usual spot where I enter the tunnel. If I watch any more, it will give me nightmares for weeks. Probably years.

I'm sorry. Good luck, I mentally whisper.

Then, as if fate has tuned in to my musings, the tiger makes his move. My breath catches as fangs bare, claws unsheathe, and the scary grey wolf, Bill, leaps for the tiger's throat. The tiger drops onto his back, and his massive claws dig into the underbelly of the airborne wolf.

I cover my mouth when Bill howls in pain as ropes of his insides rain down, splattering the ground. The tiger leaps to his feet and cuffs another wolf across the head, knocking him into the seawall with a crush of bones. With strands of bloody spit dripping from his mouth, the tiger slams between the remaining two wolves, knocking them apart like bowling pins.

I watch, astonished, as blood from his injured paw

sprays with each pounding stride as he heads towards the other shifters behind me. Behind me! *What the f...*

The tiger hits me, and we both go down like a sack of spuds in a tangle of limbs. "Get off me," I cry. The furry beast is impossibly heavy. I can't breathe! Panicked, I do the only thing I can think of, the concrete parts, and we both disappear into the dark.

CHAPTER
FOUR

WITH THE WEIGHT of the two of us, my magical hold is sporadic, and I cannot control our descent. Once again, we hit the ground in a twisted heap, with my face bouncing against his spit-covered chest and my body sprawled between his furry front legs. My fear-filled breaths echo, and the blackness of the subway is smothering.

Great, now I've got a feral tiger as a guest—a guest whose paw is lying partway across my legs. Remembering his massive teeth, I wiggle, twist, and on my bum use my legs to scramble out from underneath him.

He growls.

Oh no. Oh no. Gah. I can't see for shit. I bet the massive growling and hissing *tiger* can see in the dark. I shiver and continue my awkward bottom shuffle until my back hits the far wall. I brace against the tiles, and keeping my sore arm tucked into my chest—it's a miracle I haven't done any further damage—I wobble to my feet, then blast a spark of power at the fae lanterns. They blaze to life, and my vision takes a few seconds to adjust to the harsh, bright light.

I blink. We stare at each other.

Oh no. My eyes widen, and I refrain from frantically patting myself. In my panic, I've dropped my invisibility. Miraculously, my hood is still over my head. I dip my chin to hide the majority of my face. Here's hoping the tiger hasn't seen enough to identify me. Though I'm sure he's now picking up my scent.

His tail flicks behind him, and his ears swivel to sit flat on his head. I swallow as he gets to his feet, and with a feline hiss, he stalks towards me.

"Don't eat me!" I cry. "That wasn't my fault." The stones take this opportune time to buzz in my head, rapidly feeding me information, which I relay to the tiger in an undignified high-pitched squeak, and my words come out awkwardly fast and mangled. "The shifters outside are looking for you. To them, you disappeared into thin air. Your leap when you ran smack into me might"—I hope—"be interpreted as you activating a spell."

My entire body trembles. I'm not used to this. I'm not used to hanging around with manic shifters. I'm not used to people, and I do not know what the heck I'm doing.

The tiger's amber eyes narrow.

Oh. Perhaps, in hindsight, I shouldn't have said all that. It might rile the tiger more to think the other shifters would interpret his disappearance as running from the fight. Shifters have monumental egos. I'd rather have my teeny-tiny ego than get dead.

"Lucky for us, they didn't see me. I didn't become visible until we landed down here in a heap." Wait a minute, what did I say? *Lucky for us?* I shake my head. "Lucky for *you*." There's no us. Just a scary *tiger* shifter with big poisonous teeth who has been forced into an enclosed space with a stranger, with *me* and... he is *still* growling!

Okay, that's it, I've had enough. "Oi, Mr Tiger, have a word with yourself. Why are you growling? What the...?" My good arm flaps against my side as if flapping will help me find the words "...of all the pixie farts, why did you run into me?" I finish my rant lamely.

In response, the shifter flashes his sharp teeth, the air flickers around him, and the scent of ozone fills my nose as the tiger shifts into a giant man.

Oh heck. I should have kept my mouth closed.

I huff, as I vaguely register his square jaw, wide, full lips, straight nose, and the fact that he's wearing hot guy clothes—a black long-sleeved top and jeans.

At least he isn't stark-bollock-naked. A shifter's clothing retention spell is expensive, so he isn't a common thug. I should also be happy he hasn't got silver poisoning and isn't going to die a horrid, painful death on my floor and then end up in the rubbish bag at the end of my bed. Not that he'd fit. He. Is. Massive.

But he's alive, which is a good thing. Yay.

"I didn't know you were there," he spits out. His voice in human form is very much like his growl when shifted, a raspy rumble that comes from deep in his throat and chest. "Who hangs around on the prom in the middle of the night?" His cruel, dark blue eyes are full of malice.

Gosh, he really is enormous and... *ragey*.

My eyebrows twitch up. I'm not used to *peopling*, and where this shifter is concerned, I can't seem to keep my mouth shut.

"Um, yeah, that's what the witches would call the pot calling the kettle. You"—I point a trembling hand—"were the ones who woke *me* up." I slap my chest. "Fighting in public like animals." I finish with a tut.

My mouth instantly dries when I see his expression. I called a shifter an animal. Ah, shit. Now why in the hell did I go and say that? I really need to learn when to shut up.

The shifter moves.

One second, he's menacingly standing on the other side of the subway—taking up way too much space—and the next, he stands over me, crowding me with his bulk. I cringe and shimmy along the wall to get away, and he prowls after me.

With a feline snarl, this Hulk-sized hand snaps out, and he grabs me.

He grabs my broken arm.

I scream.

"What the fuck?" He lets go. But the damage is done. The pain is unbearable. I spin away from him with a whimper, hunching into myself to protect my broken arm as black, wiggly lines fill my vision. I wobble. It takes everything in me not to pass out. I need to go. I need to leave now.

The shifter catches me around the waist. "What happened to your arm?" he grumbles as he pulls me against his bumpy chest. Then he does something strange. He drops to the filthy floor, sweeping my unsteady legs out from under me. He lowers me onto his lap like I'm five years old and cradles my broken wrist between his massive hands as carefully as if I were a baby bird. With narrowed, angry blue eyes, he rolls up my sleeve and inspects the limb.

"It's fine."

"It's not fine. Did I do this?"

I shake my head.

He grunts.

I sniff.

One hand lets go of my arm, and he yanks at the hood, pulling it off my head. I meet his intent gaze. His dark blue eyes have lost their manic glint as the tiger scrutinises my face and observes the tears dripping from my chin.

"I'm fine," I whisper, awkwardly rubbing my wet face on my shoulder.

Another softer grunt, he pulls out a potion. "For the pain." Without asking or giving me a chance to object, he splashes the spell liberally onto my arm. "The bone needs resetting."

"No, it's—"

"Look away," he snarls.

"What? What are you going to do?" Surely he isn't going to... I try my best to wiggle out of his lap, but he manoeuvres me, and I find I'm trapped like a nut against his solid chest and huge arm.

One massive hand braces my forearm and elbow. The other hand, without even a countdown, pulls and twists. Thanks to the pain potion, I don't feel a thing, but I still gasp and gape at him in horror. My mouth flops open in disbelief as, just like that, the bones are pulled apart and then popped back into place. I stare down at my now-non-wonky wrist. I blink.

Another potion, a silver Heal Me spell, appears in his hand, replacing the Pain Free bottle, and with another generous splash, the cool tingle of the activated healing spell sweeps over me. I can taste the potent spell under my tongue, and within moments, the injury is gone.

It's gone.

My vision swims, my head lolls against his arm, and my treacherous eyes drift closed. *Oh no. This is wrong.* The pain spell, followed swiftly by the healing spell, is knocking me out. Sluggishly, my stomach flips, and my heart misses a beat, but the fear I should be feeling is overwhelmed by his body heat and the scent of freshly cleaned clothes.

No way do I need to lose consciousness in this stranger's arms. My magic grasps at the concrete, taking small bites of the power and strength from within the subway. The power floods my system like a shot of adrenaline. I gasp, and my eyes fly open.

"Pineapple."

"Pardon?" I blink at him.

"You smell of pineapple."

Oh. *Oh!* "Yeah." I slap my hand over my mouth to smother my pineapple breath. Is this shifter for real? "I like pineapple," I mumble through my breath guard.

How long has it been since I brushed my teeth?

Plaque and pineapple are not a good combination. My tongue runs along the bottom row and catches on a snag. The tusks are growing back. When fully formed, the twisted, sharp teeth are embarrassing and look messy. That's why I file them down.

I drop my hand and keep my nasty teeth covered with my lips. I'm no good at this. I am no good at interacting with the world, and the spells have made me worse. They've made me extra dopey—the only explanation for wanting to snuggle in his arms.

The shifter frowns. He's probably wondering why I haven't passed out.

I take him in. His dark hair is buzzed down on the sides but left long on top of his head, further accentuating his knuckle-breaking bone structure. He has a striking face, a rough and scary kind of attractive, with high, wide cheekbones, full lips, and a strong jaw that belongs in a magazine.

Why has it taken me until now to notice the tiger is ridiculously handsome? I don't know. Fear, I guess. I take a few more seconds of staring into the tiger's confused dark blue eyes—they have a ring of navy around the outside—for it to dawn on me.

I'm still in his lap.

I'm nestled against this stranger's chest. "Eeep." A waft of pineapple breath escapes between my clamped lips, and I clumsily elbow him in his abs as I scramble to my feet. "Sorry. Sorry." With both hands raised in a placating gesture, I shuffle clumsily away. "Thank you so much for fixing my wrist. I'm going to go back to bed. I will keep an eye out in case those shifters come sniffing around. I'm pretty sure you are safe for now, but perhaps it might be best to stay here until first light."

His intent stare drifts from me to wander around the dank subway, fixating on the ceiling's peeling paint. His top lip curls with poorly veiled disgust. "You live here?"

I try to ignore his disgust and... is that concern? I shuffle my feet. "Do you need anything?" I might as well be polite.

"Some water?"

I tug on the magic, and a water bottle emerges from the wall. I hand it to him.

He gives what I now presume is a characteristic

grunt. "Never seen anything like that before." He nods at the wall. "Your magic is powerful." He twists the cap and takes a mouthful; all the while, he takes my measure. When half the bottle is gone, he asks again, "So you live here?"

I shrug. I don't need to answer his questions, and he won't be staying long. I inadvertently saved him from getting his head kicked in, and he in return fixed my arm. Win. Win for both of us. We don't owe each other anything.

Dark blue eyes watch me as he leans back against the wall. The bottle dangles loosely from one hand—his fingers are elegant and long. He gives me a cop face. He thinks his silence is going to motivate me to talk. He doesn't know I'm the invisible girl. Stern looks and silent treatment aren't my kryptonite.

Talking is more of a problem for me. I can't recall when I last spoke so much to another person. "I think it's best if you stay here for the rest of the night, and you won't be able to leave alone. The tunnel is sealed, and you'll need my help to get through the concrete. When it's safe, I want you gone."

"I don't need rescuing." His lip curls.

I get a peek at teeth and narrow my eyes. *Huh.* Is it me, or do those gnashers look more prominent and sharper than normal? I'm no expert on shifter's teeth, but those bad boys are more than a mouthful. They're not red cap or mermaid serrated, but still... Shouldn't they be human-sized? Oh, and flashing teeth by shifter standards is aggressive and rude.

My nostrils flare, and of course I run my mouth. "Well, you are a guest in my house, so you can suck it up for a few hours until it's daylight."

The tiger glares at me.

I could just let him go... No. My gut says he needs to stay for a few hours, and the wait will not kill him.

"Are you from Faerie?"

This tiger doesn't know when to leave it alone. I've seen this type of thing play out a time or two. When you spend your life watching people in such situations, you should only ask the questions you know the answer to.

I scoff and roll my eyes. "Do I sound like I'm from Faerie?" I know I sound local. "Toilets are through the gates. The ladies are the best, and the second stall from the end is clean." The shifter has so many muscles I'm sure he can wrench the stuck metal grill open to get in.

He opens his mouth...

I turn invisible.

I stand there for a second, blocked from his senses. I shouldn't have done that, not right in front of his face. I run my fingers through my green hair. I hope I haven't made a colossal mistake.

"What the hell is she?" he snarls to himself.

The violence in his words makes my hands shake; I scramble through the wall to my tunnel. I don't need to be watching him like a creeper.

Perhaps I'll shove him back onto the street without even talking to him. Oh, now that is a good idea. It saves us from having another little chat—the nosy tiger. He has cop written all over him. Yeah, I wouldn't be surprised with all those expensive spells. It will be just my luck if he is a hunter.

When I get back, I eye the tatty bedding. Fidgeting, I debate. The pillow or the blanket? I don't want the cushion on the subway floor; the cover can take some dirt and get washed. I press the blanket against the wall and send it to him, along with another bottle of water, a precious can of pineapple, and some packets of nuts.

Then I untie and kick off my boots and fall into bed. My clothes are no longer clean, but I'll deal with them in the morning. The canvas bed will wipe clean, so it's not like I'm making a permanent mess. I also ask the stone magic to wake me as soon as it's light. It knows to wake me if anything untoward happens—or if our *guest* does anything concerning.

Lying on my back, the lumpy pillow under my head, I hold my healed arm up to the light. I twist my wrist to the left and right. No pain. It's as good as new. I'm so relieved that it was shifters and not the elves. I let out a humourless laugh.

My life is a mess.

But I'm alive.

"I'm still alive," I whisper, wiggling my fingers.

The tiger could have easily bitten me, and I am grateful he fixed my wrist, and I am glad he isn't dead or dying. I don't even know his name—which is a good thing; we don't need to know anything about each other.

Attachments aren't for me. I'm my own best friend. Time and time again, people let you down. Through the stones, I check on him. He's sitting in a corner. It looks like he's settled. With a trickle of power, I dim the fae lanterns.

Snuggling into the pillow, the double whammy of potions makes it extra hard to stay awake. Just before my heavy eyes close, I remember the borrowed bag.

CHAPTER
FIVE

Oh. Now I'm wide awake and cold. My blanket is thin, but I'm missing its weight. I huff. My eyes drift to the bag I stole, leaning innocuously against the wall. "I'll go through it tomorrow," I grumble and turn onto my side.

There might be something dangerous inside.

There also might be a lovely warm sleeping bag—an elf-made fancy one that regulates body temperature. I imagine the joy of having that kind of cover in the depths of this winter.

Groaning, I get up, flop onto the floor next to the bag, and lean back against the shelves as I tug it towards me. "Okay, what do we have?" The heavy bag scrapes across the brick as it settles between my legs. I make quick work of opening it.

I flinch as strong magic puffs out and hits me in the face. I blink. The magic makes the little hairs in my nose sting. I sniff and rub my nose with the palm of my hand as I peer inside. Tracking spells have a particular bite to them. If they're strong enough, they can even make my ears pop. I don't get that sensation with the bag or its contents. There are no tracking spells here. I sigh. Now that would have been a nightmare.

No tracking spells, but the magic inside is potent.

A trickle of fear prickles down my spine. *What have I done?* I don't make a habit of nicking things. I only took the bag because they stole all my stuff. My phone, my datapad, my coat. I puff out my cheeks, shove my fear away, and grab the first item.

It's an elemental magic water bottle. Cool. I tap it. It's the genuine article, as it sounds like glass. I spin it in my hand. It's made of a fae material way too fancy for me to know what it's called, what with my lack of fae education. Spelled to remove curses and spells, clean and filter water until crystal clear. I hum low in my throat as I slide it onto the shelf behind me. It's sealed, so it's brand-new —an excellent find.

Soft, silky fabric comes out next. Clothing. Ooh, I've seen material like this before. I wiggle, my bum scuffs against the bricks, and a wide grin pulls at my cheeks. Expensive, elf-made—magic runes in the seams automatically adjust the fit. The black trousers, top, and socks will fit any shape. The more expensive clothing will change with the environment to protect the wearer from spells, curses, extreme heat, cold, and water.

I neatly fold them and pop them inside a spare plastic storage box. I've heard that some have scales, and vampire warriors have used them to make blood armour. I roll my eyes. *Vampires.* It's always about the blood. You wouldn't see me making pineapple armour. *Bloody weirdos.*

Food. Food and more food. I pull out hefty packets of trail rations and put the feast away—no wonder the bag was so damn heavy. At least I will not go hungry for a while.

I grin when I find another set of clothing and a silky, soft cover perfect for my bed. I hold the fabric to my face. Everything in here is stuffed with magic and brand-new.

Next, I tug out a fae medical box and open the lid with a little trepidation. I groan, and the back of my head thuds against the shelves when I see a thick square book infused with potent magic—the med kits book is stuffed with ancient fae runes.

I flip the cover. Hand-drawn on handmade paper and stitched with a natural thread. There must be hundreds of them. If given the choice between potions or rune magic, you'd choose the more powerful runes. Well, you would if you had any sense. I have no training in runes or any idea what most of these will do, but the rune on the first page I've seen before, and it's for healing—it's a medical one.

I shake my head and groan again. If I'd opened the bag immediately after dragging myself back from the portal and before I collapsed and fell asleep, the rune would have fixed me right up.

The scary tiger shifter wouldn't have had to heal me.

I think... I bite my lip, and my fingertips gently brush over the book. I think my broken arm stopped the tiger from hurting me, as my pain seemed to snap him out of his rage. With that scary thought, I close it back up and slide the medical kit onto a shelf.

At the bottom of the bag is a dark wooden box. With a barely audible creak, I open the lid. *Charms.* My stomach flips. The box has dark grey foam at the bottom perfectly cut out to cradle the various charms.

Four rows of three. Twelve charms. No, thirteen. There's a metal charm in the shape of a wolf. It looks like someone had randomly dropped it inside. I grab it and place the little wolf on the floor. The metal is oddly warm against my fingers. With a small frown, I adjust the wolf so he's in the middle of a red brick and doesn't fall over. Then I turn my attention back to the other charms.

Each new charm I pull out has me more and more worried. Each one feels more powerful than the next. All thirteen are around an inch to an inch and a half high. They are worth a small fortune. I could buy a house with this lot. Heck, I could buy an estate.

Not that I can do anything about it, as selling them would be suicide. No, I can't sell these things. Talk about making yourself a target.

I sit them in a row next to my thigh. Earth-made, the ones made of stone connect to me on a deeper level, and they sweetly sing the witch maker's name. Gary Chappell. He must be a very talented witch.

One stone charm in the shape of a black cat draws my attention. It has mirrors for the eyes. It's tiny, but its magic packs a punch. Every time I try to communicate with it, it aggressively shoves my magic back. A Reflect Me spell. Handy. The cat charm reflects magic back to the user.

What to do with them? I have an idea!

Leaving the charms where they are, I stand and hunt through the shelves. There's an old bracelet around here somewhere. It was cheap and will undoubtedly go black or green with wear, but the links are sturdy and won't easily break. *Aha.* I find it, plop back down on the floor, and grab the aggressive black cat.

What is it with cats today?

"Now how to do this?" I grumble as I rotate the bracelet. Eyes narrowing, I bring the cat and bracelet together. As they get closer, the little cat charm twitches and wobbles. "Huh? What are you up to?" I tilt my hand. Suddenly, the stone charm springs from my palm and attaches itself to the bracelet with a click, like a magnet.

I stare at it. "Well now, that's handy."

I vigorously shake the bracelet, and the cat stone hangs tight. I purse my lips, shrug, and wave the bracelet over the rest of the charms. Each one jiggles. One by one, in order of their choosing—which doesn't freak me out, not at all—they shoot into the air, then *click, click, click,* they secure themselves to the bracelet.

Well, all apart from the little metal wolf. He doesn't move at all.

I shrug and slide the bracelet on my wrist. It settles warm against my skin. My magic will keep the charms from prying eyes, and it'll be safer than leaving them on a shelf.

My attention swings back to the wolf; he shows no inclination to move or attach himself to the bracelet. He must not be made by the same witch. I pick him up and press him against a spare link. "Don't you want to go on there?" When nothing happens, I bring the charm closer to my face. "What am I going to do with you?"

Huh, there's a smudge, a streak on the metal. I don't know why I do it. I use the hoodie's sleeve to give the metal charm a polish. As I rub the mark, the metal heats in my palm and... there's a puff of smoke.

I squeak and throw the charm.

It launches from my hand and bounces on the redbrick floor once, twice, and then there is more smoke and a buzz of magic. I cough as the smoke gets thicker, and then it swirls and condenses into the shape of a wolf. "What in the Aladdin's lamp is going on?" I rasp.

A charm on my wrist heats against my skin. I glance down; it's a charm in the shape of a snail, and before I can rip the bracelet off, the black wolf speaks.

My name is Eurus. I'm a beithíoch.

Whoa. He is talking in my head. The wolf is real. I

can understand him. The snail charm—now radiating a pleasant warmth on my wrist—must be for communication.

"Hi, I'm Pepper." I smile and give the wolf a weird little wave. The heck if I know what I'm doing. I lick my lips and roll with it. "A beithíoch. Aren't they supposed to be huge cats?" Fae monster cats... Rumour has it they used to be gods. I shiver.

Not just cats, the wolf—no, the beithíoch—huffs at me with wolfy disgust. And now I have offended him.

My smile wobbles. "What were you doing in there?" I point at the floor at the now inert metal charm.

Ensnared. I have languished within their trap for an extended duration.

"I'm sorry they trapped you." Perhaps playing with the charms from a stolen bag wasn't the best idea. I fidget; my bony bum is going numb. *Is he dangerous?*

I committed no crime, he says. Lifting his chin, he gives me big sad eyes. It's like he can read my mind or, more than likely, my scrunched-up and worried expression. *You freed me.*

"That wasn't my intention, but I'm glad you are no longer trapped. If you like, I can direct you to the nearest gateway so you can go home." I lean forward and scoop up the wolf charm. As soon as my fingers make contact, a crack appears along the top. "Oops, sorry," I mumble as the wolf-charm head falls off and the rest crumbles to dust in my hand. I wince as I rub my dirty palm on my leg.

You liberated me, and I am indebted to you.

"A debt?" That means he will still leave, right? He can't stay here. I don't want or need a hairy, magical roommate. "Erm..." *Okay, don't panic, Pepper. Don't panic.* What do I say to that? I open and close my mouth a few times but have nothing. Nothing comes out. The fae can be finicky with debts.

At least I can't detect any deception in his words. I'm no good at this stuff. Asking questions, small talk... by the time I work out what I'm going to say, the time to say it is long gone. I'm awkward. I don't take people's cues, and I mess up. I feel like everyone understands the things that no one says. Everyone except me. To them it's all a given, the art of communication. Add in all that body language stuff, and it's lost to me in translation. Then again, that's people. This is a wolf.

"Erm..." I focus on the beithíoch. While I was lost in my head, Eurus must have decided I'd agreed to his terms. Whatever they are. Or, more likely, he doesn't care what I think. For him, our conversation is clearly over.

I watch helplessly as the wolf turns in a circle a few times, drops, and curls up on the floor at the bottom of the bed. With a wolfy sigh, Eurus closes his eyes.

Okay then. I scratch the back of my head. What the heck do I do now?

I stare at the sleeping beithíoch—another guest. Add the tiger into the mix, and I've never spoken to this many creatures in one day in my entire life. What's going on?

At least he isn't another shifter. He'll remain a wolf and not turn into a strapping-looking man.

Okay, what do I do? Hands on hips, I turn and eye the shelves, particularly the shelf with pineapple. I've only got forty-two cans left and a few packets of nuts. What on earth do I feed a wolf? Perhaps for now he can eat the elf food.

I run my fingers in my hair—they snag on all the knots. It needs a brush. I need to have a shower, and I need to get a new job to pay for the massive wolf's dinner.

I grab the empty elf bag and fold it. Something cracks inside. *Uh-oh. I hope that wasn't a potion.* Eyes wide and arm outstretched, prepared for something horrible to happen, I hurry into the tunnel, readying my magic to whisk the danger away. Seconds pass, and when the bag doesn't immediately burst into flames, I turn it upside down and give it a shake.

There's a musical tickling as broken glass hits the tunnel floor, then a flash of purple, and a worm lands on the floor and wriggles away.

A worm with a tuft of purple hair. *What the heck?* Before I can grab it, the worm wiggles into a hole in the wall, and then it's gone. The worm disappears. I've never seen a worm like that before.

I laugh and rub my face when the stone magic can't find it. "That never happens." The little creature must be a magical null. As long as the worm doesn't crawl into my ear while I'm asleep and eat my brain, I'll leave it alone.

It's just a little worm, after all.

The worm, the wolf, and the tiger shifter—an epic start to a bad joke. Any more creatures, and I'm going to get a permanent eye twitch.

I check the bag for any other hidden surprises as the floor absorbs the glass—it'll end up in the rubbish. Nothing else is in there. I put it away, grab some clean clothes, and hide around the corner from the wolf to change. I wipe the canvas of my bed, smile at my snazzy new cover, settle back cross-legged with a hairbrush, and drag it through all the snarls, knots, and dried blood clumps. Gag.

Morning light filters in from the ceiling. There's no time now to sleep and no chance I'll be able to with the softly snoring beithíoch so near. And then there's the tiger shifter still in the subway. I need to get rid of them.

A quick check of the subway indicates the shifter is no longer content in the corner. No, he's pacing. I scrunch my eyes closed—in my mind's eye, I can see his angry, frustrated strides. The tiger has become more and more agitated as time has marched on. Dangerous. I don't want to see him again. There's no accounting for what he will do. I don't want to speak to him—he scares me. It's probably safe to let him go.

Yeah, he needs to leave.

He laps the space, his prowling strides drifting closer and closer to my usual exit spot. Priming the magic, I wait. A weird smile tugs at my lips, and like a perfectly controlled trap, I'm ready when his boots hit.

The stone snaps around him. The tiger tries in vain to spring out of the way. I push my palm, and the concrete responds to the gesture by giving the tiger a little slap in the face. The blow is just enough to stun him as the magic lifts him and unceremoniously dumps him outside.

Phew, he's out. It's easier this way.

The tiger lingers out there for far too long, studying the ground. After about ten minutes, he leaves. I can imagine him shaking his head, hands in his pockets, as he strolls away down the promenade. At least he's safe. Something tells me this won't be the last time we meet, but I ignore the premonition. It probably *won't* be the last time I see him, but fate willing, it will be the last time he sees me.

CHAPTER
SIX

EURUS CRACKS AN EYE OPEN. *I've observed that you've successfully dealt with the shifter.*

"How...?" How did he know? I narrow my eyes and nod in affirmation. I bet the beithíoch can smell him. "Yeah, he's gone."

Temporarily. His curiosity about you ensures his eventual return.

I shrug. "I hope not, though I can't control what the tiger does." The only person I can control is myself, and with that in mind, I need to stop smashing dangerous creatures in the face with concrete.

Uh-oh. I really did do that. I rub my face and groan into my palm. The tiger was rude, but I shouldn't have been rude back. I feel kind of bad for smacking him. Why the heck did I do that?

"I'm going to leave for a few hours, get cleaned up. Do you want to come with me?" I thumb the tunnel behind me. I will not let fear force me into hiding down here when things need to get done.

I shall remain here, embracing the respite of slumber. It appears rest has eluded me for countless years.

Being stuffed in a tiny charm will do that to a creature. Awkwardly, I stand, and my toes scrunch in my boots. I don't like leaving a magical stranger alone in my space, surrounded by my stuff.

But if he wants to sleep... and I need to get clean. I need to wash the blood and sweat out of my hair, and a bit of fresh air may also help clear my head.

"Okay." My hands tremble as I quietly gather my things and get ready to leave. This entire experience of running for my life has messed me up. As a troll, naturally, I'm not prey. Being scared like this, being unsure what to do for the best, is horrible, and I'm sick of it.

I'm also frightened if I don't force myself to move, to live, I never will. *Not that my life is really living.* But I do things and have helped people. I'm not completely useless.

I'm halfway out of the room when good manners prick at me. I bounce from foot to foot as I turn to Eurus. "Do you need anything? Hungry? Thirsty?" With my next thought, I feel my eyes widen. *What if he needs to pee?*

A prime cut of beef. He licks his lips, and his long pink tongue gets the tip of his nose.

I frown. "Yeah, um, I haven't got money for prime cuts of beef. I might be able to cough up a few bones?" My eyebrows rise, and I tentatively smile.

The beithíoch sniffs. *Sufficient for the present moment then.*

"Okay. Anything else?"

Eurus closes his eyes in clear dismissal.

All righty then. "I'll see you in a few hours." I grab my bags and leave.

I shuffle into the subway where the fae lanterns are still dimmed. The tiger has moved my cone, and the mesh door to the ladies has been wrenched open.

I grind my teeth. In a few brief hours, the tiger has changed so many things that have stood the test of time for years. Now this is why I don't have guests. Not that I have any friends.

I rest my hand on the forced-open grill to the bathroom, grab the cone, and slap it back on the floor in the right place, rotating it slightly to the left. There, that's better. I nod.

With a pulse of magic, the stone brings me my wash things and... I frown and check the rubbish bag I'm holding. *Huh, it's not here.* The tunic I was wearing in Faerie is missing, and according to my magic, it's not on the floor in the bathroom.

My heart skips a beat. The tiger didn't take it, did he? Why would the nosy tiger steal my dirty top? Is it to prove that I illegally used the portal? I cover my mouth. *Oh no*, he must have. Blood is dangerous in the wrong hands. It can be used against you in spells. And with his sensitive shifter nose, he'd have smelled the blood, and he would have smelled the elves.

Oh no. I slide my fingers through my hair and tug at it. "I can't believe this. What am I going to do?" Will he take the evidence to the hunters, or is *he* the hunter? I want to slump to the floor and cry my eyes out at my stupidity.

Helping him has ruined everything. I tug at the collar of my jumper. Gah, I feel all hot, and suddenly the subway feels like it is closing in.

I can't stay here.

Perhaps in a few years, I can come back, but the tiger shifter was angry and... I smacked him in the face with concrete.

Oh, Mother Nature, what have I done?

A whine of fear slips from my lips, and the plastic bags dig into my fingers as I fist my hands. It's only a dank tunnel, but it's home. A home that is now compromised. I want to kick myself for not having a secondary location set up to hide. Not that I've ever needed one. Why would I? I'm boring. There are tunnels like this all over town, but they will be the first place the hunters will look.

They will find me.

The hunters are as bad as the elves. They have magic that can strip powers away, a strip of magic called a null band. I close my eyes and take a few deep breaths. *Everything is going to be fine.* No one has ever cared about me, so why would they start now? I'm just one person in a sea of far more dangerous and exciting creatures.

It will be okay. *It will be okay.*

I hurry to the corner where he'd been. Perhaps the missing tunic is over here? No, it's not. The tunic is gone. All I can see is my blanket neatly folded on the floor with the unopened pineapple can on top. I can't even raise any excitement that he didn't eat my pineapple. I send them both back to my room and stuff the empties—nuts and the water bottles—into the rubbish bag in my hand.

I need to tell Eurus what's going on. We aren't safe. I spin, drop the bags on the floor, and run back to the other tunnel.

My feet slap on the brick floor. "Eurus, we need to go! The tiger—" I skid around the corner and barely avoid wiping out on the far wall. Panting, I continue to explain what's happened to the sleepy beithíoch. Not trusting him, I tentatively brush over the entire subject of the elves and what happened with them. I'm bouncing up and down on my toes when I finish.

Why is he not moving?

If necessary, I shall locate you, he says with a dismissive yawn, and then he closes his eyes.

What? Is he going back to sleep? "But, but it's not safe here, Eurus. We need to go."

Refresh yourself. The scent of blood and fear clings to you. Attend to that, and as you do, I shall indulge in a long-overdue rest. Eurus's lip curls, and he stretches into a different position with his head on his paws. The wolf is unhappy with my interruption. *Upon your return, consider fortifying your stone magic with a protective ward.*

My bouncing ceases. "A ward? But I can't do wards," I whisper.

While you may not possess the ability, the umbrella charm adorning your wrist can perform the task. Additionally, another of the charms in your possession will obfuscate any attempts to locate you. I shall assist after a well-deserved nap.

An umbrella? Ah. I hold up my wrist and fiddle with the charms, finding the one he means.

Cease the panic, child. Your anxiety may lead to peril. These tunnels are resilient, akin to a fortress. A ward shields the vulnerabilities—the beithíoch nods to the thick glass above our heads—*and for a lone troll, the exertion to breach the protective magic will be considerable. Rest assured, safety prevails in these confines. We will be perfectly safe.*

I nod, and then my intelligence kicks in. *How does Eurus know where we are?* He's just left the charm and is currently in a nondescript tunnel. He has gone nowhere. We could be anywhere.

Again he answers my thoughts as if I'd spoken them out loud. *Even within my confinement, awareness persisted, fuelled by acute senses. The conversations of creatures beyond and the vocal nature of the shifter during his tenure reached my keen ears. I've discerned our location. The shifter might assume you'd flee, a natural response for prey. However, you are no prey, are you? You possess the choice to either retreat or act wisely. Employ the charms at your disposal to safeguard your abode.*

Eurus is right. The elves, the tiger will expect me to run. That's what my lizard brain is screaming at me to do.

Fight or flight.

But there's a third option: *fortify* and then do nothing. Stay, make things stronger, and then only leave when I want to. I can disappear. There's no way they have the power to find me if I leave on my terms and use my magic. I huff. With my power, the only way to find me is to stumble into me. I don't know any creature that can do what I can. That means something.

"Can we do the ward and the other spell now? Please?" I'm close to dropping to my hands and knees and begging. If I have a way of keeping safe, I'll take it. Perhaps bribery will motivate Eurus to help me. "I'll get you some minced beef." I keep my smile hidden when he licks his lips. I then sit awkwardly on the bed.

The beithíoch sighs. *You are staring.*

"Yes." I tap a rhythm on my thigh and then hum a little ditty under my breath to be extra annoying.

You are making noise.

"Yes. I'm waiting to do these spells." I wiggle my wrist, and the charms tinkle as they knock together.

Eurus sits up. *An exasperating child, indeed. Modern*

creatures seem to lack respect for their elders. I, for one, am two thousand years old. He shifts his paws and shakes his furry head. *It appears I won't be granted a reprieve until I extend my assistance to you.*

"No." I grin.

Very well, troll. Let us commence. Take the umbrella charm in your hand, close your eyes, and mentally map the tunnels you wish to ward. The magic inherent in the charm will handle the rest.

"Okay." *Um, helpful.*

Map the tunnels? There are miles of tunnels, some with other creatures living in them. It makes sense that I only need to ward off the subway, this tunnel, and perhaps the tunnels that immediately connect. Yeah, that would make sense. I hold the tiny umbrella, close my eyes, take a slow breath, and empty my mind.

Slowly my second sight wavers into focus. Magic lifts the lighter strands of my hair, and a green glow immediately thickens the air, pulsing with my heartbeat. I'm sure other people using this charm don't have to use their second sight, but most users only need to do a single room, not an entire tunnel system.

I force myself to concentrate and push, allowing my magical sight to map the closest tunnels.

You have mapped the precise locations where the ward shall be established? he whispers.

I nod.

Implore. Entice the umbrella charm to gracefully unfold, enveloping and safeguarding those specified regions from any potential harm. Eurus's voice hovers at the edge of my awareness as he continues to tell me what to do: whispering, guiding, instructing me on how to move the magic. I gently tug at the blue power from within the charm, asking for its help. Like spring rain, the charm's magic is a light, refreshing blue that is cool against my hard, vibrant green.

I focus on the tunnels, seeping the blue magic over the green. My skin crawls as the ward magic joins mine and takes its place. Ignoring the creepy feeling, I pull my green magic back and ask the power of the charm to shelter the tunnels against harm. The charm's magic opens, connecting, and there's a boom inside my mind. The incredible blue magic bursts out, filling the space I've mapped with a shield of light, like an umbrella.

My lips tingle, and my hair crackles with static. With my eyes closed and with my second sight, I can see the blue light, the ward.

Good. The beithíoch praises me. *Now enact the spell of forgetfulness utilising the charm fashioned in the likeness of a fish.*

I reluctantly pull away from the blue magic, drop the umbrella, and grab the fish. Aha, memory like a goldfish. I get it. Gary, the witch who made the charms, sure has a sense of humour.

Execute a similar procedure, but this time channel the enchantment to settle precisely where you encountered the shifter. The departure point he used would be opportune. Exercise subtlety—a delicate touch. Specify that the charm's influence manifests solely when someone actively seeks you or this locale.

We aim for a discreet caress of the charm's magic, preventing a cascade of forgetfulness-induced confusion among unwitting creatures.

"Okay." I think I got all that. At the rate he's going, I can only understand every third word Eurus says. I wonder if he speaks like this to make up for being a wolf. But then why would he? It's not a negative, being furry.

I feel a little more confident this time, mapping the small area of concrete on the promenade right in front of where the magic told me the tiger had lingered. I give the charm my stipulations, and with an orange flash, the Forget Me spell activates. I grin. "I did it," I whisper, dropping the charm.

I sway. Ugh, that was hard magic, and I'm still not fully recovered, and I now feel like a dizzy, sweaty mess.

Very well, my olfactory-challenged companion. Permit me the solace of uninterrupted repose while you attend to your personal hygiene. Oh, and as for you, Pepper, opt for an exit from the tunnels quite distinct from your habitual egress point if you please.

I blink a few times, translating the beithíoch's words the best I can. Is he saying I stink? And what the hell is a habitual egress point? I fidget.

Exit the tunnels far from where you usually do.

"Oh." I nod. "Okay, good idea. I can do that." My mind is fuzzy from working the two charms, but I get to my feet. "I'll leave you to your nap. If you want to leave the tunnels, I've instructed the stone to help you." I slink out of the room. If he leaves, the stone won't let him back in, but at least he isn't trapped down here if something happens to me.

The magic brings my bags to me, and I turn the opposite way and head further into the tunnels.

CHAPTER
SEVEN

I'm squeaky clean. I sneaked in and showered at a hotel gym, and my hair now smells of oatmeal, honey, and coconut. That's a tremendous step up from sweat and blood. It took three shampoos to get all the dried clumps out, and I can only imagine what I smelled like to the sensitive-nosed beithíoch and the shifter. *Ew.* I can't help but grin.

After the shower, I dress nice for shopping, tight black jeans that hug my hips and a dark purple jumper. The colour looks fantastic on my green skin. It's my favourite. Even if only a few creatures get to see me today, at least I'm nicely dressed and clean. It's nice to feel nice.

I've dropped the rubbish in a street bin, and now I need to drop my dirty clothing at the brownie-owned launderette for a service wash—the house elves are extraordinary. I shuffle into the shadows and drop my magic. I wait a few seconds so I don't draw attention to myself, and then I oh so casually walk up to the door with Brownie Dry Cleaner and Launderette stencilled across the glass.

The bell above the door gives an annoying electric ping, and the warm air hits my face, a welcome change from the biting chill outside. With the bag of clothing in front of me, I shuffle to the counter.

The place is cosy, the walls adorned with faded posters of enchanted garments and magical cleaning spells.

I trust the brownie who runs this place. I've been coming here for years, though Jessica, the owner, can't always remember me. I don't take offence as she must see hundreds of customers daily.

Today she is behind the counter. She glances up from folding a pile of freshly laundered clothes and offers a friendly smile. "Welcome! How can I help you today?"

I heave the bag onto the counter and smile. "Good morning, Jessica. A service wash please." I rattle off my account number and nudge the bag towards her.

"Certainly!" Her long lashes sweep her cheeks as she blinks and tries her best to remember me. I internally wince when she shakes her head and grabs the business datapad. It's been a month since I was last here. At least she'll remember tomorrow when I pick my clean clothes up.

After a moment of scribbling, she finds the account. "We'll have the clothes cleaned up in no time. Would you like any treatments? We have introduced a new dirt-protection potion—this one doesn't eat the clothes—and we have a special on bloodstains, three for the price of two."

"No, thank you. A standard wash is fine."

"Got it. Just leave them here, and we'll take care of the rest. You can pick them up tomorrow if that's convenient. Is there anything else you need?"

I shake my head. "No, thank you. I'm good. See you tomorrow." With a nod of thanks and a small wave, I leave. The door does its electric ping once more behind me as I trudge back into the winter air.

I also brave the butchers, turning off my invisibility for the minutes needed to get the beithíoch his bones and a small tray of the promised minced beef.

I stare down at the white plastic bag with a frown as I head for home. I need to find a new job. The beithíoch is expensive. However, it might be best to give it a few more days for the heat to die down, especially when I have an angry tiger knowing too much about me. With my little slave rune and elf problem, the fewer people who see me, the better.

I guess it's business as usual. I scuff the kerb with my boot. Keeping myself closed off from others has always been my go-to policy, a habit that's left me in good stead since I was a kid—a necessity.

This time it feels a bit different. Hiding away from

the bad guys is forced upon me rather than it being entirely my choice. I don't enjoy feeling like a criminal or being tagged as a slave. I scowl and tug the sleeve of my jumper over my hand. The small amount of money I have stashed will see me through if I'm careful and if I can get rid of my unwanted furry guest. I like people, but I also enjoy being alone.

In front of me, a troll's wide hips sway as her heels click against the pavement. A sad, jealous-sounding sigh slips out of me. She radiates beauty. Big-boned and curvy, her skin is a deep green, and her dark green hair shines when it catches the sun. When she turns to look in a shop window, I see her bright white, gently curving tusks. They dimple her plump upper lip. The troll is what I should have been instead of what I am, and she reminds me of my mother.

A wave of sadness hits me. My mother... I sigh and brush my melancholy thoughts away. I pass the witch's shop and, once again, have the silly notion of going inside and asking for advice on the slave rune and perhaps asking them what the charms on my wrist can do—a foolish and dangerous thought. I don't need anyone's help. I can work it out on my own.

Okay, so the umbrella charm creates wards, the gold-fish charm muddles the mind, the cat reflects magic back to the caster, and the snail aids communication. That's four of the twelve charms. That's not bad at all. I can't help wondering, and I'm excited to find out what the other eight might do.

When he's finished sleeping, perhaps Eurus might tell me, especially if he really is two thousand years old. I chuckle and roll my eyes. Two thousand years, what a little liar. I need to work out how to get rid of him politely. I do not want the beithíoch as a guest. Having him in my space is beyond weird, and I'm still unsure if I can trust him. I groan. Of course I shouldn't trust him. What do I know of him? Beithíoch are known to be monsters, dangerous loyal monsters, but is Eurus loyal to me or the elves?

As if thinking about them has pulled them out of my nightmares, my heart misses a beat, and I freeze in my tracks.

The elves.

Four of them, a small hunting party, are standing in the middle of the street. I stand there staring with my mouth hanging open. Just in time, I notice the couple behind me closing in fast, and I dart out of their way to avoid impact. My crappy ankle rolls, and I bite back a hiss of pain.

Gosh, that was close. I hobble into the shadows of a closed bar and, trembling, check that my cloak of invisibility is tight around me. It's fine. Standing on one leg, I gently rotate my ankle before putting my weight back on it so it doesn't swell up like a balloon. It's always better not to baby it.

With my heart pounding in my ears and tempering the urge to scuttle away, I watch.

The elves are examining the ground.

The elf in charge is aesthetically handsome, with sharp features, long, white-blond hair, and the customary intricate elf plaits. His hair sweeps over his narrow shoulder as he squats next to the lamppost. His weapons rattle as he bends and places his left palm down in the centre of a starburst pattern of a damaged paving stone— a crack I'd caused.

How in the hell did they know that crack had anything to do with me? My eyes flick around. *There.* My heart sinks when I notice the street security cameras. They must have got access and combed the footage for any trace of me. That makes the most sense. After all, this street is close to the portal. I shake my head and vigorously rub my face.

Well done, Pepper. You kept your secrets through torture and lost them on the home straight. It wouldn't have taken much to notice the damaged pavement and to catch me flickering in and out of existence when my magic failed for those few seconds. Now they know for sure about my stone and invisibility magic. *Great. Great, just bloody great.*

The target on my forehead just got bigger.

Instead of running away, which is what I should do, I embrace the horror and the deep-down rage that is warming my blood. My nostrils flare as I glare at the elves and the pavement-touching blond. That elf—that horrid, blond-haired shithead of an elf—hurt me.

Not getting anything from the stone, the elf leader removes his leather glove with a flick of his hand and slaps against the broken slab as he tries to get a magical signature from the stone.

Good luck with that, pal.

While his fingers flex against the slab and his face twists with frustration, I get a flashback of memory. Stomach acid squirts into my mouth, and I immediately shut it down. Yeah, I remember those hands as he aggressively questioned me. I swallow the bile. Well, him and his merry band of creeps.

My eyes narrow on the three other elves, and for the first time in my life, I feel true hate. The blond likes to lead by example, and he kept punching me in the face while his colleague with the long brown hair who's standing behind him, watching his back, broke my wrist. I snarl. The brown-haired guy is also the nobhead who put the slave rune on my arm. The rune I'm going to remove somehow. These elves are slaver scum, and I've never wanted to hurt someone so badly in my life.

I mean, how hard would it be to weaken the bricks on the nearby buildings and drop them on their heads? I close my eyes and take a deep breath. That's not me; I'm not that person. Although days like today, a horrible part of me wishes I was.

Worried murmurs have my eyes flying open to see the surrounding shoppers scatter as a familiar man prowls down the street—his focus is fixated on the elves.

I groan in dismay. *Oh goody, the tiger is here.*

CHAPTER
EIGHT

I SHOULD LEAVE, but like a right plonker, I creep closer. I need to know. I need to listen. It's a calculated risk, and I need to find out what's happening between the elves and the tiger.

Gosh, the man is even more beautiful in daylight. As the tiger gets closer, his nostrils flare, he takes in their scent, and a flash of something dangerous rolls over his eyes. For a few seconds, they glow orange, and then the colour is gone in a blink.

"You lost?" the tiger snarls.

The leader stands, brushing the dirt off his palm onto a handkerchief passed to him by the wrist-breaking elf, and then nonchalantly, the blond-haired elf replaces his glove. All the while, he is eying the tiger with no small measure of disgust and making him wait for an answer.

"We are hunting a girl, a half-breed troll. She escaped from our custody four days ago. She is approximately five foot six, with green skin and hair," the leader says in excellent English, his expression blank, his body language relaxed and a passivity that screams *nothing to see here, earthling*.

Four days, wow. I guess I needed the sleep.

"A girl escaped from your custody?" The tiger folds his massive arms across his chest and narrows his eyes. His body language screams *give me an excuse to rip your head off*. "Wait, let me get this straight. Are you guys warriors working for a lord of Faerie? Got any identification? 'Cause to me, you don't look like any warrior elves I've seen."

"We are not on official business," the leader admits.

"So you're what, mercenaries?" the tiger asks with a snarl. "Ah, I get it. The girl didn't escape custody, more like she escaped capture. We have a dim view of that, you know. It's not very sporting, is it? Four strapping elves like yourselves after one tiny troll girl? Embarrassing really. So go on, tell me. What did you do to her?" His words growl at the end.

Then it all clicks. With that first big sniff when he approached the elves, the tiger knew who they were. He had smelled them before on the tunic he'd stolen from the bathroom. He had smelled their scents and my blood, and he had healed the aftermath of what they did to me. Pain, fear—it all has a scent. My tunic was saturated in it.

The blond leader lets out a haughty scoff, and the three other elves join in with their own rude laughs. "Hunter, this is a matter for your council, not you. Be on your way. We don't need any help to track our prey." The elf flicks his fingers.

"Hellhound," the tiger growls, the word low in his throat.

And my heart drops to the soles of my feet.

Hellhound. Whoa, whoa, whoa. He's a hellhound? In response to that single word, as if choreographed, all four elves take a big step back, and their hands drop to hover over their weapons.

I rock back on my feet. Hellhounds are old shifters, at least over six hundred, which is rare in itself as shifters are a violent race and tend to die young. Hellhounds are bigger, stronger, and more magically potent, with an affinity for fire.

Yeah, it's as bad as it sounds. It starts with the shifter's poison teeth, and then it's all wrapped up with elite fight training, and then the rare beasts can also set themselves on fire. Fire shifters. Hence, the nickname *hellhound* has taken on a life of its own, a fear-filled connotation over the generations. I'd already decided not to play with the tiger, and taunting a *hellhound* is suicide.

They're an army of one—death walking.

I rub my face and groan. Why me? *Why me?* I've kept my head down and nose clean all these years. Apart from my sneaky job, I've been a good girl. I've done so well for a feral latchkey kid. With my start in life, I could have died a million different ways. Yet I dragged myself into adulthood. I've done nothing to warrant a hellhound in my business. Until last night, I wouldn't have believed I'd ever seen one. Yet here he is. This is turning out to be a hell of a week.

Then the realisation hits, the realisation of what he is *really* hits me, and now I feel like a proper numpty. As a hellhound, the tiger shifter could have handled all the shifters last night—probably all the shifters in town— with his hands tied behind his back and one eye poked out.

Oh no, another thought, and I groan and close my eyes, mortified. I slap a hand over my face. I locked a *hellhound* in the subway to protect him.

I huff a weird, strangled laugh into my hand—no wonder he was pissed.

No wonder he had all those fancy spells and that scary cop face.

No wonder he instinctively scares the crap out of me. I can't believe I smacked him in the face with concrete.

Oh, Mother, what next?

"Paperwork," the tiger growls, holding out his hand and moving his fingers in a hand-it-over gesture. The tiger radiates menace. I thought he was ragey in the subway, but now I see that was his *nice* face. Oh heck, it was nothing compared to how he is now. Power, disgust, and a deep-down fury. He wants to rip these elves apart.

Even the humans on the street cross over to the other side of the road and disappear into random shops to avoid his wrath. The power he puts out would scatter the bravest of souls. I doubt there will be any other shifter sticking around within a mile radius of here. A mile radius of him. So why then am I still standing here? Yeah, I don't know either.

One by one, the elves shrink under his gaze, and the leader clears his throat and puffs his chest. "We have got no paperwork, hellhound. We didn't have the time. The girl we are hunting is a potentially dangerous suspect."

Dangerous? I chuckle under my breath. Look at that. The grotty little man is skirting the truth. They've come after me because not only did I get away, but I got away with an illegal, easily-traced-back-to-the-caster slave rune on my arm.

"Dangerous?"

"Potentially," the leader replies with a sniff as he again deliberately fudges the truth. Somewhat uncomfortable, he rubs his mouth with the back of his hand. The three other elves shuffle and drop their eyes.

It's a carefully cultivated myth that elves can't lie. Most modern elves can lie; it's just not an honourable thing to do. Beating someone when they pose no threat and whacking a slave rune on their arm is also frowned upon, but that never stopped them. I think honour and truth are goalposts that can be moved to suit the person.

"You know the rules: no paperwork, no hunting. I

will escort you back to the gate." The tiger sweeps his muscled arm so they can go ahead.

"No, we need—" the leader's snooty voice breaks off with a gasp as the tiger loses his patience and his hand snaps out, wrapping around his neck, and lifts him. The elf's gloved hands yank on the tiger's fingers as he dangles a few scant inches off the ground. The toes of his boots frantically scramble and scrape to find purchase as he chokes.

"We can do this easy or hard."

"I vote hard," says a raspy voice.

A woman steps from behind the group, dressed in black combats that fit her petite frame like a glove. Her pale pink hair is in a thick plait, so long it bounces against her waist as she moves. She prowls around the tiger and pauses, tilting her chin to stare at the captured elf. Even though the tiny woman looks up, it feels as if she is looking down on him.

I'm. In. Awe.

She smiles. It's not a nice smile. The elves sink further into themselves.

"She's a shifter," I mumble to myself.

Barely over five feet—which is strange as shifters, like trolls, tend to grow big—she looks to be about eighteen, although with most creatures it is impossible to tell. Big yellow eyes, high cheekbones, and a tiny pert, turned-up nose. Adorable. Although the mean in her eyes speaks otherwise. I would rather pull the tiger's tail than mess with her.

"Warrior Hesketh," the brown-haired, wrist-breaking elf whispers. His nasal voice is reverent and... scared.

"Hi, Forrest." The tiger greets her, his tone friendly as if he hasn't got an elf dangling from his hand—or more than likely, he does this sort of stuff regularly.

Forrest Hesketh, I mouth.

"What's up, Corbin?" Her rough, broken voice makes me wince; she must have been through some nasty stuff.

Ah, and the tiger's name is Corbin.

"These gentlemen are hunting a troll. A girl."

The elf leader lets out a soft moan as Corbin tightens his hold and gives him a little shake that sets his feet back to scrambling.

Forrest's lips twitch.

"She's not a full troll, and she escaped our custody. We want to get her back as we have further questions." Wrist Breaker answers for the leader while holding his shaking hands to ward off the pink-haired tiny terror.

"Questions, *riiight*," Forrest says with a roll of her gold eyes.

The other two elves haven't moved their feet, but their upper bodies have rocked back, and the closest guy to me... Whoa. His knees are knocking together. I've never seen that before. The elves look like they are going to piss themselves.

Who the heck is she?

"They're mercs who don't have official paperwork," the tiger shifter growls.

"No?" Forrest tuts. She takes in the red-faced elf. "You can't come to Earth, to my hometown, and start shit."

"You will leave now," Corbin says as he drops the lead elf and, with a disgusted expression, wipes his hand on his leg. "If you dare return, ensure you have the right paperwork. Otherwise, Warrior Hesketh here has the court's permission to rip you all apart."

Nice.

"Yep. Go on then, off you pop." Forrest smiles and nods in the direction of the gate.

"The paperwork will take months," Wrist Breaker objects with a nasal whine. I roll my eyes. These guys don't know when to leave things alone.

"Not our problem," Corbin growls.

The leader, a hand massaging his throat, scrambles away. The other elves rush to follow. The wrist breaker is bringing up the rear. He squeaks when the tiger grabs his arm. With both hands and with a practised twist, the limb snaps like a twig.

The elf screams.

My mouth pops open.

Did he... did he... do that for me? Noooo. No way. I shake my head and rub the back of my neck—bloody hell. I have no idea what is going on. I watch in disbelief as the elves scatter, hurrying towards the gate as if the hounds of hell were after them. I guess, in a way, Corbin the hellhound is.

Forrest doesn't bat an eye at the violence. "Why the

wrist?" she asks in a conversational tone as she watches them scuttle off.

"He hurt her."

"Ah." She nods. "Right, good for you. Though if it were me, I would've done both arms."

The tiger grunts.

"Let's make sure they leave, eh? But fair warning. Like all mercs that reek of slavers, they'll sneak back, and after today, you're on your own. I've not got time to fix this."

"Dragon?"

"Yeah, the dragon. Some kid is causing a right stink." Forrest turns and nudges Corbin towards the retreating elves.

As they prowl past me, a smirk pulls at the corners of her mouth. She scratches the back of her head, looks directly at me, and winks.

What. The. Fuck.

CHAPTER
NINE

SHE CAN SEE ME! She can bloody see me. How on earth is that possible? My heart slams a mile a minute as I hightail it back to the tunnel. As I speed past the shops, I check for a reflection in the nearby shops and... nothing. Nothing. My magic is locked down tight. The cloak of power covering me hadn't wavered. Not once. Yet Forrest Hesketh is the first creature to see me while I'm cloaked.

What the heck is she?

I thought she was a shifter, but perhaps not. That makes sense. Female shifters are exceedingly rare and supposedly locked up for their safety. Whatever creature she is, I'm unsure if she will do anything about me. Not when it sounds like she has a dragon problem to deal with. I hope she won't use the knowledge of my magic to hurt me. She would have done it already. Right? Right. Unless you count the wink that almost stopped my heart with fright, she doesn't seem to wish me ill.

My speed increases until I fall into a fast clip. With each step, my ankle spasms, but I keep moving. On the fly, when I reach a suitable spot, I throw out my hand, dark green magic hits the pavement, and I drop like a rock.

I plop into the tunnel none too gently, landing on my bum onto something squishy: moss and built-up filth. I hope. I wrinkle my nose. Huh, at least I didn't hurt myself.

Breathing fast, I duck as moisture drips onto my head, and the plastic bag in my hand crackles and bounces against my thigh as I scramble to my feet. Blind, I make my way home, trying not to touch the slimy walls. So gross.

Following the stone's gentle nudges, traversing the unknown tunnel takes me ten more minutes. I sigh in relief when the light of the shimming blue ward greets me. Just a few more strides, and I'll be safe. I hurry through and feel much calmer behind the ward. I can now breathe. At a sedate pace, I plod through the light-filled tunnel to my room. Eurus is where I left him—still sleeping.

Great.

I grab the bowls off a shelf—I only have two—and pour water into one and put the minced beef in the other. I slide them onto the floor and tip the bones out of the plastic bag. The bones roll and settle next to the sleeping beithíoch nose. He snores deeply. I plop onto the edge of the bed, ignoring my dirty wet bottom and lean forward, chin on my fist, and wait. Another deep wolfy snore, and he must catch the meat scent. His wet black nose wiggles, and a single dark brown eye opens.

"I saw the elves."

Ah, did you manage to navigate the situation unscathed? It appears you are whole and intact, a favourable outcome. I presume your elusive presence evaded their notice entirely. He lets out a little whine as he yawns, showing me his tongue and a mouthful of strong teeth.

"No, erm, they didn't see me."

Good. He stands, bows into a stretch, and then his tongue disappears into the water. He laps, and water droplets sprinkle to the floor. He then turns his head and takes a mouthful of the beef. He swallows. *Cheap processed crap,* he grumbles.

"I think I saw an eyelash and some cow snot in there." I point, leaning forward. I lift a single green eyebrow and stare into the bowl. "Yum, yum."

Eurus narrows his eyes, moves to the side so his furry bum blocks my sight, and then takes another bite.

"Not that bad then, huh?" I shake my head. Cheap processed crap. Rude, ungrateful mutt. "That mince was expensive." Yes, it was way less money compared to the prime steak he'd wanted, but meat isn't cheap. "And it was all I could afford, so unless you have some Earth money hidden away, I can't afford any more, so enjoy it while you can," I say, trying to get a reaction, perhaps rustle up some guilt.

The beithíoch ignores me.

There is a buzz in my mind, a flash of worry from the concrete and tarmac outside. Something strange is happening on the promenade. *What now!* I'm hit with some weird information. Confused, I excuse myself, leaving Eurus to his meal.

I take a different tunnel to exit so I can see with my own eyes what is happening. I have a horrible thought. I hope the memory spell I put up before hasn't gone haywire or there aren't more shifters fighting. I tug my invisibility around me and allow the stone magic to push me into the light.

Ew. I wrinkle my nose. I'm in a dirty side street beside a fish-and-chip shop and its big, smelly commercial bins. That's gross. The wind whips at my hair, and I sidestep a rank-smelling puddle to venture onto the promenade, peering to the right, towards all the commotion.

Immediately, I see the problem and who has the magic in an uproar. My stomach churns with nerves, and my chest feels tight. A slight form with pale pink hair stands across the road close to Central Pier over my favourite spot.

I sigh, wait for a bus to trundle past, look both ways, and bolt across the road. The strain makes my calves ache. I need to do more exercise. Being a hermit isn't healthy.

I'm moving towards a bonfire of poorly veiled power.

Forrest has added to her badarse clothing, wearing sparkling orange Hunter Wellington boots and a matching down jacket in the same bright colour. She leans over to give the ground a good rap with her knuckles.

"Knock, knock," she says in her distinct raspy voice.

I blink a few times. Did she? Oh yes, she did. Forrest is knocking. I rub my temples. She pauses her ground assault as I approach, and her yellow eyes lift to mine. I'm closer to her than before and notice a splash of green in her right eye. Odd, it makes her intent gaze seriously disconcerting.

"Oh, there you are." She grins. "I'm glad I found the right place, plus Corbin's scent is all over." She sniffs.

His scent? Right. Well, I'm making all the mistakes lately, aren't I?

Forrest rotates her hand, then waggles her index finger from side to side. "Naughty. Just so you know, the memory spell you used here is illegal. I'll let you off with a warning as you are frightened, but don't use it again. You shouldn't make a habit of breaking the law." She nods at the not-so-hidden bracelet of charms on my wrist.

My eyes widen with her warning, and I tug the purple jumper over my wrist. Bloody hell. Did Eurus know the spell was illegal? I hunch and pluck at my fingers, doing my best to look contrite. "I'm sorry. I didn't know."

"Meh, no harm done. The spell tickles, and the salty

air will eat away at it within the next few days. Just don't use it again." Her manner's awkward, as if she isn't used to long conversations and doesn't speak much, just like me. I have a feeling she doesn't let many people in, and I'm lucky to be talking to her.

To get out of the wind, Forrest stands in the shadow of the pier's big and bulky main building and looks me up and down, as if checking for something. "Are you okay? Corbin said the elves broke your arm. Do you need a healing potion?"

I cross my arms under my chest. "I'm fine, thank you. He fixed it. May I ask a question? How can you see me?" What the hell kind of creature is she? All my senses still say shifter—a wolf. But a shifter shouldn't be able to see me when I'm cloaked.

"Magic." Forrest wiggles her fingers, and with a wide grin bordering on manic, she turns the wiggle into a wave. Behind us, a family of humans has stopped to stare.

Well, stare at her. I'm still invisible. They must think she's talking to herself. They hurry away when Forrest keeps waving.

She laughs. "This is fun. We must do this again, perhaps to my unicorn friend, Tru. Freak her right out." Then her beguiling and innocent eyes blink. "So what happened with the elves?"

I drop my eyes at her abrupt change of topic and shuffle my feet. *Come on, Pepper, her eyes lie.* I don't believe all this friendly stuff. She isn't sweet or inno-cent. She is a big, bad predator. I must remember that

Forrest must be bad if she scared the elves who hurt me.

Forrest lets her question sit in the awkward silence between us and moves so her back is away from the wind but facing the pier. The surrounding area isn't busy as it's midweek in winter when the holiday town slows to a crawl. Still, with her senses, I bet Forrest knows where every creature is on this stretch of the promenade.

"I want to help you. I really do. But innocent people could get hurt with these elves hot on your trail. I need to know what they have on you. Why are you running?" With each question she fires at me, her body language becomes a little more threatening.

"Nothing!" The word comes out as a yell. I wince and rub my mouth. She's making me extra nervous. "Sorry," I mumble through my hand. "They've got nothing on me"—except a slave rune—"I didn't do anything wrong." Except for the bag I stole. I wince and hop from foot to foot, clear my throat, and tell her an obvious truth. "I'm from Faerie, but I've been coming here, using the gate, since I was a kid. I prefer it here," I finish in a whisper.

"From your accent, I had presumed you were local. So what happened with the elves? Come on, the truth."

I don't want to tell her. She's a stranger. But I'm at a loss for what to do, and I don't have a choice. Forrest can see me. She sent the elves back through the gate, and the tiger seemed respectful. She'll probably lock me up and throw away the key if I don't answer.

I need her help.

I might as well get this over with. I can give her the bigger truth. I rub my face. *Start with the simple stuff first.* "They wanted to know what creatures I'm mixed with, where I'm from." I nibble on my thumb. It isn't polite to ask about race, and creatures have been killed for less.

Mixed breeding is bad. On Earth, hybrids are mostly killed at birth because of their instability. They are dangerous. In Faerie, they're ostracised, left to survive without protection or a home. They die quickly.

Forrest is quiet. She doesn't push, and I'm grateful.

"Of course, after a while, I broke and gave them my clan name. I was on the border of my old clan's territory and hoped name-dropping would get me a pass." With a tug of my hair to remind myself I'm here, not there, I force myself to continue. "They wanted to know why there was no record of me being born into the clan. They had a datapad linked to the fae database and a written statement from my mother saying..." My voice breaks, but I plough on. "...the only female child in the clan had died weeks before birth and remains unnamed."

Forrest sucks in her breath. Sympathy shines in her eyes.

"I couldn't answer them." I shrug. "What creature I am, I do not know. My mother is a troll. Her mate is a troll. I have six older brothers who are all trolls." My rising voice betrays my distress, and getting a grip on myself, I lower it, pleading. I need her to understand.

"My mother and my brothers' father are true mates. She can't have a child with another." I hold my hands out to my sides. "Yet here I am."

I huff a breath full of pain, turn, and look out over the seawall to the miles of sand beyond—low tide. The ocean is far in the distance. The sand has little ripples and gouged pools of water where the waves have left their mark.

"They wanted to know about my magic and what I can do. When I refused to tell them, they continued to hurt me." My hands shake, and I hide them behind my back. Forrest is so strong, and my weakness is embarrassing. "Even through the pain, I didn't tell them one more thing, and they concluded I was a magicless half-breed. A liar. It made me fair game, someone no one would miss. I overheard them saying that the Lord of Spring might take me on as a slave. He likes *exotic* bedmates." I grind my teeth. "The elves plan on selling me to the lord's household."

That's when they put that bloody slave rune on my arm.

"Forrest, I don't feel like a half-breed. I know in my heart I'm a troll." I brush my knuckles across my chest. "My mother wouldn't have touched another over her mate. I'd only be a half-breed if someone hurt her." My face stings with the icy wind.

Someone must have hurt her to make me.

"The elves were going to drop me off on this lord's

doorstep. He would have killed me when the claim of my being a half-breed proved untrue."

I stare into Forrest's strange yellow eyes, and all the dirt of my past comes tumbling out. "From the moment of my first cry when I departed my mother's womb, the clan instantly knew I was different—a mistake. Whatever strange mix of fae creatures is in my blood, I wasn't clan to them. No. I was cursed. To them, it's as if I have never existed. They never laid a hand on me in anger. They never hurt me. Well, not physically." My voice shudders, and I take a deep breath.

"I came to this realm when I was a child. I followed one of my brothers and got stuck here for two days. When I returned to the clan, no one noticed I'd been missing. Naively, I had thought I'd be in trouble, you know, that I'd be punished. I don't know why. Hope, perhaps?"

The understanding and raw compassion I see on her face keeps me talking.

"The clan didn't care that I'd been missing for two days. Fate, they didn't care if I ate. I should have been a feral child, but I watched, learned, and tried so hard to be good. To be happy. If I were their happy, good girl, they'd love me, right?" My voice cracks.

Forrest clasps her arms around herself, gripping her elbows.

I don't know how I survived.

I remember that night, the night I left.

CHAPTER
TEN

Twenty Years Ago

I STAND AWKWARDLY in the corner, my stomach rumbling. Once through the portal, I ran all the way home. The big carved stone table is set with plates and cutlery, and my mother bustles around the kitchen, humming softly. My mother loves to cook, and she looks happy. She carefully places down a steaming bowl of purple potatoes, rotating the bowl just right. She sprinkles a pinch of black pepper onto the dish—pepper is her favourite spice; she loves it—and steps back, smiling with satisfaction at the spread before her.

"Dinner's ready!" Her voice echoes down the hall,

and the scrape of chairs and heavy footfalls indicates the others have made their way to the table.

I take a small step forward, but she almost knocks into me as she strides past, so I huddle back into my corner.

"Mother, I'm back," I whisper with a sad wave of my hand. I hunch as the clan pours into the room. My mother's mate kisses her on the forehead, and they all take their seats, laughing and joking about their day. Everyone is seated, and there is no space for me.

The girl who lives down past the woods called me some nasty names once. I avoid her now. She said I was a half-breed, and on bad days I worry she might be right. The trolls in my clan are strong, robust, not delicate-looking with wonky teeth.

I don't wanna be a half-breed.

I feel like a full troll inside, and that's what counts. Sure, my skin is a lighter shade of green, and my hair is black at the roots, which isn't quite right. Plus my build is short and scrawny.

And then there is my magic. It's all over the place. The stone magic I've been blessed with is all wrong; it's too strong, way too strong for my age. I can feel everything around me, make pebbles move, and have no one to ask why. I'm surrounded by the clan and have no one to ask.

Then there's the new invisibility power that's been plaguing me for weeks. At first, it was only when I was frightened that the power would snap over me, but then

I did it on purpose to follow my brother into the gateway that ended up being the portal. The power makes me a freak; from what I can gather, it's an unheard-of fae gift.

I know I'm not invisible at the moment—my shadow dances on the opposite wall as the flames flicker in the hearth—yet they pretend I don't exist. Mixed with my strange new magic, this makes me feel like I'm slowly going mad. Invisibility would at least explain their ignoring me.

I hop from foot to foot, wanting to scream, "Am I real? *Am I real?* Why won't you see me? Speak to me?" Most of the time I'm too confused, too busy trying to survive, and too hungry to care. My tummy whines a protest, highlighting that thought, and I shuffle towards my mother.

"Can I have a plate? Mother, please don't be mad. I'm sorry I was missing. I made a mistake." My voice squeaks at the end.

Things can get strange when she pretends not to see me, and when she finally does, she gets upset and sometimes cries. Thanks to my absence, somehow it seems worse this time. Everyone is eating, and they all ignore me.

I reach out a trembling hand and gently, ever so gently, touch her arm. My mother turns her head and looks right through me.

Her eyes are glazed.

For a moment, I see a spark of recognition in her dark green eyes, and then it's gone with a blink of her lashes.

She dismissively flicks her hand and growls, "No, not tonight."

Not tonight? Head down and with my heart breaking, I creep back to my corner like a whipped dog. Everything I feel right now is too big and too confusing. I don't understand. No one else looks at me as I slide against the kitchen wall, inching my way towards the door.

As I slip out, I grab the tatty hand-me-down coat I'd rescued from the bin two years ago. It's still two sizes too big, but it keeps me warm and almost dry from the rain. I leave. I close the main curved door behind me for the last time.

"I'm not running away," I mumble into the wind. Going back to another realm is dangerous, but I'm quick and smart. My life will be easier. I'll blend better on Earth as I'm more human-shaped. I'm at an age where, if I try, I can pass as a local and learn the language. I'll be safer there. And I like the sea.

The autumn rain soaks into my hair and trickles down my back. I tilt my head to wash away the tears from my dirty face and slink into the night.

CHAPTER
ELEVEN

I SNAP BACK from the memory. Gosh, that was twenty years ago. It shouldn't hurt anymore, but it does. Most of the time I'm reactive. I deal with things when they happen and try not to think about my past. Putting the pieces of my life together hurts even now. As an adult, none of it makes sense, and it hurts more than a punch in the face, more than a broken wrist. I keep going, one step at a time, mostly numb to the world around me and doing my best not to hurt anyone.

The sometimes troll in the magical bubble, always running away yet going nowhere. *What a mess.* All I want is to forget and, in turn, to be forgotten.

I guess fate has tired of me ignoring things.

I focus back on what I was saying, shooting Forrest

an apologetic smile for zoning out on her. "I grew up when I realised nothing I did would ever be good enough. Trolls are long-lived. We stay in our clans until we are at least fifty years old. Fifty is seen as a human young adult. I left the clan when I was eight." The wind whips my words away, and I try to smile.

We are both quiet. The silence stretches between us like a heavy, weighted thing. The lump in my throat is painful, and my chest burns with repressed sorrow. There are only so many times I can bury this pain inside.

Do I feel better vomiting out this secret? No. I feel icky, itchy, and weird. Like I've lost something precious. It seems I'm not a sharing type, and I've embarrassed myself.

"Have you had any DNA testing?"

I lift my eyes from the ground and stare at her.

Forrest tugs a datapad from a holder against her thigh. "I can test your blood now. To get you answers and find out once and for all what type of creature you are."

"You can do that? You'd do that for me?"

"Yes. We only need a drop of blood from your finger." Forrest's voice drifts off, and she squints. "Ah, shit, I'm sorry. I can be rude sometimes. I missed the peopling part of growing up."

Me too, Forrest, me too.

"I don't know your name. I'm Forrest."

I don't bother to tell her I know her name from my

earlier eavesdropping and offer instead a tiny smile. "Pepper, Pepper Sterling."

"Okay, Pepper, you ready to give this a shot? Are you going to let me help you get answers?"

I glance around, grab hold of my courage, and nod. "Okay." *Please don't hurt me.* I drop my magic, step toward her, and present a trembling finger.

"As I work for both realms, the datapad is linked to the Creature Council here and the fae system. If it's bad news, I can wipe any trace of your blood result from the fae part of the database before this thing updates. Put your finger there." She points to a small dent at the bottom.

I place my finger on the pad, and a microneedle zips out and takes a drop of my blue blood. The datapad lets out a happy chirp, and Forrest nods that she got it.

I move away.

The datapad then makes a series of beeps, and Forrest raps her fingers on the sides of the device. Her expression is closed off; she could be watching paint dry instead of unlocking the secrets of my life.

"Doing this might not be a good idea," I mumble. I spin on my toes, pace, and dig my fingers into my hair. I feel useless.

Waiting for a piece of tech to tell me where I fit into this world. What was I thinking? It's only been forty seconds, but it feels like an hour. What will the results say? I could be a stolen child and no one in the clan is related to me. This is a horrible idea.

I lean against the seawall's curved metal railing and tap the bottom rail with my boot. The temperature has dropped, and dark clouds are rolling in from across the sea, telling of a storm to come. *I should have layered on more clothing.* The wind blows between my jumper's fibres. The purple top offers little protection from the cold blasting at my skin.

When this is done, I need to eat and persuade the beithíoch to leave so I can have the place to myself and get some more much-needed sleep. Passed out sleeping doesn't equal quality rest. I'm alive. I can fix anything if I'm still breathing.

Whatever the result of Forrest's DNA test, family is what you make it. I need to remind myself I'm not responsible for the clan's poor decisions or their treatment of me. I was just a kid.

The concrete vibrates under my boots, and tendrils of magic come from the tarmac. The tarmac's magic drifts around my waist. I smile and rub the stupid wetness off my face. Both are lending me their strength.

"It's okay. I'm okay," I murmur. I can let things drag me down, or I can love myself, forgive the haters, and get my revenge by living a good life.

A wispy ball of light decides now is the time to mess with me. It zips towards me like a pesky fly. I peek under my lashes at Forrest. Thank fate, her head is down, and she doesn't see it. I lift my hand to block it from smacking me in the face, and for what must be the millionth time, it disappears when it touches my skin. I rub my fingers together. The ball doesn't leave any residue. I don't know where the light goes or what it is.

I frown and rub my hand on my jeans. The wispy lights always find me. They've done it since I was a kid. I put the phenomenon down in the column of my mind and marked it off as weird shit.

Some days, there can be hundreds of them. Some are wispy, some solid bright white, others grey, and even a few black. It doesn't feel like magic. It's a mystery. Like my invisibility, it must be linked to my other half. Perhaps the clan is right, and I am cursed.

Behind me, Forrest lets out a hiss.

"What?" I turn but don't move towards her. I can't. Fear has me in its grip. I'm rooted to the spot. I can't feel the wind. I can't feel my limbs. I'm like a Pepper lump of stone as I stand here.

"You're a full troll."

"I am?" I'd crumple to the ground if I weren't frozen solid with fear.

Datapad in hand, Forrest stalks towards me. "Parents are named Bree Brennan and Noel Brennan of Clan Brennan of the Autumn Court."

Whoa, that's my mother and her mate. For as long as I can remember, I've called him my mother's mate or my brother's father. He is my father. They *are* my clan. Why? Why then, if I was their child, did they treat me like I didn't exist? Why ostracise me when a simple test could have proven who my father was?

Oh heck, this is anticlimactic. I frown. I didn't think

it was possible, but this information hurts more. I grimace and rub my chest; if I were a half-breed, it would explain so much. But this—the test result—leaves more questions than answers in its wake.

"Is that your clan?" Forrest's intent stare over the datapad meets my frozen gaze.

Jerkily, I nod. "I don't use the clan's name as they never named me."

Forrest's eyes lose their compassion and softness, returning to a dead-eyed stare. Anger rolls off her, and my stomach tightens. I take three steps back until I'm stopped by the railing.

"Sorry." She raises her hands in placation, and her brow pinches in worry. "They never named you?" she whispers.

I shrug. "I named myself."

"What the hell is wrong with some people?"

I don't know. "So is it normal?" I wrap my arms around myself. "My DNA? Does it have any anomalies to explain why I'm different?" Why they didn't lo— I close my eyes.

"Pepper, these tests are basic." She waves the datapad. "They identify heritage but aren't set up to deal with more details. At least you know you are a full troll, and you now have your parentage." She takes in my expression. "Are you okay?"

No. I shake my head and take a deep breath. "What the elves said, is it true? Does it say in your system that I'm dead?"

Forrest bites her lip and presses the screen. She takes a few seconds to pull up the correct information, and when she lifts her eyes to mine, her bright yellow eyes crinkle at the corners with sympathy.

I brace myself. That's answer enough, I guess.

"Yes," Forrest states softly.

Wow. Something horrible happens to your sense of self when your clan hates you so much that they tell all the realms you're dead. *They said I was dead.* "Okay, so the elves had the correct information. Oh well. That's it then." My arms flop to my sides in defeat.

What did I expect? To the best of my knowledge, they never looked for me, and before I even left, they had registered me as dead.

It's okay. I don't need them. I don't need them or anyone. I don't even want them in my life.

"I can send someone to speak to them," Forrest says, righteous anger for me in her voice. "Pepper, at the very least, what they've done is fraud."

"No." My eyes almost pop out of my head, and I wave my hands frantically. "Please, please don't do that." Being rejected is soul-destroying the first time. I can't go through that again. "I don't want anyone else to know about this mess."

Perhaps my mother didn't want a girl? Or there was a baby that had died, and she got me? Stop it. I snarl at my inner voice. If you can't be kind, shut the hell up.

"Do you want a copy of the results?"

"Yes please." I rattle off my email address. I might not

be able to access it yet, but it will wait until I finally can. "Thanks, Forrest." I can't help the bitterness in my tone; I want to go back to being oblivious.

She gives me a chin lift and a small smile, puts her datapad away, and passes me a slip of paper. "It's a number for my friend, Tru. I won't be around for the next few days, but if you need help, ring her."

Again, I don't explain I won't be ringing anyone; I haven't got a phone. I take the number and slip it into my pocket. "Thanks," I mumble with a small smile.

I want to ask Forrest about the slave rune on my arm and see if she can remove it or if she knows anyone who can. She seems knowledgeable enough, and she's powerful. But I've already said way too much and am horrified; I can feel myself falling into the deep dark hole where introverts go when they overshare. I feel sick with embarrassment.

"Take care of yourself." She squeezes my elbow, and then she stalks away.

And now it's too late to ask.

I watch her go, my request for further help lodged in my throat. The words will not come out. And there it is, a once-budding friendship destroyed by my trauma dumping. Forrest can't wait to get away from me.

Head pounding, I watch until she disappears down a side street. I feel like a fool... If I'd just opened my mouth to ask. I shake my head. "Well, that's it then."

The little hairs on the back of my neck stand on end,

and I spin on my heel to see a flash of movement on top of the pier building.

Uh-oh, where did he come from? I'm so surprised I scramble backwards, trip over nothing, and land on my bum. I wince as I crack my tailbone.

The metal building shielded him from my stone magic, and he must have been concealed by a Don't See Me Now spell. He leaps and lands with catlike grace on soft feet.

I scramble back to my feet and try not to skitter away; instead, I lift my chin as he approaches.

Corbin moves like the tiger he is. Each step is careful. Rhythmic. What is he doing here? And why can he see me? I groan. I didn't recloak myself after the DNA sample. His eyes narrow at my chattering teeth, and he pulls off his coat and throws it over my shoulders.

"You don't have to."

"You are freezing," he growls. "I could hear your teeth from the top of the pier."

"Thank you," I whisper.

Corbin grunts an acknowledgement, helps me with the sleeves, and then zips the jacket all the way up to my chin. My eyes land on his lips. The coat is still warm from his body heat, and I catch his scent on the fabric and... The tiger keeps hold of his jacket as if I'm going to steal it —or disappear.

This now doesn't seem so wholesome or sweet. *Uh-oh*. The tiger has been here the entire time. "Well, this is a nice, fun get-together. What's happening?"

"The elves wouldn't talk. They wouldn't explain why they'd tracked you through the gates." *Oh.* "You are a dangerous, unknown, illegal creature in our realm. The charms and power you possess." The hint of his tiger growling is in his voice's cadence. "You're a contradiction. You live in an abandoned subway with no winter coat"—he grips his coat tighter, pulling me closer, and breathes in deep, scenting my skin—"yet you have a bracelet with a few million pounds' worth of charms."

I gasp in shock. *A few million pounds' worth of charms?* Oh, bloody hell. "In Faerie, the elves confiscated my stuff. So I took a bag." I lick my lips and wince when the hellhound raises a cop eyebrow at what is now a confession of theft.

"A bag of charms?"

"Yes, and some other stuff."

He grunts and shakes his head. "Did you admit that to Forrest in your little speech? That you're a dirty little thief?"

I shake my head.

"No? What lies were you telling her when you were invisible, and how did you trick her into conversing in secret?" He is way too close, his fist gripping the jacket, preventing me from maintaining a respectful distance.

"She came to me," I whisper.

"Something is seriously wrong with you," he says with a low growl. "Pepper Sterling, you are under arrest for illegal magic use and entering the Earth realm without the necessary paperwork." He continues with his cop stuff, but I'm stuck on his words. *Something is seriously wrong with you.* Why does that hurt so much?

"What?" I blink at Corbin as he finishes his rant and pulls out a strange plastic band. He wrestles me for control of my wrist and slaps the band down. I watch it wrap around, and... my connection to the stone magic is *gone*. No! It's a dreaded null band. I let out a small whine of fear and try to wiggle from his grip.

But everything is going hazy.

"Don't fight it." The tiger strokes my hair while my knees buckle. *Not again.* He's going to hurt me like the elves did. "It's okay. I will keep you safe. I need to find out what you are hiding."

Safe? "Liar, you're killing me." I whimper as tears swim in my vision, and as I fight the null band's power, my body convulses. My head cracks against the tiger's biceps, and I bite my tongue without meaning to.

"You're going into shock. Pepper, stop fighting." Blood dribbles from between my lips. "You leave me no choice." Wetness splashes against my neck accompanied by the lavender scent of an expensive sleeping spell, and then nothing else exists.

CHAPTER
TWELVE

My consciousness reaches for the stone magic, and I hit a wall. I have no access to my power, and the uneasiness of the situation brings me fully awake. One by one, memories of what happened trickle into my mind. I'm alive—always a good start.

I'm also warm and feeling stuffy.

I move my head, and a label scratches against my chin. I frown and angle my face away from it. I'm still wearing his coat; it's twisted around me with the zip digging into my back, and my arms are wedged against my sides. *Nice one.* I must have been wiggling around like a worm to get so wrapped up.

"I know you're awake," says a gruff voice above and behind me.

Corbin.

I freeze and hold my breath to listen. He's really close. Is he inside my cell? My eyes fly open, and... *Oh.* They widen as I take in the cream ceiling and the dark leather sofa I'm sinking into. It has to be the softest thing I've ever lain upon—if I ignore the zip of the coat. I don't know what I expected, but it wasn't a living room, a home rather than a hunter holding cell.

Gosh, I'm hot. I blow out a breath, and sweaty strands of hair cling to my dry and tight face. My eyeballs feel like they've been popped out, rolled in sand, and stuffed back into my head. The heating must be on—I'm not used to it, and it feels like I've been lying here steadily boiling away in the tiger's jacket for hours.

I wiggle. If I don't get it off soon, I will pass out. I need to get it off! Above me, there's a low, exasperated growl.

"Sorry. Am I not getting out of the kidnap coat fast enough?" I grumble. The fabric flips over my head and buries me, muffling my words, but I think Corbin gets the gist.

He responds with a soft snarl. "Let me help you. Pepper, stop moving. You are making it worse."

"Some people get sweets or puppies before they are kidnapped," I snark as I wiggle more.

"Some people wake up naked and chained to a basement," Corbin snaps back as he grabs hold of my wriggling legs. Under the coat, I gasp. "Not on a settee. Shit, I didn't think how that would sound," he quickly adds as his enormous hands snatch at the fabric. The jacket whips over my head. I wince when he takes a handful of green hair along with it.

Free at last, I scramble to sit up and point a shaky finger at him while the other hand rubs my sore scalp. "Ha, so you admit to kidnapping me then." I don't know why I sound so smug. Perhaps overheating has rotted my brain. I drop my hand when Corbin's dark blue eyes widen.

"I admit to no such thing." The tiger is horrified. I must have dinged his manly pride. "I didn't kidnap, abduct, or whatever else you have going on in your pretty little head. I'm a hellhound, not a common thug." He squares his shoulders and folds the jacket across his arm. "I arrested you, and you're here for your own protection."

I scowl. "Arrested. So where are we then, Mr Hellhound? Why here and not at the hunter headquarters? Huh?" I cough and rub my dry throat.

Corbin hands me a glass of water, and I drain it dry. "For your protection," he repeats as if I didn't hear him the first time.

My protection, yeah, right.

I sigh, rub my temple, and none too gently put the glass down onto the dark wood coffee table. The clinking sound stirs a memory of the beithíoch's bowl scraping the tunnel floor. Eurus! I hope Eurus is okay. I'm glad I fixed it so he isn't trapped in the tunnels, but now I'm worried he won't be able to find anywhere to hunker down if he leaves and can't get back in. What a nightmare.

At least it was one way of getting rid of him. I chuckle to myself. Mother Nature, I'm a miserable person.

Corbin has put his straitjacket away, and then he hovers above me. He's wearing the same clothing as when he arrested me, so I can only hope not too much time has passed. Hopefully, we are still on the same day.

"Where's Forrest?"

"She's busy."

"Yeah, I'm sure she is." Damn it. I opened up to her and told her things, things I wouldn't even allow myself to think about. All those secrets leaked out of my mouth. Was her kindness and help all a pretence? Was she only helping me, keeping me in one place to draw me out, to allow the tiger to ambush me? I thought Forrest was trying to help, to be friendly. To be my friend... Or am I just a job—something to handle? My head thuds on the back of the sofa.

Hurt bubbles in my words. "Did she set me up?"

"No. Forrest didn't know I was there." A wariness flashes across Corbin's face—fast, but I catch it—and he rubs the back of his neck.

Looks like I'm not the only one stressed; I let myself sink back into the leather. It really is a lovely sofa. I'm relieved that Forrest didn't dupe me. Thank fate, she didn't screw me over, and from the worry in Corbin's eyes, I think Forrest would kick his head in if she had any inkling of what he'd done.

My lips twitch, and I check my wrists; the charm bracelet and evil null band are gone.

"The null band made you convulse, so I removed it."

"Oh. No wonder I feel so rough." I rub my red wrist. "So why can't I feel my magic if the null band is off? What, does it take a few hours to get back to normal?" I meet his hard blue gaze, and my heart jumps with fear. I don't understand. "Why can't I feel my magic? Did the null band do permanent damage?" As I continue to rub my wrist, the sleeve of my favourite purple jumper moves, and it's then I spot the black marks on my skin. Bruises? I push the sleeve higher and gape.

It's not a black mark or a bruise. No, it's another rune. I push the sleeve past my elbow; look at that, the slave rune has some friends. A horrified, strangled laugh rips between my lips as I see dozens of runes all over my forearm.

"What did you do?" I whimper. What is it about creatures jumping out of the woodwork and wanting to own and control me? Runes are expensive, and chanting a rune to life takes some knowledge and skill. Unfortunately, you don't need a drop of fae magic, which is why the tiger was able to put them on me. "What the fuck did you do!" I lose my temper and slap my hands on the sofa.

Corbin rubs his mouth, and his voice drops an octave. "The runes will stop you from going invisible or using your magic, and they won't come off without my say-so."

I rip up my sleeve back up and drop my eyes back to

the nasty runes on my skin. I'm so mad I can't look at him. "Oh, so now *you're* the slaver."

"No. I'm not a slaver. I help people. I'm helping you."

"Yeah, real helpful. You are such a nice guy. Yay, what a hero." I pull a face, give him a thumbs-up, and continue to stare at my arm. I don't know what they mean. "Is that...?" Lighter than the others, it's almost faded. I don't know where I've seen the mark before, but the sight of it pricks at my memory, and in seconds, I know what it is. "Is that a death rune?" I stare at it in shock. "You put a death rune on me." This just gets better and better.

"I didn't put a death rune on you, Pepper." The tiger steps around the sofa and gently takes hold of my arm. "I wouldn't do that. This rune here?" He points at the mark. "It wasn't there when I placed the others."

"Yeah, like a shifter knows what he's doing. So it just appeared on its own?" I shake my head, and my lip curls, flashing stubby, wonky tusks. I snatch my arm away from his warm hands. "What in the fairy farts is wrong with you? My only defence is my magic. It's my sole protection, and you steal it from me and slap on a death rune. What a horrid thing to do. You... You are a bad person."

"I'm not a bad person, Pepper. I'm trying to keep you safe."

"I never asked for your help, *Corbin*." I say his name with a sarcastic edge. If he can keep throwing my name around in a lame attempt to manipulate me, I can do the same. I know what he's doing. It's psychological manipulation, trying to persuade me he's some trustworthy guy and that he's listening to me. It's giving me the creeps.

I'm shaking so much, and my breath sounds so loud in my ears. I turn onto my side, sink into the cushions, pull my knees to my chest, and then hide my arm. All these runes and just a few days apart. A slave mark, a handful to block my magic, and as a bonus, a death rune. This is just great.

I lick my lips; fear has whipped whatever spit I had from my mouth. This isn't fair. I don't deserve this.

Bloody Corbin, I liked him. I found him handsome. I liked him so much that I went googly-eyed on the prom long enough for him to slap a null band on me. That is me begging so much for male attention that the first handsome guy I meet, the first drop-dead gorgeous guy I talk to, and I lose all sense.

A hellhound, no less. I really should choose who to crush on more wisely.

Perhaps this is a sick joke. I pull out my arm, lick a finger, and rub. Nothing good will come from these runes. I shiver and rub harder—the tiger huffs. It's not coming off! The runes are real. Of course they're real.

But what does a hellhound know about runes anyway? *I can't take his word for it that my magic is blocked*. It might only feel that way. And they might only stop my stone magic. No one understands my other power.

I need to try. It's important. I need my magic to stay safe. Cutting me off from my power hurts me. There's a nagging emptiness inside me. I should be more powerful, and my magic should be more potent than these stupid runes.

I didn't raise myself to be a quitter. I owe it to myself to try.

With a nostril flare, I grit my teeth and pull on the magic to cloak myself.

CHAPTER
THIRTEEN

NOTHING HAPPENS FOR A BREATH, and then, like a flash fire, unseen flames scorch my skin. I thought I was hot before. "My arm! My arm is on fire!" I scream. My cries echo around the room as I flap my burning arm, drop the hold on the magic, and hit the floor with an *oof*.

"Ouch," I groan.

The tiger growls above me.

Yeah, yeah. "I didn't damage anything," I grumble. The flames were under my skin, and I still feel like I'm smoking.

"Except yourself. You hurt yourself. Why would you do that? They are powerful *fae runes* made especially to control you. Don't do that again."

"So that is what it feels like, being tased and set on

fire at the same time. It was lovely." I huff and try to get up.

I'm bloody stuck between the sofa and the wooden coffee table, on my back, wedged. And the runes have done a real number on me. I flop around like a fish when I try to get up again. This is beyond embarrassing and entering the kill-me-now territory. I can't get up. My limbs are rubbery. "Meh, the floor is not so bad."

With a disgusted grunt, Corbin nudges the table away with his massive thigh, unceremoniously scoops me up, and drops me back on the sofa.

I tremble and hunch into myself.

He rubs his face, and his eyes have a forlorn expression of a man regretting his life choices. "Would you like another drink? I need a drink. Coffee?"

I haven't had a hot drink in forever. I like tea. The sweat on the back of my neck makes me question having something hot, but my lips and throat are still dry. "Tea?" I rasp.

Corbin nods and heads off to the next room—to get away from me—into what I presume to be the kitchen. He turns at the door. "Milk, sugar?"

"Just black please." Awkwardly I wait. This entire situation is so strange. If I ignore the horror of the freaky, power-controlling runes and forget that he knocked me out with a null band that made me convulse—oh, and that he kidnapped me and boiled me alive with his jacket... Suppose I ignored all that, I'd feel like a welcomed guest. "Why is it so hot in here?" I shout. Might as well act like a welcomed guest.

"The null band made you cold."

Oh. My stomach flips. He left me in his coat and cranked up the heat because I was cold. It's a shame he didn't notice my face going bright green with the heat. "Is it possible to turn the heating down? Please?"

Is that something he can do? I've never had access to heating before—besides the radiators inside public buildings and the ones in the schools. It's not like even invisible customers or students get to mess with the controls.

"Sure" comes his gruff response as the kettle clicks.

I have to bite my lip to stop from saying thank you. I'm sure there's an unwritten rule that you do not thank your kidnapper. Right? Or perhaps you do. Will it make it harder to hurt or kill someone who has manners? I don't know... My eyes flick around the living room to a window. I want to see where we are but keep my bottom firmly planted on the sofa. I don't think he'd appreciate me moving about.

The place is fancy, designed like a hotel. I hear the pouring of water and the clink of a spoon. A few moments later, the tiger returns with two steaming mugs. He places mine on a drink coaster on the coffee table and settles himself in the chair opposite.

"Thank you." Internally I groan—*nice one, Pepper*. I guess good manners can't hurt, and maybe I need to stop winding him up. I've never been so chatty. Am I enjoying talking to Corbin? It seems I am still fangirling.

Corbin leans forward in the chair, his hands dangling between his widespread legs. The expression on his handsome face is shadowed with determination.

Oh, here we go.

The tiger hasn't even given me time to drink the tea, and here come the questions. My being unconscious must have really messed with his timeline.

I pick the tea up to hide behind. "Why did you put that horrid null band on me?" I blurt out.

His dark blue eyes gaze back at me with a shadow of concern and a big wallop of guilt.

"You didn't have to do that. No matter what the elves have led you to believe, I'm not a criminal. You've seen the slave rune, right? Well, they did that to me. If you'd asked, I would have come willingly."

An incredulous look rolls across his face, and the guilt is replaced by a smirk. The smirk makes him achingly handsome, and my brain short-circuits for a second. "No, you wouldn't. You would have run the first moment you could. Little thief."

Damn that bag! I can feel my cheeks throb, radiating a furious blush of dark green. "I wouldn't have run," I mumble into the cup. *I so would have.* I've seen the datapad footage when creatures have defied a hunter and got themselves seriously messed up. And that was a hunter. Do that with a hellhound? No way. That's a good way to end up dead. If I had known he was arresting me, I would have scarpered. Run for the hills.

"Anyway, you've got no room to talk. You stole my tunic."

Corbin's face is static. "I collected evidence. There's a difference."

"Oh right. Well, that's okay then if my personal property was *evidence*." I tap the cup. "Do you really think I'm a criminal?"

"I'm only interested in what I can prove."

Diplomatic. Okay. I nibble on my lip. I should shut up, but I can't help myself. "You're a hellhound." Hellhounds can do whatever they want, it seems. "Why are you behaving like a hunter? Isn't dealing with fae troubles far below your pay grade?"

"I have autonomy in picking what I do." He stands and opens a window.

Oh, thank the Mother. A breeze! A breeze, that's great.

"How long have you been creeping around, spying on people?"

My mouth pops open. "What?" I sputter. "I don't creep around"—much—"and I'm not a spy."

"There is something more going on with you. You are a mystery that I want to solve, and I'm intrigued." He sits and hits me with his cop face. "You're dangerous." He leans forward, picks up his cup, and takes a gulp of coffee while watching me intently.

All this time, I've presumed he's a good guy. What if he's working with the other side? I've enjoyed talking to him, bantering back and forth, but now it all feels way too real. Dangerous. I didn't sign up for this hellhound crap. Even without the runes keeping me visible, I'd be in deep doo-doo.

The tiger sits there. He isn't twitchy. He's relaxed but looks ready to act, and he's not the type to get caught unawares. So no boinking him on the head and running away. What a shame.

"So are you holding me here for the elves? Is that why you brought me here and why you didn't tell Forrest what you were up to?" My voice is thin and wobbly. "Before I met you, I'd been unconscious for a time. After chatting with the elves, I got away, healed with a potion, and passed out. You just saw the tail end of what they did to me. The broken wrist." I sit forward in my seat. I'm not too proud to beg if it will keep me alive. "Please, Corbin, don't send me back to them."

He stares at me as if I've gone mad. "I'd never send you to those animals. If it were up to me and Forrest, they'd be dead. I'd rip them apart. As it is, the Lord of Winter has been informed, and for now you are under his protection."

The Lord of Winter, I mouth. I'm floored.

This is bad. Really, really bad. Fear floods me, and my hands tremble. "I-I am? W-w-why? Why would Madán" —my voice cracks—"the lord of the aes sídhe warriors, help me?"

Madán is a warrior elf, the top, scariest warrior elf.

"Surely you're not that naive."

I don't like the patronising look Corbin gives me.

"He's not helping you. Why would he? Don't think he's doing this out of the goodness of his heart. He's not." Corbin adjusts his cup. It must be frustrating to have such gigantic hands. "What you can do is unusual and very useful, and he wants to ensure you're not a threat. Pepper, I don't have to point out to you that you're in an awful lot of trouble."

The Lord of Winter wants to control me. Welcome to the club. Let's hope he doesn't also like *exotic* bedmates.

I make a *pfft* sound. "I'm fine, I'll be fine. I can look after myself, and I'm not a threat. Me? A threat." I laugh painfully. "You know if I could just go home, you'd never have to see me agai—"

"If looking after yourself includes being held by elves, tortured, and escaping with a slave rune, then yeah, you're doing great." It's his turn to give me a thumbs-up.

I scowl at the big oaf. The tiger is a dick.

"You can be completely invisible and still interact with the world. Plus your stone magic is remarkable. You're an unknown threat. We use and control threats, or we eliminate them."

Eliminate them, nice. "You told all this to your boss, the Lord of Winter?"

"I didn't tell him. I was sent out to find you." They sent him to find me? I put the tea down and sit back on the sofa. "The elves were not circumspect in their hunt for you. He saw the CCTV footage of the gate and when you cracked the paving stone. Also from the night on the promenade when you rescued me."

I wince.

"Your actions put you here. Anyone with an ounce of understanding of magic would know you are special."

Special, yeah, that's great. Aren't I an extra-special snowflake? I wiggle and draw my socked feet closer, wrapping my arms around my knees. *They are powerful fae runes made especially to control you.* That's what he said before. I move my arm to the side, and the runes peek from under my sleeve. "Madán gave you these runes." The tiger doesn't even have to nod. "So I'm here 'cause you made a deal with the Lord of Winter. You sold me out. Why couldn't you have just left me alone?"

"If I let you go now, the elves will grab you. They won't stop. At least this way, you have a chance," he gruffly says.

"Why does it matter to you?"

"I'm going with my gut. You need help, and I'm going to help you."

"Yeah, only because you're getting a big pay cheque. You're not helping me; you are like everyone else—you're only helping yourself." He's no better than the elves. "I was wrong about you."

The sound of traffic comes from the open window, and the curtains rustle in the breeze. Thinking my legs might be steady again, I drag myself to my feet, and Corbin doesn't stop me when I pad across the room and peek out the window.

I blink.

We are in the middle of a city I've never seen before. "Where the heck are we?" I whisper, pressing my cheek to the glass.

"Sligo."

"Sligo? As in County Sligo, Ireland?" A different country. Wow. My stomach flips, and I turn to face him, my back against the sill. In this realm, I've never been out of the one town, and now I'm in Ireland.

Ireland.

I glance about at his place with fresh eyes and realise this isn't, in fact, his home. I was right when I thought it was designed like a hotel. It's a bloody suite. I feel a little stupid. Why did I think he'd take me to his private space?

"How can we be in Ireland? How can you be here? Aren't shifters banned?" The fae aggressively hold the entire country. Since a long and bloody war, Ireland has been strictly human and fae. It is one of the safest places for humans to live. Shifters and vampires don't come to Ireland if they want to keep breathing. Then the answer hits me. The west of Ireland, with its beautiful beaches and rolling hills, is Madán's domain. His territory. "This is bad, very bad."

"You're safe here."

"Safe." I slap at the runes. "Yeah, right. So safe. I'm in the Lord of Winter's territory. In *fae territory*. I don't think you quite understand the feelings I conjure with them." I might be a full troll, but I'm still a freak, and now, with these runes, I can't disappear.

Corbin shrugs. "I told you what you need to know. You are under his protection." He clears his throat. "Under my protection."

He smoothly avoids answering me. "But how are you here?" I ask again.

"You didn't think all hellhounds live in your tiny holiday town, did you? There are other places that need our help, and we gate to where we are needed."

"I've never met another hellhound."

He looks at me as if I am an idiot and shakes his head.

"So you are a mercenary."

"No."

I don't believe him. I turn back to the view. I'm stuck. If I leave, the elves will find me. I sure did a lot of bleeding while in their company, and it doesn't take much blood to work a tracking spell. Not for them. They will track me down, and without the hellhound's protection and my magic to hide behind, I'm a dead troll walking.

CHAPTER
FOURTEEN

"WHAT WERE YOU DOING IN FAERIE?" Corbin asks.

I tut and firmly keep my lips shut. I've had enough heart-to-heart chats to last a lifetime, and I've decided that telling anyone about my business gives them ammunition to use against me. I've seen it play out time and time again. The more information you provide, the more people dislike you. Creature nature is shocking but not complicated. Talking to people and interacting with the world is pointless and... painful.

Yes, it might be very unhealthy to have no friends, but why bother when no one cares about you, not really? All anyone cares about is themselves. Having said all I'm going to, I pad back to the sofa, sit, and fold my arms.

Corbin gives me a look of pure frustration. "Don't,"

he says on a warning growl. "Don't you dare. You can wipe that stubborn expression off your face, little thief. I don't want to make you answer me. But I will." He rubs the back of his neck, and his biceps bulge with the movement.

The tiger is not playing around; his cop face is back and at full force. I wiggle in the chair. "I just want to forget about everything, go home and be left alone."

"The runes will make you talk."

Oh great.

"I'd rather not use them. Answer the question, *Pepper*. What were you doing in Faerie?" He bites his back teeth, and the movement tightens his jaw. I'm guessing he doesn't want to hurt me, but he's a hell-hound, and that's what they do. They are killers, and what's one little troll?

I lick my lips and hold my elbows tight to my chest. The pain I felt before was no joke. The phantom pain still sears across my nerves. I never want to go through that again. Okay, here we go, some more truth. "I run messages."

I'm the messenger. But he doesn't need to know that. "I run messages for creatures who live on Earth. Most were born here but still have family in Faerie. They don't have gate codes, and even if they did, they are at risk of getting caught."

Trust me, no one wants to get caught. The portals might look unguarded, but they're heavily monitored and spelled.

You can't find a portal on Earth unless you know exactly where to look. They don't advertise them with big signs. Rich people can have them in their homes, but that's rare, and they need a lot of nasty magic to keep uninvited creatures out. That's why I was so frightened I'd got the wrong code the last time I used the portal. Killer wards are there for a reason.

Faerie, it's a little easier as the gates are out in the open, but they are in dangerous places. Places with creatures that you don't want to cross. The gate I use is in my old clan territory, and if I got caught, no questions would be asked; they'd just rip me apart.

For some reason, the gateway doesn't record my passage when I cloak myself, and I can slip in and out undetected. That has nothing to do with the gates, everything to do with me and the odd magic hidden in my blood.

Well, unless rabid slaver elves are tracking me.

The local fae leave messages with Tilly, a dryad who owns a coffee shop. The dryad emails me a form the client completes with the terms and the fee details, and then it's up to me if I take the job or not. I'm careful creatures on this side of the lines never see my face. I pick up the messages from the café. Near the back door, next to the toilets, there is a drop box. The system has worked well for years.

With the gateways and vastness of Faerie, I only travel to Autumn. I have trusted creatures that will take the messages to the rest of the realm. It pays a lot, and sometimes it pays very little, but you try telling a brownie no when they must announce the birth of the first male child of a generation.

They might pay in favours, which is why I have a hundred years of service washes at the launderette. I feel like I'm contributing to something greater than me. It's good for my soul, and it keeps me busy. I don't want for much. I have everything I need. Well, I had everything until the elves jumped me, branded me, and stole most of my stuff.

I realise I've been quiet, and I smile sheepishly.

"You're a messenger?" Corbin is frowning like he doesn't believe me.

I shrug. I don't care if he believes me or not. What does it matter? Who is he to me, apart from my kidnapper? "Yes, I'm a messenger, and the last run seemed normal enough until it wasn't." I guess somewhere along the way, I dropped the ball and made a mistake, or it was just plain bad luck that the elves caught me.

"That's how the elves got you. They hired you?"

"No."

He lifts an eyebrow.

"Oh, I don't know." I shrug and throw my hands in the air; my palms hit my thighs with a slap when they land, and I shake my head. "It would explain a lot."

I've been cocky. The invisible messenger will take your message to the other realm for a nominal fee. I'd done the job for years and gained attention, and the elves, well, it looks like they found out about me.

"Perhaps they set me up." Maybe they saw an opportunity, and as I delivered the message directly, I got myself caught. "I don't know. No one sees me; everything is done electronically, and I'm cloaked when I pick up a message. The message this time was for a troupe of pixies in the Autumn lands."

It was a straightforward message to deliver and was supposed to be a quick in and out.

"No, I don't think anyone sold me out. It was just bad luck. The pixies hadn't known who I was. I'd drop my cloak to give them a verbal message"—no sound comes from me when I'm all cloaked up—"and the pixies got their message. It was all normal, and they wanted to return a message. While I'm there, I usually do it for free. It was a simple thing. The elves passed by just as I was finishing up.

"They grabbed me before I could react, not that I'd be able to do much. I'm not a fighter. They knew I was a messenger but didn't know my power level"—I lock it down tight—"or that my messages were from another realm. I was frightened, and I kept my mouth shut." Mostly. I made the mistake of telling them about my clan.

Corbin taps his thumb under his chin while intently watching me. If he were in his tiger form, his tail would be swishing. "And the message?"

"What type of messenger would I be if I told you?"

He sighs. "Do you keep any information from your runs?"

"No, nothing." Nothing for him to see, nosy tiger.

Corbin grunts. "Do you want some food?"

"No." My stomach whines in protest. I pull a face and stare down at my belly, *shut up*. I hunch over and cross my arms in a poor attempt to cover the sound.

Corbin shakes his head, and without asking, he gets out a datapad and orders what looks like a load of food. Then he goes to the kitchen and returns with a bowl and a can of something.

"Start on this." He rotates the tin so I can see the black label. Oh wow. A deluxe can of pineapple. It's bribery I can get behind. With a flick of the wrist, he holds the pineapple like a high-class sommelier with an exorbitant bottle of wine. His grin is smug. I give an approving nod, and the can opens with a burst of sweetness. He tips the fruit rings into the bowl, all 435 grams of deliciousness. Yum. Corbin hands the bowl to me, followed swiftly by a fork.

"Thank you." I spear the pineapple and stuff my mouth. I groan. I don't know how I'm going to go back to my usual brand. This fancy black-label pineapple is to die for. The tiger is watching in fascination. I don't know what's wrong with my eating. I swallow and this time, take a small, dainty bite. He looks away, but I catch the twitch of his lips and a barely hidden smile.

When the food comes and he eats, I will stare at him.

"Now I've answered your questions. Will you let me go?"

"No."

"Why did the Lord of Winter give you the runes to hold me?" With my fork still in my hand, I shiver and brush my fingers against the death rune.

"I don't know. Elf magic is beyond me. How do you get the jobs?"

His questioning is giving me a headache, and now the last bite of pineapple tastes like ash in my mouth.

"They leave the job with a contact, and the contact emails me with the terms." There, that's simple enough. I don't want to sell the dryad out. I put the empty bowl and the fork on the coffee table.

"Show me." He hands me a datapad.

I push it away with a glare. "No. I delete them."

He thrusts it into my hand, and when I refuse to take it, he slaps it down onto my knee. It wobbles precariously. "Log on, Pepper. I want to see if you've had any more messages, maybe from the elves. Log on." Corbin gives me a look that screams *or else*. He really is a mean man. I snarl. I bet Forrest would smack him in the face with it.

I'm not Forrest. I sigh and move the datapad closer, hiding it against my chest so he can't see my password. I log into the system I use to check my mail. Three messages. One from Forrest with the DNA results. I roll my eyes at the second one, block the sender, and the message wizzes off to the junk folder. It was from my non-existent child telling me they were stranded and needed cash to get home.

The last email is from the dryad. Tilly's messages are

always encrypted. The encryption on them is simple and easy enough to remove, but the clients like that we treat their messages as important.

Corbin's datapad doesn't have the necessary stuff to turn the message into a readable format. But I'd linked the translator software to my message account, so that isn't a problem. The subject line is usually very simple, but this time it has the words *urgent run, big payday* and quotes a number that's triple what I usually get.

Hmm, that's not suss at all.

CHAPTER
FIFTEEN

Before I can click it open, Mr Impatient snatches the datapad out of my hand. "Oi," I grumble.

"Forrest did a DNA test on you?" he murmurs as his big fat tiger fingers tap the screen. "What did you delete? Ah, I get them too. They also call me mum." He looks over the datapad and grins—my heart pitter-patters like crazy. The man is seriously breathtakingly hot.

I push down my attraction and glare at him. I bet he's sent himself a copy of the DNA results. Even with his threats, I shouldn't have logged in. I wiggle in the chair and pick at a hangnail on my middle finger.

The nosy tiger continues to go through all my old emails. I'm not a violent person, and until recently I've wished no one serious harm, but if I could get away with it, I'd love to at least punch him in the nose.

"What does this code mean? What does this email say?" He points to the screen, tilting the datapad ever so slightly towards me. "It's encrypted."

No shit, Sherlock.

I don't even try to read it. "I don't know," I say as I tilt my head back and stare at the ceiling. That light fitting is lovely, and I quite like the pale colour. It's so different from the red bricks at home.

"How do you not know?" he snarls.

"Well, if someone hadn't grabbed the datapad out of my hand, I might have been able to finish reading it. Rude cat," I snarl back. Using the datapad to bludgeon him to death sounds quite good right now.

He hands it to me. "Fix it and tell me when and where the pickup is."

I click on Tilly's email and tap the correct button. To annoy him, I hum and rhythmically tap the sides of the datapad as I wait—the lines of gobbledygook whorl, letter by letter, then turn into readable text.

Corbin growls.

I smile smugly at the tiger and drop my eyes to read.

We know what you are, and if you want to discuss the terms of your surrender, pick up our message at the usual place for further instructions. If you do not appear, we will kill the dryad. You have twenty-four hours.

My smile drops off my lips, and I gasp. Are they really doing the old "your colleague will die if you don't do what we say" thing? I click the green button at the bottom of the page, and message delivery terms are accepted. "Shit." I drop the datapad onto the sofa. Corbin grabs it midbounce and reads the email.

Arm over my head, I grip the back of my hair and take in a deep breath so I don't scream. *Oh no, what have I done?* I should have told her, warned her. She should have been the first person I told. I went out shopping and never thought of speaking to her. Instead, like a selfish idiot, I looked out for number one. My only option now is to hand myself over, and somehow, I'll need to get past the tiger.

Without access to my magic, I'm powerless.

But I don't care. Tilly can't get hurt because of me; there is no other option but to do what they say. In my head, I'd put the dryad firmly in a colleague category of my relationships, but now I think about it, she's worked herself into the cracks of my psyche and, without my knowing, became my friend. Being my friend has put her in danger.

"The elves will kill your friend if you don't surrender," he mumbles.

I jump to my feet, ready to head to the door. I need to find my boots. Frantically, I search the floor.

"Pepper? Pepper?"

He must have been calling my name for some time.

I glance up at him. "Have you seen my boots?" Of course he has. He took them off me. "I need my boots."

"You don't need your boots."

"I do. My friend needs me." *My friend.* What have I done? I'm freaking out, and I can't find my boots. The evil bastards are going to hurt Tilly, and I can't find my boots.

He gently takes hold of my forearms. "You aren't going anywhere. You need to sit down."

"But Tilly—"

"I will get someone out to your friend to do a welfare check on her. These elves are more than likely bluffing. You need to calm down and let the professionals deal with this mess." His voice is cajoling.

I focus on his warm eyes. "You promise to send someone to keep her safe?"

"Yes, a welfare check."

"She won't be in trouble for the messages?"

"No, she won't be in trouble. Brokering messages to pixies and lower fae is not a crime. Crossing the realms without the paperwork is, and you should be more worried about yourself."

"But she's the one in trouble. The elves—"

"So are you," he says with a low growl and a light squeeze of my arms, pushing me to sit back down.

"But they hurt people." I drop my voice to a pleading whisper. "I don't want them to hurt Tilly." The memories of what they did to me are a recent horror that make me shiver.

"Pepper, do you not understand your situation? *I* hurt people." He doesn't say it but implies he'll hurt me if I push this.

"But you're not like them. You're a good guy. Right? You are a nice person." I blink up at him.

The heat of his hands bleeds through my jumper, and his thumbs brush against the fabric as he sighs. "No, I'm not a good guy. I do what I'm paid to do."

"Like a policeman, a hunter?"

He shakes his head.

I frown. "So I'm not under arrest? You really kidnapped me?" I can't believe my words. He's a good person, right? He's just a little rough, like you would be when dealing with creatures that need a hellhound.

He lets go of my arms and tucks a wispy green strand of hair behind my ear. "You're a naive little thief. You shouldn't believe everything that you are told." His voice is rough and unkind. My lower lip trembles, and he looks away. "Do you want more pineapple?" He heads to the kitchen. His voice is sad, but when he turns, his expression is shut down and blank, and his eyes have lost their sparkle.

He has the dead-eyed stare of a killer. I don't know if that's a mask to protect himself or the real him.

I remember a quote by Maya Angelou: *When someone shows you who they are, believe them the first time.* Even with the threats and the kidnapping, I chose to believe he is a nice person.

Do I want more pineapple? "No, thank you." Even

pineapple will not fix this mess. I sit, head in my hands, and my left leg bounces with the need to run.

He comes back from the kitchen with two more steaming cups. "So where do I pick the message up?" He waggles his phone. "I promise to help you with your friend if you tell me."

"You've promised already. Ring them, and then I'll tell you. Tilly owns a café in the centre of town." I rattle off the complete address and nod at his phone.

He scowls and leaves the room to make the call. "John, I need a favour. I've got an issue with some elves, and I need a welfare check on a dryad—" A door down the hall slams, cutting off his words. I fidget. Let's hope this John can help.

The elves' twenty-four-hour countdown had already started when they emailed. Ticktock. Corbin has left the datapad on the sofa. I drag it towards me and check the timestamp on the message. It was sent two hours ago at noon, so the deadline is tomorrow afternoon. That's not so bad. But the time frame means they've had plenty of time to grab my friend.

The message, or in this case their directions, should already be in the box. But Corbin doesn't need to know that. I need to use this information to my advantage. If Corbin thinks I must pick the message up myself, perhaps I can find an opportunity to escape.

"Okay, that's done. I've sent a buddy to check on your friend. When and where do I pick the message up?"

"Tomorrow morning at ten. I must go, and I need to go alone."

"The hell you are—"

"If I don't go myself, we'll never get the message. That's how it's set up. I'll bring it straight to you."

"You better," he growls.

CHAPTER
SIXTEEN

After eating—he ate; I pushed the food around the plate—I thought we'd go back and prepare for the imaginary meeting I had lied about, but no. It seems we are going to see the Lord of Winter. He wants to speak with me, so it looks like my day is about to get worse.

The tiger guides me down the hallway with his hand on my lower back. "Do we have to use the lift?" I eye the metal door with distrust.

A teeny-tiny electric-powered box. I know it's somewhat hypocritical as I let the stone magic suck me through walls, swallow me, and move me about, but I shudder at metal. On the other hand, it is something I can't control, and it's bad for my health.

"Yes." Corbin presses the call button.

"Great." I bounce from foot to foot. If it were made entirely of silver, you'd bet we'd be using the stairs. The doors open with an unhealthy grinding sound, revealing a box the size of a wardrobe. I gulp. I'm sure the floor dips under our weight as the tiger helps me inside. I close my eyes as the doors whoosh shut. My stomach dips, my head spins, and it is the longest thirty seconds of my life.

When the doors open, I rush out, and Corbin, seemingly not even picking up his pace, is still beside me. His heavy hand finds my waist again. His fingertips guide me through the hotel's wide glass doors and towards a white car with a green hire sticker in the window. A car, really?

"I don't do cars." My hand hits the neck of my jumper, and I scratch the skin I can reach.

"Are you deliberately being obtuse, little thief?" Corbin opens the passenger door and shoves me inside. He waits for me to settle and then slams the door closed.

"I don't do vehicles!" He walks around the outside. I continue to gripe when he gets in next to me. "I've never been in one before."

"Yes, you have. I brought you here in this car from the portal."

I grind my teeth as I glare at him. "All right then. *Conscious.* I've never been in a car while I've been conscious before. Creep." I finish with a mumble, scratching my left leg, which is closest to the door.

"Seat belt."

I give him a confused look. He gives me a sceptical look. With a sigh, the tiger twists his bulky frame, and with an impressive amount of dexterity and manoeuvring, he leans across the controls and pulls the seat belt across my body. He smells nice. I watch as the fabric pulls tight, and the metal end clicks into the plastic holder—seat belt, of course. I've seen them before in films.

The tiger settles back in his seat. There's the click of his seat belt, and then he twists his hand, and the car growls to life. It moves. I let out a squeak and grip the edge of the seat, my nails digging into the fabric. I don't know what I fear most: sitting in this car or going to speak to the Lord of Winter.

The tyres thud, thud, thud against the road, and next to me the door and window ever so gently vibrate. I eye the door, not trusting it will not fly open, and I bum shuffle away. I bet it would go unnoticed by most passengers, but I can feel the wind outside, the movement echoing and pushing against the metal frame and plastic panels of the vehicle. I swallow and turn my head to gaze out of the window, and the world whizzes by in a blur of colours and shapes.

Corbin's communication skills are lacking. He has not said anything after the demand to put on the seat belt. In dealing with me, the tiger has reverted to grunting. I move, he grunts. I squeal, he grunts, not saying a word after he bundles me into his death trap of a car. In strained silence, we drive. The tiger is a skilful driver and leaves space between this car and the one in front. His hands, strong and capable, confidently guide the wheel through the labyrinth of streets.

If I'm pointing the finger, I have to admit my communication skills aren't any better. Instead of demanding to know where we're going like a normal person, I keep my mouth shut and sit in the passenger seat in an anxiety-driven haze. My body is stiff as a board, and my muscles are beginning to protest. With a face of pure misery, I let go of the seat and twist my hands in my lap to get some feeling back.

If I kick up a fuss, Corbin might shove me through the nearest portal to Faerie and be done with me. We could still be doing that, but why would Corbin bring me to Ireland if we were just going to Faerie? He wouldn't.

My self-enforced silence doesn't stop my internal monologue—which is on the fritz—from screaming and silently freaking out, repeating *this isn't happening* over and over again, to worrying about Tilly. Nothing I've seen so far in my life has prepared me for this. I watch other people. I don't join in, and I don't have the skills to deal with what's happening now.

I'm so confused.

I side-eye Corbin. I like him. I really like him.

When the tiger broke the elf's wrist in what I thought was retaliation, my silly heart did a little pitter-patter—as if breaking someone's arm was romantic and not messed up. Then the same guy, who I like, the man I'd convinced myself was a hero, *arrested me* and, to control my magic, slapped on a null band, then power-stealing runes, and now he is throwing me on the mercy of his boss. The boss, Madán, who is the scary lord of the aes sídhe warriors.

My lower lip wobbles, and I swallow the stupid, girlish lump of attraction in my throat. Yeah, the best and safest thing I can do is shut the hell up. Go back to watching life pass me by.

I. Do. Not. Trust. Myself.

A handsome face and I've lost my ever-loving mind and all common sense.

I fidget with the unfamiliar belt that hugs my frame and digs into my breasts. Everyone says Madán is generous and kind and has done sooo much for the fae living in his court. They make out he is such a benevolent lord. *Yeah, right.* No powerful man with the Lord of Winter status is kind. Powerful creatures don't do things out of the goodness of their heart.

No, they do it to control the masses. They do things to earn alliances and favours. They gift things that are worthless to them but everything to the gift recipient, and that's it—the giftees, their lives and loyalty, are bought. Bought for a bargain price.

We leave the main stretch from Sligo and go onto narrow, winding roads until we reach the coastline. I watch in awe as the scenery shifts and the landscape transforms. Green hills surround a sandy inlet with just a few loose stones. The seawall here is almost non-existent compared to the one at home.

Peeking between thick trees on the left, I see glimpses of the vast expanse of the sea stretching out to meet the horizon, the wild Atlantic. The setting sun makes the deep blue sea shimmer. It is beautiful. Breathtakingly beautiful.

Corbin turns the car into a driveway, the sound of the tyres changes to crunching, and the solid wrought-iron gates ahead make me cringe. Iron. Those babies are dangerous. The skin on my neck and arms begins to itch in earnest as the nose of the car stops near them.

A buff-looking vampire steps out of a guardhouse and peers through the window. The tiger nods, and the vampire eyes me suspiciously, then nods back, waving us through the opening gates, revealing a grandiose driveway lined with ancient oaks.

This must be Madán's estate—his home. It feels oppressive. The wards surrounding the house and the grounds are impressive; the power sets my teeth on edge. I blow out a breath and swallow my fear as the car approaches a big fancy house, and the tiger parks. The house is old. The back of the building must overlook the sea. It's probably built on a good bit of rock and has been standing here for hundreds of years. I can also see a peek of an iron perimeter fence. It isn't just the heavy gates that have fae-killing power.

Not so benevolent, after all, is our Lord of Winter. And I don't know what he is thinking; prolonged exposure to iron can harm even him.

Corbin sighs and gets out of the car. His door clicks softly shut as he prowls around the front of the vehicle.

I click the seat belt off, and beyond that, I can't seem to move.

Madán. I huff. I should call him the Lord of Winter in my head. If I slip up and call him by his first name to his face, I'm dead. I bet for my insolence, he'd make my skull into a candleholder.

Corbin opens the passenger door, and I climb out on wobbly, stiff legs. "Lord of Winter, Lord of Winter," I mumble under my breath as I grab the doorframe with trembling hands to keep from stumbling.

"Are you okay?"

I shoot the tiger an incredulous look. Um, is he taking the piss? As if he doesn't know or smell my hurt, confusion, and fear.

"Am I... okay? No," I whisper harshly. If I could spit green flames from my eyes and set him on fire, I would. "No, I'm not okay." *Arsehole.* I'm far from *okay*, but I don't say that. Now that we're here, anything I wanted to say to him has passed. I can no longer control who is listening. I peel myself from the car door and slam it closed.

Corbin grunts and ignores my angry, whispered words. The cool, calm tiger takes my vitriol on the chin, and not for the first time; I wish I'd ignored the stone magic and stayed in bed that night. I wish I'd never met him.

I follow as he makes his way to the front door. He's confident I won't run. Otherwise, he'd be behind me. The six steps leading to the black Edwardian-style door are like climbing a mountain. With each step, my soul cries out. I feel like I'm missing a vital part of myself; the runes locking my magic down tight make me feel like a huge part of me is missing. I can't feel anything: the ground, the stones, the carboniferous limestone of the house. The modern hotel wasn't so bad, but being here is torture.

The door knocker is a troll's head with a huge ring coming from its mouth. Corbin knocks and, without waiting, opens the heavy door. He gives me a nod of encouragement, waving me to move ahead of him and inside.

I stare at him blankly, refusing to go first. With another grunt and a roll of his dark blue eyes, he steps inside.

The house is gorgeous. It has a substantial double staircase right out of a period film or heritage postcard. I creep over the threshold, and the wooden floor creaks beneath my hesitant steps.

The hallway is in various shades of red. I frown. No, perhaps more burgundy than red. The deep colour should be garish, but it is not. It's rich-people fancy. I glance down at my old boots. Maybe I should take them off? I don't want to track in my filth.

Corbin has continued down the hall a few strides ahead of me. "Pepper," he says softly like he's talking to a prey animal that will bolt. "Come on, you're okay."

What he doesn't say is that I'm safe. I'm not safe, and the tiger won't be watching my back. He'll be looking after his boss. And then the tiger does something to make my heart go all squashy again—holds out his hand. I don't know why, but I shuffle forward and take it. The heat of his hand engulfs mine.

"You're freezing," he grumbles.

Yeah, my fear has turned me into a block of ice, and I was shitting myself, but with his hand in mine, *now* I feel safe.

Stupid. So stupid. I smile bitterly, and even as I feel like a fool, I cling to him as if he is a safe harbour in a storm as he guides me to the back of the house and to the Lord of Winter.

CHAPTER
SEVENTEEN

I GRIP CORBIN'S HAND, and his sleeve rises as my other hand curls around his wrist. The oak door in front of us opens on silent hinges, and my anxiety spikes. I hide behind his bulk. I'm filled to the brim with fear and my entire body trembles.

The tiger makes no sound as he prowls into the room, pulling me along. My boots squeak as I brace against his thick, corded forearm, the soft hairs prickling against my skin. The room smells of vanilla and clove oil. When the door to the office clicks closed behind us, I jump.

Panic hits me in waves, threatening to send me to my knees.

I can't do this. I want to go home. I want to go home!

Corbin acknowledges the elf with a rumbling greeting. I can't hear his words over the ringing in my ears. Each breath I take rattles in my chest, and my eyes swim with frightened tears.

I'm out of control.

One step at a time, Pepper. I can do this—*one step at a time.*

First, I need to steady my breathing so I don't pass out. The only problem is breath control isn't my thing— I tried it before in a long-ago teenage meditation phase, and if I try, I'll make myself worse. I wince. Meditation either makes me giggle or hyperventilate.

Instead, I give my brain something else to think about. I take in the room, one exit behind me. Windows. The office looks out onto a perfectly level lawn, like one of those infinity pools you see on the datapad reels, but with bright green grass instead of water. Grass that sharply drops away till all you can see is the sea. I bet there's a hidden fence and a path you can walk to the beach.

If I had my magic, I'd know. I'll never get my magic back if I keep on acting like prey in a room with two predators. Anger flashes through me, beating down my other emotions. My breathing slows as determination fills me.

I *will* get my magic back.

I tune back into the conversation to see the Lord of Winter's eyes narrow at our clasped hands. I let go, but Corbin doesn't. Holding my hand safely in his grip, he leads me towards the big wooden desk Madán sits behind as if the elf is a businessman and not one of the Faerie rulers. I dig my boots into the thick carpet to stop my momentum; I don't think the tiger even notices the extra drag.

Influential, powerful, older fae. Madán, the Lord of Winter. I only know about him from his reputation. He's been in this role for about five years, after killing his predecessor in a bloody battle. The rumour is he had help from a silver dragon, which must be nonsense.

Enormous pale blue eyes and pointed ears betray him as a full-blooded aes sídhe, a warrior elf. His black hair is shiny and long, styled into the usual elf-style intricate plaits. The style makes the blond elf leader look like a poor imitation and not just the hair. Comparing both elves together is like comparing two different creatures. The aes sídhe warriors are something else.

Black fae warrior markings like human tattoos start at his right hand and disappear underneath his shirt to lick up his neck and fan under his jaw. They link him to his court and give him crazy powers. I'd expected Madán to be suited and booted, but he's not. He is wearing black combats that fit his lean, muscled form like a glove. It is a surprise he's so casually dressed. But it shouldn't be. The outfit hints at his proud warrior heritage. It's not that I expect him to dress up to meet me, but I thought he might for his station.

No wonder Corbin likes him. If you ignore his pretty face, the elf is down with the peons. Where Corbin is rough and handsome, the Lord of Winter is beautiful, a deadly, delicate beauty.

The worst kind of evil is wrapped up in pretty packaging.

"Hello. Pepper, is it?" he says with a musical Irish accent.

I nod. Madán is so closed off, his power so tightly controlled, that to me, while I have no magic, he feels human. Scary.

Scary, scary man.

He indicates with a pale hand for me to sit. "Thank you for taking the time to see me. Please take a seat."

Yeah, like I had a choice.

He's watching me as intently as I am him. This is weird. So weird. This meeting is all so ordinary, yet we all know it's not. The entire exchange is unequal; we all know he's trapped me. I shouldn't be polite. Yet I must tamp down the urge to scream and rage. Out of fear and pure self-preservation, I keep my mouth shut, and whatever I feel, I hope to keep it off my face. I can't react.

"Would you like something to drink?"

"No, thank you," I rasp.

"Did the runes work?" Madán asks over my head.

Corbin grunts. He lets go of my hand and pulls out the offered chair, nudging me to sit. Without the tiger's warm hand in mine, I feel adrift.

"Good. That's excellent." The Lord of Winter's attention turns back to me.

I robotically sink into the chair, perch on the edge of the seat, and politely fold my hands on my lap.

"Did you try to use your magic?" he asks.

"I did. It hurt." It hurt a lot.

"Quite." He stares down at me, his eyes taking me in from head to toe like he is appraising a prize cow, a cow he finds lacking. Almost nervously, his finger runs across the desk, tracing the wood grain. "I have been told a recent DNA test appeared in the system for you. In direct contrast to the results, both your biological parents claim you're a fraud, dead, and want nothing to do with you."

Yeah, yeah, I've heard all this before. If he is waiting for a weepy response, he'll be waiting a long time. I sit there like I'm made of stone.

Internally, I sigh. *This is all your fault. Your bad choices led you to this very moment.* A hellhound at my back, the Lord of Winter at my front, both men analysing the micro-expressions that flitter across my face.

What was I thinking, jumping between the realms with pointless feel-good messages? None of this would have happened if I hadn't chosen to be a messenger, if I had kept myself safe. Easy money has a way of biting you on the arse. Why didn't I get a safe job working online? That's honest work. Why didn't I get a position walking dogs or working in a supermarket?

I know why.

Corbin keeps snidely calling me a thief, but I've never been a thief by choice. As a kid, I had to steal to live. It was that simple. But after a while, I didn't want to live off others to feed myself. It always left a weird, nasty taste in my mouth. Pride. I guess pride is my sin.

I had to buy food when the schools closed for the holidays, and even though the world we live in doesn't care about starving children or slave labour, people would have talked. They would've wondered why a child needed employment, and that would have made me a target. There's a big reason creatures and humans are tucked into their beds at night and there are no homeless. Monsters eat them.

Hiding in plain sight and playing the messenger with the dryad at the coffee shop was an ideal solution. It meant I had a good income for a kid, and when I grew up, there was nothing else I wanted to do or could do. Invisible children don't get certificates of education.

I realise Madán has asked a question and is patiently waiting for an answer while I've been stuck in my head. I wince.

"The runes are making her dim-witted," he mutters. Madán continues to look at me, a curious expression on his face. "Perhaps I shouldn't have used so many to contain her magic. I must have miscalculated."

Perhaps the mysterious death rune is bleeding me dry, killing me slowly. It feels like it. I adjust my arms, and my nails dig into the flesh of my forearm and into the runes. I've been an independent creature for as long as I can remember. No one has told me what to do. Never. Being trapped by the runes makes me want to chop my arm off in the hope I'll regain my magic and while still bleeding pull all the strength from the building and surrounding hills, then make a sinkhole where His Lordship and the tiger will disappear without a trace. *So sad.*

Losing patience, Madán leans forward in his chair, and a blast of his power hits me. A wind whips across my face, so cold I wonder if ice will flutter from my lashes when I blink.

"Tell me," he says. "Do you know what you are?"

The chair is hard, and the wood digs into my thighs as I stare at the elf in disbelief. Is that a trick question? I must stop myself from dropping to my knees and searching under the desk for a hidden big buzzer, the one which he'll press when I get a question wrong. Is he starting with the easy ones first?

My face is chilled from his blast of power, and my jaw aches. "I am a t-t-troll."

Where is he going with this?

Madán sits back, smugly satisfied, and brings his boot up to rest on his knee. "No, you aren't." And with those three words, he drops an explosive red spell on my life. "Maybe at conception, but you've never been a troll. I never thought I'd meet one of your kind. It's so rare. But it seems someone messed up your transformation." He looks down his nose at me.

Transformation?

"Tell me, girl, do the strange lights always follow you around?" He nods at the dozen lights bouncing off me like annoying flies. He can see them then?

I wish I couldn't. I've been ignoring them since I woke up at the hotel.

The tiger moves next to me. "What lights?" he growls.

"The runes, your runes, are stopping them from doing their thing." Whatever that is. Ever since I got the runes, they've been unable to sink into my skin. "Will you remove them? Please?" *I feel like I'm dying.* I finish in my head.

"Interesting."

So that's a no *then?*

"What lights?" Corbin asks again.

Madán raises his eyebrows. "Ah, you can't see them. Don't take it personally, dear boy. Few creatures can. I can see them, and I'm guessing anyone with a touch of my power will also be able to. It was a long-ago gift that I continue to pass on to my warriors." He smiles at me while tucking his hair behind a pointed ear. "It must be annoying for them to keep bouncing off you like that."

"Yes," I grumble. Annoying is putting it mildly.

"I know what the pretty lights are. Would you like to hazard a guess? No? All the information I'm about to give you is freely given. They aren't magic. Well..." He wiggles the foot on his knee and tilts his head. "Not conventionally so." He sits back in his chair, folding his arms across his chest as if he has all the time in the world. "They are souls."

"Souls?" both the tiger and I say at the same time.

Madán drops that information bomb as if he is

talking about the weather. His eyes never leave mine. His lips twitch, and his voice changes to a lecturing tone. "You are one of Death's rare chosen. I never thought he'd take a fae, least of all a troll." He sneers, then chuckles. He can't seem to help himself from looking me up and down. "It looks to me as if you've only been transitioned halfway, enough to rip you from your clan, convincing them of your death before birth, but not enough to move you to the training stage—a pity."

My words come out stilted. "The *magic* convinced the clan I was dead. It was all because of magic?"

He taps the arm of his chair. "It's unnecessarily cruel. I'm guessing your early years were hard. Sometimes Death has a peculiar way of training his people. The threads of fate are only seen by him. Perhaps your soul hadn't learned a lesson, and the hardship of your early years might have taught you a valuable one. Perhaps empathy." He shrugs. "He also might have forgotten about you. He's very old. Ancient. You might be an easily rectified mistake." He smiles, his blue eyes cruel. "Death might just kill you. I don't know. You'll have to ask him."

Ask Death? Death, as in a person? Yeah, I'll just pop over to the other side and talk to him, no problem. "I'm not... I can't speak to the dead."

"No." That one word holds so much disdain, like he doesn't understand why he must talk to someone with such an inferior mind. "You aren't a necromancer, girl. You are death-touched. Tell me, does the invisibility magic that I've been hearing so much about feel like you're wearing a cloak?"

I blink.

"That's because you are. You're putting on a cowl. You naturally accessed a little of your magic, somehow." He flashes that smug, beautiful smile, taking great joy in the frightened and dumbfounded expression he can no doubt see on my face.

"Let me put it another way, Pepper. You're a *reaper*. A lost reaper. Who would have thought you of all creatures? I've sent a message to Death informing him of your existence, and I'm sure he will collect you soon."

Oh yay, that sounds grand. I think... I think I'm going to be sick.

CHAPTER
EIGHTEEN

WHOA. There's a name for what I am. A reaper. I'm a *reaper*—a half-transitioned reaper, whatever that means. Is that really a thing? I shake my head. A reaper with a cowl that gives me the power of invisibility and the power to absorb strange lights that I've learned are souls. *Souls.*

It's like I'm a portal for the dead. Even with my magic locked down tight, they still find me. Researching all this would be handy, as I've never heard of reapers as a race.

Perhaps a reaper is a breed of angel? But angels are born, not made, and Madán talks about a botched transition.

The Lord of Winter says a lot of things, and when a

lord of Faerie tells you to get your affairs in order, I guess you listen. Death is coming for me, and when he meets me, he might not like what he sees, and if he doesn't, he will put me down—like a bad pet.

It puts being hunted by the elves in perspective.

And it makes what Madán is doing with the runes all fun and games.

All the elves and all the aes sídhe have nothing on Death. How can I run from Death? I can't. Maybe Death is a senile old man who will continue to forget about my existence. Perhaps a blip in time for him is like oodles of years for me.

Madán claims all the information he knows is *freely given,* but you know you're in trouble when old, powerful creatures mouth off like that. I think he's angry, livid, that a lowly troll has got this curse, and I bet Death will owe him a favour for finding me.

His lost reaper.

Madán explains nothing else, not that I will ask. I'm in shock. He sits there all smug on his chair like it's a throne. Talking over my head to Corbin. The tiger is like a solid stone fortress at my back, and I just sit. Dumbfounded. I can't find any words. All the while, my previous angry bravo has dried up. I swallow, working my throat so I don't puke all over his desk, and my mind continues to pick holes in everything Madán has said.

I was a troll at conception, and according to the DNA result, I'm still a troll. So what did Death do? See me all warm in my mother's womb and kill me? Or did I die naturally, and he brought me back to torture and half-transition me into this thing? Is that Death's magic or reaper?

I must have died then as a baby as my clan had continued to insist. Death did his thing, and instead of taking me, he left me there to... what? Be a real-life ghost baby. Someone must have looked after me. My clan didn't forget me all the time. I must have had some care to make it out of the baby stage alive.

But if I was already half-dead, who's saying I didn't die a thousand times? No, that can't be right. I bleed, I eat, and I need sustenance to survive. What I do know is I am alive, I am here, and I do exist. I'm real.

None of this makes any sense, yet it explains so much. It explains a lot. To the creatures left behind, the reaper has never existed. It's like I don't exist.

I flop back, and my head bounces against the seat. Magic has a way of doing weird stuff. Being death-touched, the magic must muddle the brain, like the goldfish charm, but worse if it can stop relatives looking for their loved ones when they disappear into the realms as reapers.

My stomach flips, and I wrap my arms around my waist as I realise something significant and hugely obvious. *My clan doesn't hate me.* They didn't get a chance to hate me or love the person I am because magic made them forget. I take a deep breath that burns my lungs on the way in, and as the breath leaves my lips, it lifts the weight that had been on my shoulders. It is gone, just like that.

The pain-filled memories I can now see with new, experienced eyes, the hints of things not being quite right in their glazed eyes. The note of surprise in my mother's voice when she spoke to me, her tears and confusion. It wasn't rejection. It was powerful magic at work. Madán was right. What Death did was incredibly cruel not only to me but to my mother and my clan.

And... and I can't do a thing about it.

This is something I'm going to have to live with on my own. There's no magic wand to fix this even if Death took the magic away and they remembered me. I can only imagine what it would do to them to know the truth about how I grew up. I can't do that. It would break them. It would hurt them all so much.

What parent would want to know magic had made them forget their child? They had thought I was dead. They had grieved for a child, and for them to discover I'd been right there in front of their noses. Dirty, hungry... No, no. I can't do that to them.

That knowledge hurts something deep inside me, yet the validation that it was not my fault cracks the solid scar tissue inside my chest. It crumbles away, with a solid lump of pain clawing at my throat. I feel that lightness. I wanted the DNA results to prove I was a part of the clan. I am, and I have the answer to why I'm so different.

I've lived with this pain for so long. I could use the

reaper thing to get angry, fill myself with hate, or I can let it go.

For me, let it go. It takes more strength to forgive and to understand than to hate blindly. To give forgiveness even if they will never know.

Mother Nature, I pray that they never find out.

I wish, I wish I would have known them. Death has a lot of explaining to do.

"Is that why Pepper has a death rune? It appeared by itself," Corbin says.

"Let me see." The Lord of Winter reaches for my arm, and when I don't hold the limb out fast enough, he leans across and drags me almost across the desk. His slender fingers bite into my skin as he rips my jumper up and takes in the death rune. "Faded. Ah, it looks like he got my message." He lifts his eyes to talk to the tiger. "Death is tracking her. It shouldn't be long now, and the mark will get darker the closer he gets." His stiff fingers brush over the other runes, and he hums under his breath with sick satisfaction. That is until his eyes land on the slave mark, his fingers tighten in a punishing pinch. *Ouch.* "What is this? Who marked her?"

"The elves, the ones who hunt her."

"You let them put a rune on you? You silly girl."

I didn't *let* them do anything.

"Why didn't you tell me she'd been marked?" he snarls at Corbin.

"She kept her arm covered and didn't say a word. I

didn't know until I put the runes on her a few hours ago."

"Why are trolls so damn difficult?" Madán slams my arm on the desk, and before I can move it, he pins it down with his forearm as his index finger brushes over the slave rune. Power flashes in his eyes, and... he must be chanting an incantation in his mind. The slave mark burns, and I whimper.

Sensing a pending meltdown, Corbin rests his heavy hand on my shoulder. I shrug him off. I don't need his pity or his help. I grit my teeth as Madán continues to trace the rune.

We watch, my skin burns, and the rune fades.

When the elf lets go, I cradle my arm to my chest and slump in the seat, my body wrecked from aftershocks of pain. I'm exhausted.

But if the elf can remove a rune, then so can I. One rune down, a dozen to go. And now I've got an idea of what to do. I just need the counterspells to get them off me.

I want my life back. He doesn't even need to know. I've played the good girl, and I can play her again. I'm not trapped, just temporarily indisposed.

I drop my chin to my chest. "I don't feel well," I mumble. "Can you please remove a few of the other runes so I can breathe?" I let a bit of honesty creep in. "Without my magic, I feel like I'm going to die."

"So dramatic. No. I don't think I will, sneaky girl." He widens his eyes at me mockingly.

I bet he usually hides his personality better than this. I bet everyone thinks he is such a nice guy. Kind. If I turn, will I see confusion in Corbin's eyes? Or does he see the real man?

The door to the office flies open, and the handle cracks against shelves jutting out from the wall, hitting a well-developed dent in the wood.

"Madán, we have an issue," says a brown-eyed shifter at the threshold. I'd hazard a guess he's a wolf. Without my magic, I'm blind to my magical senses, but he looks like a wolf. Another shifter in Ireland, fancy that. The Lord of Winter is really breaking all the rules.

The man in question gets up from his chair. "All right, Mac. I am coming." He goes to the cabinet on the other side of the room and pulls out a dozen different weapons—sliding them into various holders on his body.

"See yourself out," he says to Corbin, then stalks out the door. The wolf, Mac, trails behind him down the hall.

After dropping a bomb on my life, he smugly walks away just like that, all the while rubbing his hands together and patting himself on the back for a job well done. I hunch into myself as we head out of the house and back to the car.

"You're quiet," the tiger says beside me.

I'm quiet, he says, as if I want to chat with the man who set me up—the man who ruined my life. Everything wasn't perfect before he came along, but it was better than it is now. Locked with runes, waiting for Death to get me.

"I'm sorry. That didn't shape up how I expected."

I keep my lips firmly closed. He isn't feeling guilty. I'm just a job to him. I get into the car without being told and put my seat belt on.

The other day, after my time with the elves, I said my life had hit rock bottom. A bitter smile pulls at my lips. Yep. I'd been mistaken. It hurts more when you've got further to fall.

CHAPTER
NINETEEN

"Pepper, I have lots to explain," Corbin says when we walk into the suite. Again, he's using that sad voice.

I refuse to look at him. "Is it okay if I sleep? I don't feel right," I mumble. It's not even seven, and my head is throbbing. It's been a hell of a day.

"Okay, little thief, we'll talk about this later." Corbin shows me into one of the bedrooms. It has an on-suite. "If you need me, my room is the one opposite. There are some clean clothes on the bed and shower stuff in the bathroom so you can freshen up. If you get hungry or thirsty later, help yourself to whatever is in the kitchen. Also, Pepper, I'm a light sleeper, so don't try to sneak out. It won't end well for you. We leave early tomorrow."

I nod, close the door in his face, grab the clean clothes off the bed, and head into the bathroom. I don't want to talk to him and don't care if it makes him uncomfortable. I don't like him very much right now. I use the toilet and wash my hands and face. Feeling broken and lost, I lean against the sink.

I wish we were going back home. I should have said I had to pick up the message tonight. I don't like all this delay while Tilly's waiting for help to arrive. I hope Corbin's friend John finds her safe and sound and that the slaver elves had lied.

I need to set the tiger on the elves, get these runes off, and find somewhere to hide out until Death gets bored with looking for me. I grip the sink. I can't even look in the mirror. The small bathroom is teaming with balls of light—no, get it right, *souls*.

The bathroom is teaming with souls. We are all squished in here together, and if I even wanted a shower, it would make me feel icky getting into the shower with them. I need to get this mess fixed.

What has my life become? I wonder if the elves know what I really am or if they think they are getting the mythical messenger. My lips twitch. Heck, they're in for a shock. I'm a reaper. *Surprise!* What did the Grim Reaper have in the stories? My fingers strum on the cold marble as I think. A scythe, a magical weapon to poke at them. Yeah, I'd like one of those please.

There is a *pop,* and I see black fur. Suddenly it's no longer just me and the souls in the bathroom. I let out a squeak of fright, my legs tangle, and I go down, ending up in the bathtub with a bang. The hotel's mini shampoos follow, boinking me on the head as I lie there dazed.

"Eurus!" I hunch and cover my mouth. *Oh no*, did Corbin hear that racket? When nothing happens. I lean forward, peeking over the rim of the tub. "What are you doing here?" I whisper. I can't quite believe Eurus came to find me.

The beithíoch wrinkles his nose and stares at me, but... Ah, I can't hear him. I haven't got the snail charm on.

"Sorry, the tiger took the charms when he kidnapped me." I wave my bare arm and tug up my sleeve to show him the runes. "Bloody blocked me from my magic. Hey, hey, wait a minute. How did you get here? I know you said you'd track me down if you wanted me, but... Eurus, did you Step?"

The wolf's tongue flops out.

I can't believe the beithíoch has that level of magic. I'm impressed. Very old fae, powerful fae, can Step. It is, in basic terms, magic teleporting. It's a rare gift, and I was led to believe if a fae Stepped, it had to be somewhere they'd been before. "Whoa, you're lucky you didn't end up in the middle of a wall."

Eurus shakes his head and gives me a wolfy look of disgust.

"Okay, fine," I lift my hands in submission, and my arm with the rolled-up sleeve squeaks against the bath. "I don't know anything." Things I thought I knew have been messed up, so why not that information too? But my head hurts with all that's been going on. "You have no idea, Eurus, what's been happening."

It looks like the beithíoch doesn't need any help to get in or out of the tunnels if he's been able to come to me in Ireland. He did say he'd be able to find me. He is one powerful wolf.

Eurus stands on his back legs, swipes his front paw on the handle, and the bathroom door clicks open. He wiggles his paw and then his nose in the crack of the door, then he shoves himself through, and he is off prowling.

Panic floods me. "Where are you going?" I whisper. "Eurus?" I slip and slide out of the bath and stumble into the bedroom. The wolf has gone into the hallway!

Eyes wide and heart pounding, I follow. I can't hear or see any signs of Corbin. I'm so worried he's going to catch us. Did the tiger leave me alone? The man probably thinks I'm useless without my magic, and he'd be kind of right.

The beithíoch is snuffling inside the other room off the hallway.

Crap, he's in Corbin's room! My bowels twist, and I let out another squeak as Eurus's head pops out of the door. He lets out a yip for me to follow. I shuffle across the hall and stick my head into the room. I gasp when I see his entire face deep in the middle of Corbin's bag.

Uh-oh. "Eurus, he'll be able to smell you've been in there." I grip the doorframe, my nails digging into the wood, and frown. There is something in the beithíoch's mouth. Eurus pulls his head out, and the thing makes a clinking sound as it knocks against the bag.

With shining, triumphant eyes, he pads to me and presents me with the charm bracelet, spitting it into my hand.

Ew. I ignore the spit, and with a grin slide it onto my wrist. "Come on. Let's go back to the other room before the tiger returns." I hurry back across the hall. Eurus follows me, and I gently push the bedroom door closed. The snail charm immediately heats against my wrist.

Ah, the feline pilferer absconded with you, Eurus grumbles in my head. *I harboured suspicions that he might and did forewarn you. I've spent the entire day in search of your elusive presence.*

"Eurus, I can't believe you came looking and found me."

Yes. I am hungry.

A laugh slips out. "I'll buy you the very best steak, Eurus." I lean forward and ruffle the fur on his head. "Thank you."

His face is as grumpy as ever, but his fluffy black tail wags, and he tips his head so my fingers can better scratch behind his ear. I oblige.

Tomorrow, I shall indulge my carnivorous cravings, and you shall procure a fine cut of steak. He licks his lips, and his tongue lolls out in a wolfy smile.

"If I can, I will. That is a promise. Hey, do you know

what to do with the runes?" Still scratching, I move on to his other ear and wiggle my forearm of runes.

He moves, and my hand drops to my side as he pads further into the room, heading toward the bed.

The barriers obstructing your magic are relatively simple to dispel, he remarks, his gaze sweeping across the room. *This den surpasses the inadequacies of that dysfunctional storm drain. It would be wiser for you to establish your abode here instead.* He rubs himself against a chair in the corner. *As for the book of runes within the metal box, it should contain the majority of what you need. Unravelling the counterspell for the runes impeding your* reaper magic *will pose a greater challenge, and the removal of the death rune is a formidable task. Only Death himself possesses the capability to eradicate it.*

My mouth pops open with a gasp. "Eurus, you knew! You knew that I'm a reaper this entire time, and you didn't say anything."

Of course, the beithíoch utters with a dignified sniff. *Do you take me for a mere pup? I am two thousand years old, child.* He narrows his eyes, fixing me with a scrutinising gaze. *Rest assured, I shall not unveil your secrets or highlight your imperfections. Such behaviour would be uncouth. I understand the delicacy of your stalled transformation, and there is no need to draw attention to any potential embarrassments.*

I groan and rub my face.

"What about Corbin?"

He's outside, talking into the box.

"Box?" Box? "Oh right, he's on the phone."

Come along, child. We possess the essentials you require. Let us proceed.

"Proceed?" I'm sounding more and more stupid every time I open my mouth, but I can't help repeating his words like a weirdo.

Should I leave with the beithíoch? Perhaps I should ask myself whether I trust Corbin enough to help me. I believe deep down, way deep down, the tiger is a good man. But he has a parade of red flags a mile long. He wouldn't have made me defenceless if he really had my best interests at heart, and it would be remiss of me to think he is doing any of this to help me. It's more than likely he's helping himself.

If I'm with the tiger, perhaps he'll watch my back until he gets what he wants, and there is a small possibility he will remove the runes blocking my magic after I rescue Tilly. Perhaps I can get the information myself out of one of the elves. They must know about runes to have a stack of them in a bag.

I might find Corbin incredibly attractive, but I know I'm just a job to him if I ignore his small kindnesses that make my silly heart ache. The only person I can trust is myself, and I'm doing a terrible job.

I'm done hiding, running. I think it is about time I fix this mess myself. At least I'd be doing something proactive instead of waiting.

Waiting to rescue Tilly. Waiting for Death to come and get me.

Bloody waiting.

I have two priorities: use the book and Eurus's knowledge to remove as many runes as possible, and save my friend.

I'm going.

"Wait, let me..." I turn on the television. It should mask the lack of sound from me not being here, and hopefully it will give us a head start. I then open the door, scamper down the hall into the kitchen, grab the box of pineapple pizza, and stuff a bag full of meat. A steak, some burgers, and some chunks of chicken should help Eurus's hunger pangs. "Okay, let's go." I scamper back into the room.

Eurus's paw touches my knee, and just as I worry about all the souls and if they will be able to find me again, the dizziness hits me. Whoa, I feel like I'm being magically dragged backwards through a hedge. The air around me feels as dense as stone, and my poor skin feels like it's getting sandblasted. I smell the sharp scent of ozone right before a storm.

And then everything stops.

CHAPTER
TWENTY

I open my eyes. We're standing beside my canvas bed. I'm home. Wow, what a trip! Stepping is even better than the portals.

"Thank you, Eurus." I place the pizza on the bed, drop all the meat into his bowl, and rub the weird goosebumps on my arms.

Fired meat is not so bad, the beithíoch says while shoving his head into the bowl and scarfing the food down.

Whoa, he's eating fast. "That's good to know." I smile, shake my head, and glance down at the pizza box. I need to eat. I've not been taking care of myself and haven't eaten a decent meal in days. Sick with worry, the thought of eating makes my stomach churn. Later. I'll try to eat later. I've still got so much to do.

Better grab what we need to remove these runes. I hurry to the shelves and find the medical kit with the book of runes inside. "Okay, Eurus, which ones?" I turn back with my hand hovering over the book and see the beithíoch in a wolfy doughnut on the floor. Asleep. "Eurus?"

With the book in my hands, I creep towards him. He lets out a snore loud enough to flap his lips. Stepping to Ireland and then back with me must have tuckered him out. I wince as I give him a poke. I feel horrible for trying to wake him up.

He wakes with a snarl and snaps at my hand, and I stumble back. "Damn it, Eurus, I need your help with the runes."

Impertinent child, recall that I mentioned the book of runes would remedy your situation. However, I never claimed expertise in their application. I am a beithíoch, not an elf. Allow me my respite. He covers his nose with his tail, and within seconds, he's out and back to snoring.

So what do I do now? It's only a matter of time before Corbin finds our ruse and comes hunting for me, and he'll be angry I gave him the slip. I swallow. Okay, I can wait for the beithíoch to wake up, or I can pick the message up, find out where those elves want to meet, and come right back.

Easy-peasy. All I have to do is walk into a café and get

a message from the box. Nothing can go wrong doing that.

The clock is ticking.

If I don't go now, the café will be closed for the night, and while I'm there, I can check on Tilly. She is always working. Then, when I get back, I'll have a crack at removing the runes. I can figure it out after watching the Lord of Winter.

I drop the book of runes back on the shelf and pause. If something happens and I can't get back here, is it wise to leave them out in the open? My hand hovers. Yeah, I'll take them and a few other things I might need in case things get hairy.

Layering up clothing to keep myself warm, I put on an oversized hoodie—the black fabric hits the top of my thighs—and replait my hair. I need to be presentable, after all. Feeling awkward, I tug the hood over my head to shield my face, and I'm ready to go. Being a troll isn't that unusual. The fae come in all types, and no one will bat an eye at my green skin. Yet I feel vulnerable. I've become lazy using my magic, always hiding myself away as it's easier.

If I could do it all again, I would have lived a more adventurous life, put myself out there, and made more friends. But if wishes were horses, I'd have a stable full of dreams.

I head into the tunnel. As we can't communicate, the stone is sluggish and unhappy in its response to me. It recognises me enough to help me leave, but it takes longer for me to rise into the night. Outside, it's dark. Troths of sea-foam catch the wind. The storm that was threatening earlier in the day has rolled through and left the night cold and damp. I wrinkle my nose, hunch, and stuff my hands in my pockets. Tucked under my layers is a small leather bag resting tight around my waist, holding the book of runes, some cash, and a few potions I dug up from my stash. None are of great quality, but they'll do in a pinch.

I hope I don't have to use them.

As I get closer, I eye a black-and-grey telephone box, and as I go to walk past, I stop. Patting my jeans pocket, paper crinkles, and with a sigh of relief, I pull out the number Forrest gave me.

This situation constitutes a need for help.

The phone box door is stiff and makes a horrible creaking noise as it opens. I get a big waft of urine as I shuffle inside. Gross. Gripping the number, I dig into the bag for some change.

I call the number.

I TAKE A FURTHER ten minutes to get to the coffee shop. The scent of cakes and coffee fills the outside air as people rush past. Café trading is drawing to a close, and the display for late-night shoppers that takes over an entire stretch of one window and is usually packed to the brim with treats is almost empty.

What's left is still mouth-watering to most people, and during daylight hours, I've seen many children press their noses against the glass.

The bell over the door chimes as I step inside. The subdued hum of quiet conversation mingles with the occasional clink of a teaspoon against a cup, the comforting aroma of freshly brewed tea, the rich scent of roasted coffee beans, and the heavenly scent of blossoms in full bloom.

A spelled tree clings to the ceiling. The big pink flowers bloom all year round, and the twinkling lights intertwined within the branches make the tree even more magical.

It's Tilly's tree.

My eyes scan the branches. Relief fills me when I see that the dryad's tree is perfect. The health of the tree reflects on the health of the creature tending to it, and Tilly's tree looks great. I know, looking at it, she is still alive. Healthy. Perhaps Corbin was right, and the elves were bluffing. I hope so.

Tilly had owned this café long before I came stumbling through the door, longer than I'd been coming to Earth. When I turn, I catch sight of the PENDING FOOD AND DRINK board on the far wall. I smile, and pure nostalgia fills me. The white receipts attached to the board flutter when customers walk past. I've eaten my fair share of meals from the generosity of that board. The sign on the board states:

If Any Person (Creature Or Human) Cannot Afford To Eat Or Drink, Please Pick An Item(s) That Someone Has Kindly Bought In Advance.

Tilly didn't say a word when kid me came into her café all those years ago. It was that first day in the realm, and ravenous hunger drew me inside. I had thought to come out of the cold and use the bathroom. I came in to smell the food. I remember not being able to speak or read English, and once I'd used the toilet, Tilly caught my eye.

In our language, the dryad had carefully explained what the board meant. I couldn't believe it. Who gave away food? When she asked me what I wanted to eat, I thought it was a trick, and I couldn't answer.

So the kind dryad took it upon herself to pull two receipts off the board. One for a drink and the other for a sandwich. She gave them to me with a soft smile. I'd run out the door with my prize so fast, worried she'd change her mind and take them off me. That sandwich filled my belly for two days.

When I left the clan and returned to the realm for good, it wasn't long before I learned about schools. The magic I embraced kept me invisible and safe, and I ate in their cafeterias. There was plenty of food, and most of the time, that filled me until the next day. One meal a day, I'd never eaten so well, and sometimes, if I were quick, it would still be warm.

Yeah, I ate like I was queen. Most of the time, I'd sleep in the school, and sometimes I'd go home with other children—me, the real invisible friend. Nobody knew, and all I needed was somewhere warm to rest and hide. I'd get a sofa, sometimes a spare bed or even a soft carpet to sleep on. I wasn't bothered as long as I was out of the way and didn't trip anyone.

It was fine. Good even. But I found it best not to eat their food. People seem to notice missing food more than the odd dirty towel.

Weekends were challenging, but school holidays were the worst. It was then when I had a problem. Yeah, Tilly's board saved me a time or twenty.

The dryad at first, when she realised I had no one, tried to get me a safe place to stay, but that was too much trust for me to give even to her. I was a feral latchkey kid and didn't trust easily—I still don't. I've seen with my own eyes what happens to grown adults on the streets. Trusting the wrong person is a death sentence.

But Tilly's kindness made me come back, and one day, I promised myself, I would have enough money to fill that board with receipts. No one should go hungry. When she asked me if I wanted a job, I jumped at the chance. She knew what I could do, and the guy she'd previously used as a messenger had gone and quit on her without notice. I think he probably got himself killed. But I didn't mention that to Tilly.

That was when I learned the dryads small cut of the proceeds went onto that board, and I've also tried my best to add to it over the years. I'm proud to.

Behind the counter, a girl expertly steams milk. The menu board, adorned with a handwritten chalk script, showcases an array of yummy sandwiches and tantalising desserts, from flaky pastries to indulgent window cakes. She gives me a tired smile. "What can I get ya?" I'm so good at hiding that even the staff don't know me.

"A pot of tea please."

"No problem." She presses the buttons on the till and takes the money.

"Keep the change for the board," I tell her softly.

"Thanks."

"Erm, is Tilly working?" *Please be okay, please be okay.* I angle my body and tilt my head to look into the staff area.

"The boss lady is shopping with some friends, although..." She glances at the big round clock on the wall with a frown. "...she's late. Tilly should have really been back now to help close."

My heart skips a beat. *Surely that's just a coincidence.*

"Oh right." I rub my eyebrow. "Did... erm... Did she tell you that herself? Did she look okay?" Or was she dragged away kicking and screaming by violent, evil elves? I grip the counter with sweaty hands and lean closer.

The girl flinches and takes an alarmed step back. Crossing her arms under her breasts, she sends me a worried look. "She sent a text. Who are you again?" she asks, her voice full of suspicion. "Why do you want to know about Tilly?"

Nice one, Pepper. You're acting like a proper weirdo and scaring the staff. I force myself to move my upper body back to my side of the counter, and I oh so casually cross my ankles in an awkward lean.

"She had a horrible cold last week, and I was worried. I'm glad she's all right and out having some fun. Tilly works too hard." At least that's the truth. The last time we spoke, Tilly was feeling under the weather. I tilt my head back to search the tree branches. "Poor thing. I think her tree even shed a bloom into a customer's drink."

"Ah, yes, her cold." Her arms drop, and she instantly relaxes. "I remember the moaning." We grin at each other. The girl leans forward on the counter with a chuckle, and I smile widely back, full of relief. I don't need to get thrown out before I've collected the message.

Everything is going to be okay. Tilly is busy with her friends, but she should be back soon, and we will laugh about this someday.

"I'll bring your order over to you."

Customers are waiting behind me. I sheepishly smile. "Thank you."

I weave between the wooden tables and go to the right, slipping into the corridor with the toilets. I don't have my key to the message box. One more thing lost to those blasted, thieving elves. But the box is a cheap metal postal box with a wide mail slot and enough room, too...

I stuff my hand inside, and my wrist scrapes against the metal with a tweak of pain. I angle my hand until my fingertips brush the message, pinch the paper awkwardly, and fish the sealed envelope out.

Success!

I stuff the unopened message into my leather bag to read somewhere safe and head to an empty table at the back of the café to wait. Along the back wall are shelves full of books. I grab a seat closest to the window, with my back against the shelves, and watch the dark street outside.

The café's large window frames the rare passers-by as they hurry along, wrapped in thick coats against the crisp evening air. The cold and storm earlier are keeping all but the bravest souls away tonight.

Let's hope I don't see an angry tiger stomping this way up the road.

I glance at the clock. I should have a few more hours. I check out the other customers. In a corner, a small group huddles around a table, engaged in a lively discussion; their laughter occasionally punctuates the air. And an old couple nestled in a cosy nook near the toilets share a pot of tea and exchange affectionate glances.

"Pepper?" One of the table's spare chairs scrapes against the tiled floor as a pale hand pulls it away, and a tall girl with rainbow hair sits.

CHAPTER
TWENTY-ONE

THIS MUST BE who I called from the phone box, a girl with rainbow hair. It's impressive.

"Yes, Tru?" It's best to double-check these kinds of things before begging a complete stranger for help.

She nods. I smile.

"Thank you for coming out so quickly. Forrest told me if I needed any help to call you. As I explained on the phone, I'm in a real mess."

A fairy with beautiful rose-gold wings flutters down to the table. She must have been hiding behind the mass of Tru's colourful hair. No, not a fairy. I narrow my eyes. The sapphire-blue creature is a pixie—a pixie with faerie wings, fancy that. Well, now that's a good sign. It shows Tru is forward-thinking.

"Hi." I grin and wiggle my fingers at the pixie.

She beams me with a smile and wiggles her fingers right back. "Hi, Pepper," she says in a sing-song voice. "I'm Story."

"Hi, Story. Nice to meet you. It's nice to meet both of you. Thank you so much for meeting me on such short notice." I lick my lips, drop my voice, and lean forward. "As I said on the phone, I have a problem with slavers. Elves. They caught me in Faerie, beat the snot out of me, and marked me with a slave rune before I escaped." I wiggle my still-covered arm—no need to show them or wave the other runes about. "I got the rune removed, but they tracked me down through the blood I left at the scene."

Embarrassed by such a schoolgirl error, I pull a face. I open my mouth to continue, but the girl from behind the till comes and places a pot of tea and tea things in front of me. "Thank you."

"Sorry it took a while. I had a rush, and I'm on my own tonight." She slides a hot chocolate in front of Tru. "Here you are, Tru. Are you sure you don't want anything, Story?"

The pixie hasn't taken her eyes off me. She waves a sapphire-blue hand. "No, thanks, Jen. I'm all right."

Jen smiles and walks away.

"Are you getting some cake?" Story asks.

"Me? Oh no. I, erm, I don't really like cake."

Story gasps, affronted, and Tru laughs into her drink. "Don't mind her. She decorates the wedding cakes, so she has a thing for sponge, butter cream, and fondant." Tru's eyes sparkle as she teases her friend, then harden when she looks back at me.

I shrink back into the seat.

"So these elves?"

Okay, the rainbow lady is kind of scary. "They found out where I worked and emailed me with a threat. They said they would hurt my friend if I didn't hand myself over. They gave me twenty-four hours to collect a message with further directions to meet them. I haven't spoken to my friend, but the girl at the till said she's safe and is out shopping. That she should be back anytime now." I glance at the clock and fidget with the handle of the teapot. "Tilly—"

Story gasps, and Tru holds up her hand for me to stop talking. "Tilly, as in the dryad who owns this place?" She prods the table with her index finger, and her tone makes the little hairs on the back of my neck raise. Have I done something wrong? Maybe they think I'm wasting their time?

I wiggle in my chair and nod. "Yes, and she is a lovely person." *A really lovely person. Please help me.*

Tru narrows her eyes. "These slavers, what do they want with you?"

"At first, to be an exotic bedmate for the Lord of Spring."

Tru's upper lip pulls back with a smile of pure malice, revealing lengthening canine teeth. Vampire, huh? I couldn't tell.

"Then, when they were hunting me down, they found out I'm a messenger. I ferry messages to and from Faerie. Tilly is my contact. My friend." I don't want to say the next part.

What I'm about to propose without any of my magic is suicide. But I will do it for my friend. I swallow, fiddle with the teaspoon, and with a deep breath, return to what I was saying. "Look, let me be honest. I'm going to go to the elves, but I need someone to keep Tilly safe when I do."

Tru's phone comes out, and her thumbs rapidly tap against its keypad. Story leaps into the air with a puff of pixie dust that sprinkles the table and lands on Tru's shoulder.

I sit there feeling awkward. I've messed this up. Tru must not want to work with me—or worse, she doesn't believe me. To do something with my hands, I pour the tea with a sad-sounding sigh.

After a few seconds, Tru's phone pings, and both she and Story read the reply. She taps the screen and then meets my gaze. "Tilly is missing."

My heart sinks. Tilly is missing. I close my eyes to the horror. Tilly is in trouble because of me.

"Her mate is a shifter, and he's searching for her. He's got a hellhound with him. Know anything about that?"

I keep still.

"I've told him I'll handle the café, wait for Jen to close, and put up a strong ward so these elves can't touch

Tilly's tree." Tru bangs the table. "When and where are you meeting these elves?"

The cup and saucer in front of me rattle, and drops of tea splatter onto the table. I wipe up with a napkin and take a sip of the black tea—the cup trembles. "I don't know. I've not opened the message yet. I was waiting to speak to you."

Tru gives me a get-on-with-it gesture.

I nod. The cup clacks and rattles as it hits the saucer, and out of the bag, I pull the envelope and use the cleaned teaspoon to prize open the flap. The letter is written in English.

Messenger,

By now you've realised you cannot contact your friend. That's because she's in our company. Do not spoil things by asking anyone for help, or the dryad dies. If you seek us out early, the dryad dies. You will meet us at Bloomfield Road football ground car park at seven p.m. on Thursday.

Alone. If you don't come alone, yes, you guessed it, the dryad dies.

Be a good girl,

Vivanti

That must be the blond leader's name, Vivanti. I pass the note over, and Story leans against Tru's cheek as they read it.

"Be a good girl. What a dickhead." Tru snarls. I nod in agreement. "So we've got until tomorrow night before we meet these yahoos."

"Us? But the note says—"

"To come alone. Yeah, yeah. Well, we aren't doing that. There's no way they will exchange Tilly for you. That way of thinking is total nonsense. They are *slavers,* and these elves won't let her go. If we're lucky, they have yet to offload her into Faerie. But if you play by their rules and go alone, you'll both be lost." She leans forward and absentmindedly traces the word L<small>IZ</small> that some moron has gouged into the table. "Pepper, did you wonder how I had Tilly's mate's phone number?"

I blink at her, not feeling very bright. I didn't catch that. I really need to have something to eat and sleep for a few hours.

"I know the number 'cause Tilly helped me. She helped both of us." With a soft smile, she nods at Story. "Tilly is our friend too. And I think Story will agree; we are not about to let Tilly or her messenger get hurt. She talked about you, you know. When we were kids, she was so worried about you. She even wanted my grandad and me to give you a place to live, but in the end, you looked after yourself. Shit, you're the messenger. I respect that, Pepper. I respect you even if we've only just met. You're a good person, and I want you to know nobody will blame you for what's happening. This is not your fault."

A tear rolls down the side of my nose. I wipe it away with my sleeve. Tru has no idea I needed to hear that, but I can't help the guilt. "I should have warned her when I got back."

"You got the shit beaten out of you and few broken bones?"

I nod.

"On the phone, you said you only just woke up after spending four days in a healing sleep. Yet you are here now, willing to sacrifice yourself for her. Look, Tilly will be upset if we don't help you, and to be honest, so will I. I think you need some friends."

I discreetly dab at my eyes. I blame the runes that are overwhelming my senses for being so weepy. Story flits from Tru to me, sitting on my shoulder, the weight of her almost non-existent. I smile when she pats my cheek in a motherly *there, there* motion.

"Drink your tea," she says kindly.

"The elves are full of tricks and magic," Tru grumbles.

Magic. Something inside me sings; I immediately know what I can do to help. I need to give Tru a charm to keep her safe. To highlight my thought further, the charm I'm thinking of heats. I don't even have to pull it from the bracelet as the thing jumps off and drops into my palm. "Here is a gift." I shove the black cat charm with the mirror eyes at Tru. "The charm wants to be with you. Please take it as a thank-you for helping me. It's a Gary Chappell magic reflection charm."

"Thanks." Tru takes the charm off me gingerly. "You don't need to give me anything to help." She holds it up to the café lights to study it. Even without access to my magic, I can feel the contented hum of the charm from across the table.

The black stone cat doesn't like me. I don't think it likes my stone magic, but I feel it will be happy with Tru, keep her safe, and no doubt save her life. I think the cat will have a good home.

Tru wrinkles her nose, shrugs, and drops the cat charm into her pocket. "You got a phone number?"

"No. I haven't been able to replace my phone."

"Here, use this." Tru gives me an opaque spell ball. It's the standard size of a marble. "'Cause you haven't got a mobile, this will do in a pinch. It's a basic communication spell. It will light up clear when it's time to make your way to the exchange."

It's no longer a meeting but a prisoner exchange. I bite the inside of my lip.

"If it goes red, I am coming to you. Blue, sit tight; I've got Tilly."

I nod.

"Repeat it back to me."

"It lights up clear, go to the elves. Red, you are coming to me. Blue, Tilly is safe. Sit tight."

She nods her head. "Good. I'll do my very best to kill these elves and keep both you and Tilly safe."

"Thank you." I slide the communication spell into the bag.

"I guess you can still call me from a telephone box. I need to get ahead of this and track these elves before tomorrow night." Tru rubs her face.

"Would something of theirs help?" I ask. "For a spell?"

Tru's amber eyes widen. "Yes."

As Tru watches, I angle my hips and dig back into the bag. It should be at the bottom. Story takes to the air so she can get a better view of what I'm doing. The attention makes me all fingers and thumbs.

After a small amount of panic—*please, please don't tell me I've lost it*—I pull out a small plastic zip bag. Inside are a few long blond hairs. Feeling a little like a drug dealer, I push it across the table to Tru. The little bag sticks on the old scratched name.

Tru leans forward, focusing on the baggie. "Is that elf hair?" she whispers almost reverently.

I tap the table next to the bag. "The leader's hair."

"Mother Nature," Story says with a flutter of her wings. "That's amazing. Well done, Pepper!"

"Where did you get these?" The vampire is rightly suspicious.

"The elf wears his hair down, and when he was hitting me, he must have got a few strands tangled in the top button of my tunic." I tap my throat and circle my index finger. "When I got home, I noticed them, and for some reason, I kept them instead of throwing them away.

I was careful not to contaminate the hair with my blood, but there still might be traces. Do you think the hair will still be good for a tracking spell? That is if you know of a talented witch."

"Is it my birthday? Two gifts and all you got was a lousy communication spell. We know a witch who will help," Tru says.

"Jodie?" Story asks.

"Jodie." Tru pounds on her phone, and her eyes twinkle with the promise of oncoming revenge. "Done. I can help Jen ward the café, and then we're meeting Jodie at the shop for a kick-arse tracking spell. Thirty minutes."

A purple coat hits the back of the spare chair next to me, making me jump, and an enormous hand follows, slamming down and holding it in place.

The tiger has found me.

"You forgot your new jacket," he growls, looming over me and the table, his dark blue eyes glaring.

Bloody hell. I don't know how he sneaked up on us.

Tru points at him. "You stop that now. Either sit down or go away." From her unconcerned expression, she already knew about him. "Is he with you?"

I nod, then shake my head. I don't know what to say.

CHAPTER
TWENTY-TWO

I LIFT my eyes to his. "They have Tilly," I say in a weird, squeaky whisper.

"I know. I'm sorry about your friend, little thief. John called to tell me before you disappeared. He's working with Tilly's mate to find her." Corbin leans closer until his facial hair tickles against the side of my cheek. "Don't think we won't be talking about you disappearing into thin air."

His whispered words tickle the shell of my ear and make me shiver, and my poor overexerted heart misses a beat.

He moves back, but he's still way too close. "So what did you do to get the big guns from the Creature Council involved?" Corbin's voice is accusing, but for some reason, his eyes gleam in approval. The tiger is a walking contradiction. He slides the brand-new coat over the back of my chair and sits—the wooden chair groans with his muscled weight.

Tru's eyes flick between us as if we're playing a game of tennis, and Story has this weird little grin on her face. "The elves want to meet Pepper at the football ground at seven p.m. tomorrow for an exchange."

Corbin lifts his chin to acknowledge Tru's words, and a muscle ticks in his jaw as he continues to stare at me.

I wiggle in the seat, feeling like a naughty schoolgirl.

"So you collected the message. That's *great*." He smiles at me while his eyes scream *liar, liar.* "I must have misunderstood and got the wrong time."

Gah. I feel guilty for no good reason. I don't owe the kidnapping tiger anything. I guess it's too late to show the girls my arm full of magic-suppressing runes and tell them about him slapping a null band on me and bundling me off to Ireland.

"Tru, Story. This is Corbin," I say instead of smacking my head against the table. I politely introduce them, drop my eyes, and pick up the teacup.

"Corbin, you here to help?" Tru asks.

"Yes."

"Good. Well, it's nice to meet you. As I was saying, Pepper has enough elf hair for a tracking spell. So we should get this mess sorted before the end of the night."

"Hair for a tracking spell," Corbin repeats.

I peek at him to see his eyes haven't left me and his jaw is tightening.

"Lovely."

As if I tell him anything.

"If you guys will excuse us, we need to go help Jen close up." Tru gulps down her hot chocolate, and she and Story leave me alone with a fuming tiger.

I watch as Tru grabs a cloth from the staff area and cleans the surrounding tables. She's quick, like she's done the job a million times before.

"You could have been hurt leaving like that. I smelled a wolf; he'd been in my room and had his dirty nose in my clothing. Who was it?" Corbin speaks through his teeth, and his voice rumbles with barely contained fury.

I don't think it will do any harm to be honest. "Eurus. He is a beithíoch." I don't need to tell him we Stepped.

"A beithíoch? So let's get this straight. Not only are you messing with the Creature Council's pet unicorn, but you now owe a favour to an unknown, dangerous creature. Did you do this within the past few hours, or have you been planning this for weeks?"

"Unicorn? Who's the unicorn?"

Corbin gives me an *are you effing kidding me* look, throws both hands in the air, and slumps back in the chair, his gaze on the ceiling.

I feel like I don't know anything. I smile nervously with all my teeth and shrug.

He groans and rubs his face. "Hours then." He lets

out this weird chuckle. "Fuck my life. I must be mad to like you." The tiger scratches the stubble on his jaw and drops his hand onto the table.

He *likes* me?

"Okay. Tru, the chick with the rainbow hair, works for the Creature Council. She is a half-vampire-and-half-unicorn shifter."

"Whoa. Tru's a hybrid, and she's alive? A sane hybrid working for the Creature Council. That's so cool. My estimation of her fortitude has now gone sky-high."

Across the room, Tru pauses in her cleaning and smiles. Then Jen appears carrying a plate, blocking my view. In its centre is a huge toastie that's oozing cheese. She lays the plate before me.

"I didn't order—"

"I ordered it for you," the tiger grumbles.

"Oh okay." I smile at Jen and say thank you. Jen widens her eyes at Corbin, winks at me, and then hurries away to finish cleaning. I have no idea what that means.

"You have eaten nothing but pineapple for days," he says. "I could hear your stomach grumbling from across the room. You are dropping weight. Please eat the sandwich. You aren't good for anyone if you pass out from hunger."

"Okay, thank you." I pick the toastie up, which is the weight of a brick, and take a big bite. Hot and delicious. I eat the sandwich in a dozen massive bites. Licking my fingers, I look up to see Corbin softly smiling.

The tiger is watching me eat again.

"What?"

"Nothing." He smirks and passes me a paper napkin.

I must eat like a pig. I dab my mouth with the napkin and take a mouthful of the now-tepid tea.

Corbin leans across the table. "What were you planning on doing? Huh? Hand yourself over to the elves that hurt you?" When I don't say anything to refute his words, the tiger lets out one of his low growls. "Pepper, that's suicide."

I also lean forward, meeting him across the table till we are so close I can feel his breath on my lips. "You think I don't know that?" I say in a harsh whisper. I don't care that he's getting a noseful of cheesy breath. "But what choice do I have? They took my friend, and I'm cut off from my magic because of you." I slap my arm on the table just to make a point. "What would you have me do, Corbin? I will not stand by and watch them turn my friend into a slave. Hurt her—" My voice cracks.

"So you'll be the Lord of Spring's bedmate instead?" he hisses.

I scowl at him. How long had the sneaky, nosy tiger been listening to our conversation?

"I will help you." He prods the table with his index finger to highlight his words.

"Sure, like you helped with the runes? Good men don't stand by and watch... no, not watch. *Help*. Good guys don't block other people's magic, leaving them defenceless. I have done nothing to you, Corbin. I've never hurt anyone. Heck, I tried to help you with those shifters, and you did this to me. I don't trust you, and I don't need your *help*. You've done enough."

"I saved your life."

I let out a disbelieving *pfff* sound. "Oh yeah? When? When did you save my life?" We are so close I'm in danger of booping him with my nose. "Go on, I'm listening."

"Believe me or not, Pepper. I did save your life. If you had just let me explain before you ran off with your wolf, we would have had this conversation hours ago. It would have been easier, and you wouldn't be running around town putting yourself in more danger. Please don't make me force you to listen."

"Again with the threats. That's all you're good at, threatening and forcing." I snarl. "I said I'm willing to listen, so spit it out. Make it good." I don't know where this boldness is coming from, but I enjoy telling him off and holding him accountable. He makes a fire burn in my chest.

Corbin drops his voice to a pleading tone, but it's his hurt expression that finally keeps my mouth closed. "You frightened Madán."

Me? I frightened the warrior elf? I flop back in the chair with a disbelieving laugh. He can see I'm flabbergasted. Why does the tiger even care?

"You don't understand." He reaches out and takes my hand. "The Lord of Winter's magic is almost omnipotent. The man is one of the most powerful creatures in the realms, but you scare the crap out of him."

He waits for a beat to let that sink in. "How can you not see that's a huge problem? I smelled his fear when he found out about you."

"But how? Why? You're right. I don't understand how anyone so powerful can be frightened of me." I glance down at myself, dressed in a hoodie and layers so I don't freeze. A piece of loose hair tickles my cheek. "I can't even keep myself warm without charity."

I flick the arm of the new and pretty purple coat. I'm not even going to think about the fact the tiger went out and bought me a jacket in my favourite colour. If I did, confusion would blow my mind.

Still holding my hand, Corbin leans across the table, tucks the strand of hair behind a pointed ear, and with his thumb rubs my cheek.

"Buying you a coat isn't charity. I wanted to. I don't enjoy seeing you cold. Like I don't want to see you hurt. Putting the runes on you myself gave a very powerful man breathing room. I encouraged Madán to meet you in person so he could see for himself what type of person you are and see that you're not a threat to him.

"Pepper, there's only ever one reaper. There aren't hundreds of them out in reams all going to reaper school to learn how their magic works. You're it. You are death-touched. Death's chosen. One of a kind. Unique. Madán is frightened because there's never been a fae reaper and he doesn't know what you'll do. If you want revenge on your clan, revenge on Faerie—"

"I don't want revenge," I sputter and let go of his

hand, pushing from the table and into the chair. "Why didn't he just ask me? The answer would be no. I don't want to hurt anyone."

"I know. I know. I spent five minutes with you and knew that. Look, I'd rather see you hate me than watch you be killed for something beyond your control."

"So you blocked my magic for my own good 'cause I scare the Lord of Winter with my freaky reaper powers. Power I have no idea how to control and didn't have a clue about until he told me a few hours ago. Now you're telling me because I scare him, he wants to kill me. He wants me dead." *Fabulous.*

I suck my bottom lip between my teeth. It makes a sick kind of sense. The tiger is so confusing; what's it to him if Madán kills me? "Why do you care?"

"I've asked myself that question, oh, a hundred times or more today, and I've concluded that I *like* you."

"You like me?"

Corbin drops his chin and gives me a beautiful smile that transforms his face and takes my breath away.

Uh-oh.

"I like you, even with all the crazy baggage of you being the reaper. I'm willing to outwit fae lords and kick Death's arse so that I can get to know you."

He likes me. He must be joking.

I don't know what to say. I'm not experienced enough to deal with this. I puff out my cheeks with a shaky breath. The tiger seems genuine enough. Right?

"I-I, erm, like you too." My face heats. "I don't know

why. It might be just your face." I wave a fluttering hand to encompass him. "These feelings will likely go away, and I must add the caveat they go against all my common sense. You know what? With the null band, the kidnapping, and the runes? Stalking? Can we look at this later? Please?"

The tiger continues to smile.

"Okay. For now I need you to let me rescue my friend."

"Pepper." He takes both my hands. They look so small and green in his massive grip. "You have a team of trained professionals who will rescue your friend. Qualified people will get the job done if you stay out of the way. If you interfere, you'll likely get someone—Tilly or perhaps yourself—killed." Again he does that strange pausing thing, letting the words sit between us.

Deep down, I know he's right, but how can I wait at home while everyone is put in harm's way? Shouldn't I help to clean up my mess? Why change the habit of a lifetime? Waiting is what I do best. It's not like I have a queue of creatures banging down my door to do fun things like hunt creature-trafficking elves.

I frown. Yeah, he's right. "Okay." I nod.

"I will do my best to save Tilly, but I can only do my job if you promise to stay home *safe*."

Safe. "Okay." I shuffle forward in the seat and softly caress one of his hands. "So if we are talking about me keeping safe, when can I have my magic back?" The tiger drops his eyes to the table and takes a deep breath.

Oh, that's not good.

"To stop you from freaking out, I kind of misled you earlier when I said I could take off the runes."

I slowly shake my head. "You lied," I whisper. *I feel sick.* I tug my hands from his grip.

He rubs his eyebrow. "Madán has the reversal spells, and as soon as we've dealt with these other elves, I will speak to him. I give you my word. Giving him time to re-evaluate you as a threat might be best. I didn't even tell him you'd left Ireland without me."

And this is how villains and rebels are born. When people in power get scared and let their imaginations run riot, they stop acting with any common sense. Punish the people who don't deserve it and who aren't their enemies. Yet they mould them into one. This is how they create their own downfall.

My hands slip onto my lap, resting on the lump of the leather bag, the bag with the book of runes. Let's hope I can save myself and not have to wait for the grace of an overprotective tiger and a scared elf.

CHAPTER
TWENTY-THREE

WE OFFER TO HELP, but they wave us away as they clean up around us. It doesn't take long, and then Tru is mopping the floor, almost mopping over Corbin's feet as she glares at him.

"Okay, you two, out you go. Go wait on the street, and then give me a second to finish this, lock up, and activate the ward."

"I'm going to escort Pepper home."

"No, you're not. I need her for about ten minutes. Jodie, the witch who's doing the tracking spell, will need to make sure the sample isn't contaminated with Pepper's blood. Ten minutes tops. Then you can drop her off at home."

Corbin grunts.

We wait outside. Corbin zips the new jacket to my chin and holds my hand as if I'm going to do a runner. If I wasn't so concerned about Tilly, I would. It isn't long before Jen's boyfriend comes and picks her up, and Tru locks the door and, with no chanting required, throws a vial against the wall. The glass disintegrates as the spell ignites, and the expensive ward springs into place.

Story flits between us while we all troop around the corner to Tinctures n Tonics. Ah, this must be Jodie's shop. I'm excited to finally see inside. The shop is closed for the evening; the lights are off, and the door is locked. Tru gives the wood a good rap with her knuckles, and from inside, I can hear approaching footsteps.

"One second," comes a muffled voice.

The lock clicks and turns, and what sounds like two deadbolts, one at the top and the other at the bottom, slide.

When the shop door swings open, the air is thick with an enchanting aroma, the scent of dried herbs, ancient books, and mystical potions. I feel the magic. It bites against my skin, but it's nowhere near as potent as it usually is when I walk past.

The blinking runes. It feels like how I'd imagine having a human cold would. A magical cold where everything is bunged up and muted. Still, the walls seem to hum with the echoes of countless spells cast and potions brewed. I let Corbin's hand go to rub the goosebumps on my arms.

"Tru, Story! Come in, come in. Corbin, it is lovely to

see you." The pretty dark-haired witch beams a smile at him.

Jealously bubbles inside me. I smile politely. Corbin glances down at me and grins. I pull a face at him. And jealously has a scent, that's just great.

"Oh, and who is this?" Jodie beams another smile— the same smile she hit the tiger with—and now I feel like a right twit.

"Hi, Jodie, I'm Pepper. It's lovely to meet you. Thank you so much for helping us so late in the day."

"Nonsense, it's no bother, Tilly is my friend, and it's lovely to meet you too. Come in. Please come in."

We all shuffle into the shop, and Corbin closes the door behind us. The old wooden floor creaks underneath my feet. The main store lights are off, but globe witch lights bob over our heads—along with the now fine mist of souls—lighting our way.

Jodie's shop is packed to the brim with magical items. Shelves line the walls that seem to go on forever, heavily laden with jars containing exotic ingredients, spells, and spell books, each item whispering tales of its magical potential.

Some shelves are piled so high I imagine if I even attempt to get something, I'd cause an avalanche, while others hold fancy glass cabinets with a single item on display.

Where would you start? Trying to find anything in here would give me a headache, and a shot of anxiety forces me to look away.

In one corner, an open door leads to a cosy green room where a cauldron bubbles gently on the stove, and a row of colourful candles flicker on a long wooden table, each imbued with its own unique enchantment. The flames seem to dance in response to the magic that lingers in the air.

"Are you all right? If you need to get rid of your furry problem, I can take him, probably." Tru smirks at me while Story rolls her eyes.

"Jodie will have a potion to take him. It'll be fine," Story says. "He'll go down like a tree."

Tru makes a tree-falling noise along with an arm gesture and finishes with a *boom* and a wiggle of her fingers. They both grin. I stare back at them both, a little horrified; they aren't even quiet. The tiger has heard everything, and across the aisle, he scowls. Tru gives him a double thumbs-up. He expects me to think they can work together.

"I have everything ready to do the tracking spell. Tru, did you say you had some hair?" Jodie asks diplomatically, steering the conversation.

"Yes, although the hair might have traces of Pepper's blood. That's why she's here, in case you need to do anything to rule her out." Tru hands over the baggie of hair.

"Okay. Well, let's have a look." Jodie's long skirt sways with the movement of her hips as she moves around to the other side of the shop's counter, and at a wave of her hand, an orb drops to give her more light.

Jodie then pops on some thick glasses and thin, latex-style gloves like she's doing a science experiment. She opens the bag and, with some tweezers, gently teases the hair out.

"I see the blood, but it hasn't affected the sample. I have a clarifying potion that will clean the hair right up." She glances at me over the glasses. "Well done, Pepper. It was good thinking to put the hair into an air-sealed bag. I'm happy to say that it will be perfect for our tracking spell." She carefully puts the hair into a beaker and adds a solution. "There. It just needs five minutes."

Frowning, Jodie removes her glasses, places them on her desk, and throws away the gloves. She looks back at me. "Pepper, may I have a word?" She waves me closer, and I shuffle to her side.

In a soft, caring voice, Jodie asks, "Are you okay?" I nod. She pats my arm. "I'm so sorry that creature hurt you. Tru and Corbin will sort this mess out and stop these dangerous elves from hurting anyone else. If anyone can get our Tilly back, it's them. Don't you worry. What I wanted to say is trauma hits us all differently. If you ever need anyone to talk to, you are welcome here anytime. I'm a nurse, and I've been trained in mental health. I'm a good listener, and"—she smiles brightly—"I make wonderful tea."

"Thank you. That's very kind."

"The charm on your wrist. You should use it tonight to get some sleep."

"Oh." My bracelet of charms is hidden underneath

layers and layers, but not hidden from this powerful witch. "Would it be okay if you pointed out which charm that is? I've only had them a few days, and I don't know what they do. Well, not all of them anyway, and as they are on my wrist, it would be handy to know."

"I'd love to." Jodie wiggles her fingers, and trusting her, I dig the bracelet out, slip it over my wrist and into her waiting palm. She lets out a gasp. "It's rare I get to see such master craftsmanship." She glances up with an excited grin. "The charms sing their magic to me, so I can even write the incantations for you if you want."

"Yes please. That would be so helpful."

"It's no bother. But with these charms, it's less about what you say and more about your intention. You gave one to Tru?" she asks with a small frown. I nod. "I can feel it in her pocket, a magic reflection charm. That was *very* generous of you."

"I had a feeling the charm would save her life, and it might sound odd, but the charm doesn't like me."

"That's not odd at all. Magic can take on a life of its own."

I smile gratefully. "It doesn't gel with my stone magic, and the charm almost felt as if it didn't trust me not to unmake it. Does that make sense?"

"Yes, it does. You've done a good thing, and the way that girl attracts trouble, I think you're right about the charm saving her life." Jodie flips to the first charm. "The fish is highly illegal. It's for memory confusion, so I wouldn't use that at all if I were you. Snail, that's a good one; it's for communication. You will talk to animals and understand people speaking in other languages and speak mind to mind. The umbrella is for powerful wards and is a difficult charm to use. Ah, there it is. The sleep charm is the pillow. This will help to clear your mind and give you a nightmare-free sleep without compromising on safety, and you'll wake naturally and not be groggy. The glasses" —Jodie drops her voice and has a quick glance around; Corbin is talking to Tru and Story on the other side of the store—"will help you see hidden spells and magical text like incantations written on runes." She eyes my middle, where the leather bag with the book of runes sits around my waist.

I get what she is saying. I grin. With the glasses charm, I might be able to remove, if not all, some of the runes on my arm.

When Jodie is sure I get her meaning, she continues. "The sea horse will help you breathe underwater, and the fly is a fly-on-the-wall charm. You can send it to listen to conversations. But you'll need to be close, or you might not get it back. They are pesky little things. The carrot— how fun—that will help you see in total darkness. The lightning bolt, be careful with this one. It's not illegal, but if a hunter sees it, they will confiscate it. The charm gives you a burst of focus and energy. It burns through calories and natural stores of energy like you won't believe, and it is best used as a last-resort option 'cause if you do use it, you'll sleep for a week on top of feeling like you've got human flu."

Creatures do get poorly, like with Tilly and her cold, but with dryads, it's in their nature to be affected by environmental things. I've never had a cold. Trolls are a sturdy, healthy race, so the human flu side effects sound horrendous and not something I want to deal with.

"Last but not least. The feather, as in light as a feather. Sad to say, it doesn't make you fly, but it can make you float or make someone who is heavy light enough to move. Levitation is perfect if a shifted friend needs help and they're the size of a pony. What a wonderful collection! Thank you for letting me examine them. I'm very jealous." Her eyes twinkle with joy and a deep-seated kindness. "I wouldn't give any more away or sell them, and I'd keep the charms out of sight. There's enough priceless magic on your wrist to make you an appealing target."

She hands the bracelet back. I'm somewhat overwhelmed. I didn't think the charms did all that. Priceless indeed. "Thank you so much for your help."

Jodie grabs a pen and some branded sticky notes. "Let me jot down the incantations. They are simple, and it will give you an idea of how to use them. But like I said before, you'll be fine 'cause it's all about intention. Now you're aware of what each one does, you shouldn't have a problem." The pen flies across the page, and I have a dozen helpful notes within a few minutes. "Oh, give me back the cat one, and I'll give that one to Tru."

"Thank you."

A warm arm nudges my side. "So you've got everything you need?" the tiger asks Jodie.

Jodie, in a sudden panic, glances at her forgotten jar of hair and gives the glass beaker a swirl. "Yes, yes, I'm ready to do the spell. I have the cauldron all set up." She comes back around the counter with the hair and heads into the back room. "Come on back if you want to watch, Pepper. I don't mind. I enjoy the company."

Wanting to watch Jodie work, I widen my eyes at the tiger and give him big puppy dog eyes. "Please?" He shakes his head but doesn't stop me when I scamper behind Jodie and into the back room.

I pass a big stockroom on the left, and I almost sigh with relief at the calm difference in here compared to the shop. This is nice.

Jodie points to the table. I take the closest seat, put my elbows on the table, and rest my chin on my hands. I watch as Jodie thoroughly washes her hands and uses a paper towel to dry them; she dons another pair of gloves.

"Have you seen magic like this before?" she asks as she cracks open a bottle of witch water and pours a few glugs into another beaker.

"Yes, I have." My eyes fixate on her movements. I don't want to say that I spent years invisibly hanging around at the local academy and watching the young witches blow things up while eating food Jodie's family possibly paid for.

But Jodie doesn't push. She smiles again and uses a clean pair of tweezers to remove the hair and pop it into the witch water. Her movements are precise, and watching her work is a pleasure. I can certainly understand why her spells are so valued.

She hums under her breath as she checks the cauldron, and with a nod, another new pair of tweezers emerges. She gets the elf's hair and drops all of it into the pot. It floats on the surface for a second, and as soon as it sinks, the prepared spell flashes a bright purple.

"Perfect," she murmurs.

Both sets of tweezers and the used beaker go into a saltwater solution on the other side of the room so as not to contaminate anything.

Jodie takes the pot off the heat, and then washes and dries her hands and changes her gloves again.

A clear glass marble is on the counter; Jodie removes it from its sterile packaging and drops the empty ball into the cooling liquid. Then, holding her gloved hands above the pot, she begins to chant.

The magic is complex, and the language is beautiful. The candles on the table flicker with the rising power, and all the flames of the candles point in Jodie's direction. The purple in the cauldron fades after a few more moments, and all the liquid inside disappears.

I lean across the table and peek in. The clear glass ball is now purple and sits on the pot's empty bottom. It glows just like the liquid did. Jodie dips her hand inside and confidently pulls it out. She holds it up to the light. "There. That's perfect. Tru?"

Tru walks in, giving me a smile, which I return and

then promptly yawn. My jaw cracks and makes my eyes water. Jodie hands the spell over to Tru. "That's perfect, Jodie. It's the best yet. I'll be able to track him no problem and bring Tilly home."

Jodie pats her hand. "You do that."

I yawn again, and a warm hand touches my arm. "Come on, Pepper, let's get you home safe."

I scowl.

"Look, you're not the only one not facing down the elves. Story isn't going."

I'd love to tell him he's wrong, that I don't need to sleep, but I can't stop yawning. I'm at that tired stage of feeling extra cold and floaty, which isn't good. "Thank you for letting me watch you work, Jodie."

"My pleasure."

Corbin steers me out of the room, through the shop, and towards the door with friendly shouts of goodbye from Tru and Story.

"Don't be a stranger, and once Tilly is home, you both must come for tea!" yells Jodie as we are about to walk through the door.

"We will. Night!" I hope we will.

CHAPTER
TWENTY-FOUR

I RETURN HOME, stumbling into the stinky chip shop side street with its rotten potato bins and putrid puddles. Corbin waits at the mouth of the street. Vulnerable and my heart pounding, I stand there in the dark for five minutes like a lemon as I rack my brain for a way to communicate with the stone. It's not working. *Uh-oh, am I locked out?*

"Are you okay, Pepper? What's taking you so long?"

I wave my hand for him to go away, and of course he steps closer. I grind my teeth. *Be nice, don't be rude, be nice.* It becomes a little mantra to keep my temper in check.

"Pepper, what's wrong?" asks the damn tiger, moving a little closer still.

"Just a minute. It's hard to communicate without my magic."

"Oh, I didn't think of that. I'm sorry."

"Whatever," I grumble.

Under my feet, the stone stirs as if it recognises my voice. Of course! I've spent a lot of my time within its depths, feeding my magic into the walls and talking, lots of talking. Who else am I going to talk to?

I shuffle. "I got it. It's working. Please be safe. I'll see you tomorrow." I give Corbin a wave and then aim all the positive intentions I can muster into the ground. Dropping my voice, I plead. "It's me. Can you please let me in?" I toe the tarmac with my boot for a bit of encouragement.

The magic is sluggish and unwilling, and for a moment, I worry I'll be locked out forever. But too much power, too much of me, has gone into this ground.

I'm let in.

When I get back to my room, I can hardly lift my feet. My body is so weary, yet my stomach is flipping with nerves and worry for my brave new friends and their coming mission to save Tilly and arrest the elves.

Ah, you've returned. Alas, my pangs of hunger persist, and your venture yielded no delectable snacks to satiate my appetite, says a grumpy wolf, followed by a big sniff.

"I'm sorry, Eurus, I didn't think. We have some pizza..." What I'm saying fades away as I spot the shredded pizza box and bits of cheese-laced cardboard all over the bed. Oh great.

I ate the cheese disc.

"I see that. I'm sorry I didn't think to get you more. The elves have taken my friend, Tilly, so my head is all over the place."

The lingering scent of the tiger clings to you. Has he, perchance, crossed paths with you during your absence?

"Yes."

However, this time he permitted your return. It seems you're progressing admirably in your training. He nods, his shaggy head conveying approval. *Every male benefits from steadfast female guidance to steer clear of perilous ends. I shall go hunt for a snack and return come morning.* Eurus disappears.

I bet he goes somewhere good. I hang up my new coat, wrinkle my nose, and clean the cheese and spit-covered cardboard off the bed. Then I change clothes into some comfortable jogging bottoms and a long-sleeved T-shirt. With my fancy new elf blanket, I no longer need to wear any more layers than this to sleep as it will regulate my body temperature like a dream.

I grab the leather bag, take out the communication spell, and pop it on the nearest shelf so I can see it from the bed. Tru said it would also ping. Eyes heavy, I force myself to do one more thing. I pull out the book of runes and hold it carefully in my lap as I sit.

I rotate and flick my wrist until the charm shaped like a pair of glasses is in my palm. I whisper its incantation. A prickle of magic zips up my arm and into my skull, settling behind my eyeballs in a whoosh of pain. I rapidly blink, and my eyes feel dry, but when I look back at the paper, I notice that the top rune of the book has two neat handwritten incantations—one to place the magic and the other to remove.

The charm works. I smile.

While thumbing through the book, I rest my arm on my leg, rune side up. I yawn. My eyes are burning. I'm two runes past a rune that I need when my brain catches up, and I realise I missed the first one. I flick back, and there it is.

Carefully I compare the rune to my arm, and it's a match. It matches perfectly to the mark in the crease of my elbow.

I need something to hold the page. My eyes flick around the room and fall on the shelves. I jump up, peel a label from a can of pineapple to use as a temporary bookmark, and then, with more vigour, continue my search.

The burst of surprise woke me right up, and with new determination, I eventually find another three runes.

Four runes are not bad at all. *Now, do I try to use them?* My stomach flips. I'd been unconscious for Corbin's runes, but I'd been wide awake for the slave rune the bad elves slapped on me, and I'd watched Madán remove it. If I stick to the written incantation, it shouldn't be that hard. You've got to love magic for being consistent.

Some practitioners draw on the skin with a pen; others can chant in their minds and trace the skin with barely a fingertip like what Madán did. I've also heard lazy creatures wet the paper and put the rune ink side down, like it's one of those fake transfer tattoos, and chant, ruining the entire thing for future use. No one should do that.

I have visible, neat marks; Corbin must have also used a marker to seal the ink into my skin. But to reverse it, I only need to trace the outline and say the reversing words. Simple.

It should be simple. I wiggle, and the canvas bed groans and creeks, highlighting what a bad idea this is.

The first problem is I don't know if the runes are built on top of each other, like a game of Jenga. So I've no idea what will happen if I remove the wrong one at the wrong time. The magic might come tumbling down and fry my brain. Yep, that will be fun. I stare at my arm. I'm hoping that's not the case and they work independently. That would make the most sense.

I poke my arm and then glance back at the book. A deep, shoulder-moving sigh leaves my lips. I've always been prone to flying by the seat of my pants, why would I stop now?

My thigh jiggles. I'm used to rescuing myself, and the endless lessons I observed at the witch academy must be good for something. I suppose the most logical way to remove them—without a random pick—is to start with the rune closest to my wrist and move up the arm. I leaf through the book using my torn pineapple-label markers and find the closest one.

I could magic myself into a frog. I rub my tired face and get to work.

Holding the rune, I say the magic in my head repeatedly until I'm confident with the rhythm of the spell. Finger poised on my arm, softly I speak the words. The language is older than this realm. It dances from my tongue, and with each rolling word, I trace the outline of the rune, adding my will to the magic.

Remove, remove, remove.

The skin on my arm burns, and the rune fades and then disappears, leaving just the ink outline. "Ow." My breath trembles as I exhale and swipe at the nervous sweat on my hairline with my arm, and then I shimmy my shoulders.

I deliberately ignore the prickling of magic on my skin and lock myself away from any magical changes happening inside me. I don't need any distractions.

"Wow. I'm definitely not tired now." My heart is crashing against my ribs, and I'm so hopped up with fear and adrenaline I could run down the promenade and back. I won't. That would be weird.

I take another deep breath and turn the page to the next labelled rune. I chant and trace, forcing myself not to get cocky and go at the same sedate, careful pace. I do the same for the next rune and the next until the last of the four fades.

I did it.

I mentally let go of the glasses charm, and the hidden writing fades to nothing. The helpful adrenaline has long been absorbed into my system, and now I'm left shaky and exhausted. My chin sinks to my chest, and I slump for a second. Then I make myself move, place the book back in its box, and slide it all back on the shelf. I'll recheck the book in the morning in case I missed a rune.

As a precaution and inspired by watching Jodie work, I grab a bottle and a rag and wipe a mixture of saltwater onto my arm to clean away any leftover spell fragments and all the remaining ink. I glare down at the horrid collection. *I still have ten more runes to find.* I use a pack of cleansing wipes to wash my face and hands. I feel better and more confident, more like myself than I have in days.

I don't reach for the newly released magic. I'm too frightened to try and too tired to deal with any more pain. As I climb back into bed, and before I lift my socked foot from the ground, the stone magic brushes against my toes, and the power zings up my leg. My surprised gasp is loud, and my throat hurts from the harsh sound.

It's back! The stone magic is back! I have access to some of my magic, and the stone is eager to communicate with me. Cautiously, I open myself to the stone magic in increments. Now it's being heard, it rushes through me, giving me a pins-and-needles sensation in my hands and feet.

Then it floods my mind.

With no pain, happy and grateful to have such a big part of myself back, I snuggle into bed as the ecstatic childlike magic bombards me with information. I let it flow, not at all bothered. It can shout all it wants.

Once the magic drops to a trickle, I hold the pillow charm in my hand, and just before whispering the spell, I ask Mother Nature to keep all my new and old friends safe from harm.

CHAPTER
TWENTY-FIVE

THERE IS an unfamiliar ping that has me bolting upright in bed. My eyes flick wildly around the room as my heart beats like a drum in my ears.

What was that?

Then I see the soft, shining blue of the communication spell. Blue! What the heck does blue mean? Dizzying panic rushes through me and stops me from thinking clearly. I should have written it down. *Why didn't I write it down?* I'm not the best at remembering things.

"Okay, Pepper, calm down. What did Tru say...?" *Uh-oh.* I've slept since then. I rub the back of my neck, tug at my loose hair, and take a deep breath. *Come on, come on.* I close my eyes and remember sitting in the café opposite Tru. "Clear means go to the elves. Red means

Tru is coming to me. Blue means sit tight, and Tilly is safe."

My eyes snap back to the spell. *Blue.* "Tilly is safe." I drop my head into my hands and press the base of my palms against my eyes to stop myself from crying. At least this time if some leak out, they will be happy, relieved tears—Tilly's *safe*. I sniff. "They did it. They bloody did it."

From the light filtering through the ceiling's glass bricks, it's pitch-black outside—still in the middle of the night.

I hope everyone got out safely and they locked the elves up. I cringe. It's probably more likely the elves are dead. But I'm not in control of their choices; whatever happens to them is on their heads.

I will never have to see those damn elves again.

Of course things still aren't safe. I have a warrior-elf problem, the Lord of Winter. I groan and settle back into bed, eyes on the light coming through the glass bricks as I wait for the day to start.

Not for the first time, I wish I'd replaced my phone, but my gut instantly rejects the idea. Technology, the first thing they'd look for, is easy to track and trace. But it would be nice to speak to Corbin to check that he's all right.

Gah, have you heard yourself? The man's a hell-hound. He can shoot magic fire out of his pores. He'll be fine. They all will be fine.

I close my eyes and drift off towards sleep. Exhaustion clings to me. There's another ping, and I open one eye. The communication spell shifts from blue to red.

Tru is coming to me.

I sit up, the bed cover crumples around my waist, and I throw my magic out to the tunnels to check in with the stone magic. The concrete on the promenade and in the subway hums happily. The promenade is wet and clean from the sea spray, and the tarmac is settled and cold, with traffic down to almost nothing but an odd taxi.

I put the magic on high alert to warn me when Tru or Corbin arrive and to let them inside. I get up and do my morning routine, changing into dark grey leggings and a matching jumper. Then I return to the room, glug some water, and check on the tunnel's ward by closing my eyes and finding my second sight.

The blue ward, I see, is healthy and solid.

While waiting, instead of pacing, I grab the rune book and methodically recheck it. I find out I hadn't missed any, and then I'm back to waiting. My boots tap out a rhythm on the floor with impatience.

Then the stone tells me there's movement. Not outside. It's at the tip of my senses, almost a mile away and inside the tunnels. Whoever they are, they're closing in fast.

Something tells me it isn't Tru or Corbin. They are both too polite to come through the tunnels, and why would they? The only person who can navigate down here is me, a professional with a detailed survey map, or more likely, someone using a spell to track me down. It'll have to be a mighty strong spell, a blood spell.

The only creatures with my blood are *the elves.*

Shit.

We didn't have a colour on the communication spell for "the elves are coming; run like hell." I groan as my memory returns to the warnings I received in the email and the handwritten message left at the café. I wonder if anyone followed me when I picked up the note and watched as I talked to Tru and Story.

That would be a simple thing to do, and I just waltzed in there, grabbed the message, and proceeded to meet with a renowned hybrid who works for the Council. All in sight of a massive window. I groan. *Nice one, Pepper, mega sneaky.* They must have seen me hand the message over.

I try to recall if someone was watching while I made goo-goo eyes at Corbin and when we all went to the witch shop together and when he walked me home.

Had we all been too cocky?

I was exhausted. I'm sure Corbin knew what creatures were around; he's a hellhound and would have been trained to spot a tail. The elves are sneaky. Perhaps a few got away from their assault and they are heading this way through the tunnels to get their revenge.

The ward will stop them, but where will they go instead? *Who* will they go after if they can't get to me?

I take the umbrella charm and reinforce the ward in this tunnel. When Eurus Steps home, I don't want him to be at risk and land in the middle of a fight. I also refill his bowl of water before I hurry into the subway. If the presumed evil elves are heading my way, they will come directly to me, and the subway is perfect. The space is bigger and darker, and there are more places to hide.

With a quick check of Jodie's notes, I chant the incantation for the carrot charm—so I can see in the dark. As the spell begins to work, the burning in my eyeballs feels like I'm using my nails to scrape the lenses off my eyes, and for a giggle, it also adds in some ground-up glass shards.

Yep, using the charm is so comfortable. I wonder if it's like that for everyone or if I'm just special. Ha, I bet the damn runes are attempting to block all magic. Hence the extra-special amount of pain I'm getting. I rapidly blink, my eyes lubricate with tears, and the scratchy pain fades.

I extinguish the fae lanterns to see if the carrot charm is working. I can see the subway clearly for the first time and can't help wrinkling my nose at the horrid sight. The place is a mess. The fae lanterns sure soften the area. Perhaps I will invest in a cleaning potion and a fresh coat of paint for the walls. Make some changes. There's no point in pretending I don't live down here. Not anymore.

The intruders are getting closer; I follow them with my magic as they turn in to the last tunnel that will lead them directly to me if I make a hole for them and allow the ward to let them in.

Now comes the magic juggling.

I keep the carrot charm going and attempt to use the umbrella simultaneously. I sigh when both charms work well together and cause no extra pain—just the usual ice-pick-to-the-brain headache. The ward once again sits a bright blue space of power in my mind, and with a mental poke, I peel it away to let them in while my stone magic makes a careful hole between the tunnels. I don't need the elves making their own.

Then I wait.

CHAPTER
TWENTY-SIX

I SIT in the far corner, where the tiger hunkered down when I locked him in here. Was that only yesterday? Wow. It feels like a lifetime ago. The corner gives the best view of the room, and the angle of the wall provides a natural shadow. My grey outfit works well, almost as if I'd planned it. I once read that grey and brown clothes are best for sneaking about and hiding in the dark and that wearing black makes you more likely to stand out.

Let's hope they are using human torches rather than light spells.

Focusing on the spot on the wall where they will come out, I remind myself I can slip through the wall to the other tunnel at any time.

I can't do my usual trick of being invisible, so I still

feel like I'm missing an arm, but I do have the stone magic running through my veins.

I'm still pissed that the tiger, in his wisdom to keep me safe from the Lord of Winter, put the runes on me in the first place. He should have trusted me to behave.

Like you are behaving right now?

Meh, I haven't broken my promise. I haven't gone anywhere. I'm defending myself and my home and not letting them hurt anyone else. Tru and Corbin asked me to sit tight and that they would come to me. That's what I'm doing.

I admit I'm not cracked up to be a fighter, and half of me is screaming obscenities and that I should leave or hide under the bed. But the other half of me wants justice for Tilly, justice for me. Not that I can do anything. I have no weapons. But I'll think of something to keep them busy while I wait for the cavalry to arrive.

I can feel their footsteps.

I glance down at the array of charms. Perhaps... Still channelling the carrot so I can see, I take the feather between my fingers and from the bag around my waist grab the note for it. This time I chant the spell in my head.

My entire body tingles, and the force of the magic has me slamming back against the blue tiles. With blood streaming from my nose, I wiggle tight into the corner to keep myself stable as my feet leave the ground.

Oh heck. Trolls are not meant to fly. My boots scramble, and I almost drop the connection to the charm. But I'm not just a troll. I'm a half-transitioned reaper.

I rise like a Pepper balloon, and when my head hits the crumbly paint of the ceiling, I wince as little bits of grotty paint get stuck to my hair and sprinkle down the back of my neck into my jumper. I twist and force my upper body to lie flat, with my legs dangling so that if I lose control of the spell, I won't plummet to the floor and splat on my face. Instead, I should land on my feet or my bum.

A lump of troll on the ceiling. *This is the worst idea I've ever had,* runs through my head. This is something you practise a lot beforehand. You don't do this kind of thing off the cuff. *Oh, cuff.* I use the jumper's sleeve to stem the bleeding from my nose. I observe the far-off floor—or I attempt to. While I was sleeping, the souls went from a fine mist into a swirl of thick fog. From here, the ground doesn't look so bad.

An alert chimes from the concrete as six elves appear from within the labyrinth of tunnel passages. My pulse quickens, and I dare not move. *Six. Oh, bloody hell.* I roll my eyes when I see each elf has a light spell.

The spells only reach so far, and tucked into the top corner, I'm still in shadow, thank the Mother. I hope the shadows continue to be my ally and that they remain oblivious to my presence.

Now I feel foolish for not running away when I had the chance. *Silly, Pepper.* I press myself against the cold, crumbly plaster, barely daring to breathe as I watch. I can hear them murmuring to each other in elvish, a melodic symphony of foreign words. Their voices are hushed, yet the tension in the air is palpable. They seem determined, driven by a purpose that sends shivers down my spine.

They want me.

"What a shithole," an elf with red hair says in a loud, obnoxious voice. Even though I'm comfortable with the language, the snail charm warms, translating their words into English.

Oh heck. I hope my brain doesn't leak out of my nose. That's three charms I'm now using at once. Can I keep myself up here and simultaneously use all this magic? Well, I'll give it a good try. Not that I have much choice.

"Do you really want the girl, Vivanti?" The elf who speaks next has unusually short, white hair cropped close to his skull. His face is thin and all angles. He moves like a professional killer. Dead eyes. And he addresses the elf leader by his given name as if they might be friends. "Is she worth all this? That was a hellhound and the Executioner back there. The rest of our team is dead, and for what? One troll girl. This is madness, and from a monetary standpoint, it doesn't make any sense."

"Are you challenging me?"

"No, never."

The elf leader, Vivanti, lets out a petulant noise. "It's not about the girl. It's about the principle. If one slave escapes, then they all will. They are already talking." He hunches his shoulders and wiggles his fingers. "Whispering about the green girl who ran. Mutiny."

My inner voice can't help shouting out an *ooh aaarrr* pirate noise as Vivanti straightens.

"And then it's the start of them thinking they have any chance of freedom. We do not want that. What I do want is for her to be a lesson. I want to break her entirely, horrifically, to make sure no one ever thinks about running from me again. That running and being brought back is worse than death. It's a life lesson, gentleman. I want that green bitch so broken that no one will think I'm anything but a monster.

"The tracking spell says she is here. I want her on her knees." He cups between his legs and thrusts his hips. "Hey, little green mouse, I know you can hear me! We are coming for you. You shouldn't have run. You should have taken your beating and gone to the Lord of Spring. At least then you would have been able to hobble after he was done with you." He smiles, amused. "Now you'll have to drag yourself around like a slug. I'm going to rip your insides out with my fist." His laugh echoes, and the four other elves laugh along with him.

The short-haired elf doesn't make a sound. He stares into the dark areas of the subway.

"Are we sharing her then? Never had a troll. This is going to be fun," says the redhead.

I swallow down bile and allow myself a second to close my eyes. This is a nightmare.

"Isn't she powerful?" says another.

"The wolf said she has runes all over her arm blocking her magic, courtesy of the Lord of Winter. It took her ten minutes to get in and out of her den. He also said he'd let us in, and he did; here we stand. So do what you're paid to do—spread out and find the bitch," Vivanti snarls with a wave of his hand.

Eurus let them in. My soul shrivels.

No, I let them in. I moved the ward, but the beithíoch told them about the runes, my lack of magic, and where I live. He must have Stepped me home just to get me away from Corbin. That's why he misled me about being able to remove the runes.

How could he not be able to remove them but know how to talk me through setting a ward with a charm even Jodie said was hard to use? The rune removal is simple in comparison. How could I be so blind? He was probably there in that box guarding the charms, or maybe he was a slave, a prisoner, and he sold me out to get his freedom.

I'll probably never know.

My heart hurts, but on top of that, a little piece of growing hope and happiness inside me dies. Creatures like me don't get to have friends, and this happens when you don't interact with the world. You become an easy target for men like them.

"Are you sure that's what the wolf said? I couldn't understand a word that came out of that strange creature's mouth," the redhead whines.

"Spread out and find her!" Vivanti yells.

In my corner, I brace myself.

CHAPTER
TWENTY-SEVEN

I WATCH the six elves spread out and do my best to think no more about Eurus's betrayal, no more about the vile words of what the elves will do if they catch me. I don't need that sick stuff in my head. *I can't freak out,* even if every fibre of my being screams at me to run.

If I lose it now, I might as well hand myself over to them and call it a day. That's not going to happen. I will not let that sick elf hurt me like he is insinuating. He's a monster, and by the time I finish, he will be incapable of hurting me or anyone else. The elves will remember Vivanti as the idiot who tried to play chicken with a troll.

No, worse. He tried to enslave Death's chosen reaper.

Reaper. I scoff. No wonder I'm only half-transitioned. I make bad choices. I listen and let the professionals pat me on the head and send me home to bed; all the while, they tell me they'll deal with the bad guys, and look how that turns out. The elves are down here hunting me without a scratch on them.

I'm so mad.

I'm willing to embrace this scary, strange, weird reaper destiny if I can just find a way to eliminate the runes imprisoning my reaper magic. I will take everything fate has to throw at me and be glad about it just to stop that horrible man and his nasty elf henchmen.

And as if Death is listening to my thoughts, or I simply had the power within me all this time and needed an extra push, the runes on my arm *burn*.

Stuck to the ceiling like a fly, the rough paint scratches against my face as I slowly, silently turn my head and stare at my covered arm.

The pain worsens, and I must grit my teeth and close my eyes against it so I don't make a sound as what feels like acid eats away at my skin. All the while, I desperately scramble to keep mental hold of the feather magic. It wouldn't do much good to fall on my arse in front of the elves.

The pain disappears as quickly as it starts, leaving tingling skin and a stronger connection to my reaper magic than I remember.

And the souls... Bloody hell, the souls silently rush me.

Like a never-ending wave, hundreds of them, maybe thousands... a torrent of impatient souls crashes into me.

My upper body jerks at the impact of so many; the thick fog of them pushes me hard against the ceiling. My joints crack, my bones ache, and my body twitches with excruciating pain as the power of the dead floods me.

When the pain stops and all the souls have gone, the magic buzz they leave behind bolsters me. Almost in a dream—a trancelike state—something takes over. The need for retribution pulses through me. The steady ebb and flow of my combined magic fills me and makes me feel invincible, like granite. My agreement to embrace fate has lit a fire, and I feel powerful, strong, and *furious.*

I gather the reaper cowl to cloak myself with its invisibility, and gradually I let go of the feather charm to gently slide down the wall to land on the balls of my feet.

"Pepper!"

That's when they call my name.

"Pepper pot, come out, come out to play!"

Oh, I think I will; it's playtime, you say? One thing Eurus was right about is they've come into my den. My home. My world. I'm a part of the concrete under their feet. They breathe under my whim, and all the dirt and stone surrounding them is mine to control. I'm not totally naive in letting them in.

I smile when they split up.

One elf pauses, head tilting slightly as if catching a scent. He heads for the corner and moves a little bit too close for comfort. I must have made some noise while battling with the return of my magic, or he smells the blood from my recent nosebleed.

Let me start with you. No one else is watching him. *Now this is more like it.* I roll my shoulders. I'm back to myself, more than ever, and I feel confident as I stalk out of the corner towards him.

I've never used my power to hunt before. Always hiding or observing, never going after another creature, and I have to say there is an odd sense of empowerment to not feel like prey.

It's as if this is how I'm supposed to be.

I tip the floor when he takes his next step, and with an almost soundless grunt, elf number one stumbles. His left side hits the subway wall, and the wall wraps around him and swallows him.

Eats him.

Oh, and there's no way he'll pop out on the other side and... *no way he'll be able to breathe!* My eyes widen with a burst of panic, and I push a pocket full of air around him. Phew, that should keep him alive for a few hours, or I'm likely to find bits of him in my rubbish bag in the morning. I wrinkle my nose. Ew, I hope not. I don't want to kill anyone.

No one notices that first missing elf, too busy hunting for me. I step around the elf leader, ignoring him. If I can, I'd like to leave Vivanti for last.

Instead, I go after the redhead elf who just threw my orange cone like he's doing the Olympic hammer throw. The cone smashes into the far wall with a plume of plaster dust and flops to the side, broken.

My eye twitches.

I follow him as he enters my bathroom. He barges into the space with zero respect and dares to shove the weighing scales. I watch in horror as they fall apart, clattering onto the tiles. I step over the mess.

He leads his search for me with his feet, and with a grunt, he spins and back kicks the nearest delicate stall door. He knocks it clean off its hinges. Bits of rotten wood splinter, raining down onto the floor and hitting the porcelain. One door after another. When he hits door number four, I've had enough. He'll be breaking the mirrors next.

When both feet land on the ground, I encourage the pink floor tiles to part and suck the redhead into the ground. With a flick of magic, I stick a thin, crumbly piece of the concrete to his mouth, hardening it so zero sound can come out. He can still breathe.

I'm so cross, but I try my best not to hurt him. At some point, my anger will fade, and anything I do now, I will have to live with.

I drop the cloak on my invisibility power, squat before him, grin, and wiggle my fingers in a wave. "Anytime you make a noise, I will drop you another foot into the floor. Since you need oxygen to breathe, it might be best if you keep it down. Vivanti isn't worth dying for. Sit tight now." I pat him on the head and snuff out his light spell, leaving him trapped in the dark.

I slip back into my cowl and, careful where I place my feet, leave the ladies' bathroom. My attention flips to elf number three. The short-haired, dangerous one. He is in the gents' next door. At least this guy isn't kicking anything. He's more professional than the rest of the elves; he stalks across the pee yellow tiles. His light spell is brighter than the others, and the iron knife gripped in his fist screams he knows how to use it.

He's a silent type. He didn't laugh or jeer with the other elves. This job isn't personal, and if the others got hold of me, he wouldn't save me, but he wouldn't join in. He'd walk away, have a coffee, and return when I'm quiet or dead. A paid professional. Keeping him awake, like I did elves number one and two, would be a mistake.

Methodically, he checks all the stalls, and while he works, I loosen the concrete in the ceiling. I drop the slab on him when he approaches the far wall. It hits his shoulder, and the elf crumples like wet cardboard under its weight. He drops his knife, and it spins away from his hand. *I'll take that.* There's no need to leave it lying around. The floor swallows it.

I don't even uncloak.

Before he can do more than groan, I hold the pillow charm and whisper the spell. Asking for a longer, deeper sleep for him means I don't have to knock him out with more concrete. Brains are squishy, delicate things, and I have no experience. I don't want to make a mistake that I can't fix. What I'm asking the charm to do is a little bit of a stretch for the pillow's magic. It doesn't want to be used as a weapon, but it does what I ask, and he slumps to the floor, fast asleep. Just in time too, as the massive crash of the concrete brings elves four and five running.

CHAPTER
TWENTY-EIGHT

THIS IS GREAT. Now I don't have to hunt them down. They're coming to me. Shock freezes them to the tiles as wild-eyed elves four and five stare at the crumpled, sleeping number three and then at the hole in the ceiling.

"The ceiling caved in."

Oh, what a terrible accident.

"This entire place is a death trap."

He's got that right. They both admirably work quickly together to move the slab and drag their unconscious colleague towards the bathroom door.

I can't have that.

Elf number five's foot sinks into the floor. When four attempts to help him, he sinks to his knees. As it worked so well last time, thin strips of concrete fly out from the rubble and seal their mouths and drop them both down to their chests, trapping three out of the four arms. Not bad.

I'm still cloaked, and on a whim, I now check the sleeping elf's pockets. I wasn't able to do this with the others, what with them being encased in concrete. The elf has a ton of equipment stashed on his person. I find his wallet—it has cash but no identification. I don't know what I expected. It's not like he'd carry his passport or driving licence on a kidnapping mission.

I carefully sink him into the floor next to his pals, leaving the three sunken elves without speaking or showing myself.

The two awake are in a state of shock, breathing fast through their noses and on the edge of panic. They keep staring at their badarse unconscious colleague. Perhaps they're thinking if he got caught and sucked into the floor, there's no hope for them. I can tell they will stay nice and quiet. I extinguish their lights and leave the men's bathroom.

The elf leader is waiting for his men in the centre of the subway. He adjusts his sleeves, taps his foot, and looks mightily impatient.

I blend into the darkness for a second, take a deep breath, and then drop my cowl. It's time for us to have a little chat. "And what do we have here?" I whisper in elvish. "A pack of uninvited rats." I might be a tad pissed that the elf leader called me a mouse. "You've gone from six rats down to one. It looks to me like the rat king is all alone. It's just you and me now, rat boy."

The fae lanterns flash bright white—the reaper power is making me a tad dramatic—and I strut into the light. "What did you think would happen coming into my home, making a mess? Have you seen what one of your rodents has done to my bathroom?" I angrily point to the ladies.

Vivanti smiles at me. It's a creepy, wide, blocky-tooth smile. "There you are, mouse. What took you so long?" He looks me up and down. "What's with all the confidence? The last time I saw you, you were a bleeding, snotty mess, begging me not to hurt you. What a difference a few days make. Have your new friends injected a backbone into you? I will thoroughly enjoy ripping that out." He looks around the subway mockingly as if the tiger will appear. "They're not here to save you though, are they? They've left you to me."

The last time we came face-to-face, this elf hurt me, and it throws me off balance. A tiny sliver of doubt creeps into my mind, paving the way for fear to fill me. Eurus sold me out; what's to say the others didn't do the same? I don't know them. They care about Tilly. I'm the creature they'd exchange to get her back. All my "I'm a reaper, hear me roar" goes out the window, and I feel intimidated and frightened.

What the hell am I doing?

The elf holds his hand out, palm up, not dropping that creepy, toothy smile. "Come with me. Now."

"Have you not noticed you're missing something? Like five henchmen?" My eyebrows rise, and I try to pull out my newly formed cocky side. *I can do this, finish this mess.* I removed the runes. I'm strong enough to deal with one nasty elf.

"They are unimportant."

There is something wrong with his head. He isn't listening.

"Where is Tilly?" This time my voice wobbles. *No, don't you dare.* I lift my chin and glare. I'm okay. I'm perfectly safe, ready with my magic. It's just on the end of my fingertips, already prepared to suck him into the ground. I'm willing to end this any second now.

"Oh, she's fine. All rescued. We didn't touch the dryad; she stinks of her wolf. We just locked her in a room and didn't harm a blossom on her head. Unlike you." He smiles that creepy smile again. "She was only a means to get to you."

I force myself to keep my ground and not back away.

"It surprised me when three big hitters and her mate tracked me down. With a tracking spell no less. I wonder how they got a sample to track me so well. Perhaps a little bit of blood under your nails, a hair?" He nods when he sees the answer on my face. "You've been a very naughty girl. No matter. They won't find you where you're going. And let's be honest—they don't care enough to look. Come on now."

"No," I squeak.

Now I'm closer to Vivanti. I remember how big he is

compared to me. He's over six feet tall and has a solid, athletic build. He's used to hurting creatures, and I'm untrained. I need to stop chatting and finish this now. I realise I'm not going to get any closure from this man, and I won't ever see an ounce of fear in his eyes.

"You were lucky to escape, and you dared to steal my bag when you ran. You freed the beithíoch, a recent and expensive purchase, you made me look like a fool in front of my employees, and all the while, you somehow gained the negative interest of the Lord of Winter. Stone magic and invisibility are such an interesting power combination. Shame you can't use your powers." He laughs. "Mouse, you are a fuckup. How can one creature make so many mistakes in such a short time? I'm doing you a favour in taking you away from this horrid life."

The elf moves towards me, and I realise my mistake. I should have secured him before I showed myself. I've no idea what I'm doing. He flicks his wrist, and I notice a nasty-looking orange spell ball in his hand.

Shit, Pepper duck! I dive out of the way; I hit the floor with an *oof*, and my chin scrapes the dirty ground. Head spinning with panic, I forget I have magic as the orange spell flashes with a heated *boom*, turning the spot where I stood into a pool of dark orange goo that eats at the floor. I scramble away and get to my feet; a hand grabs my arm, and a null band slaps down onto my wrist.

"A null band." *Oh no!*

CHAPTER
TWENTY-NINE

I HAVE only microseconds before the band's magic blocks my power and knocks me out. I desperately pull on the umbrella charm to protect my mind. Even though the null band can take away my magic, using the ward charm, I hope to at least prevent myself from passing out.

If I fall unconscious now, I'm as good as dead.

All my focus is on the charm as I battle the null band's magic. It will be handy if the bad guy can let me deal with this first, but he doesn't. I twist to the left, avoiding his fist, but I don't elude the next one—duh, he's got two hands—and I do a poor job evading the one after that. His elegant hands turn to weapons as he pounds my face like a punching bag.

My left cheekbone throbs, and the eye above is

rapidly swelling as he circles me. I finally get my hands up, covering my head. I groan when the next vicious punch gets my elbow. All the while, I mentally fight with the band's power that is sucking the magic from my blood and the vitality out of me.

"Stop! Stop it!"

He doesn't stop, and his leg shoots out. His shin kicks me, catching my ribs. The kick knocks all my air out of my lungs, and my diaphragm feels stuck.

I can't breathe.

I can't think.

"You deserve this. I'm going to enjoy this immensely," says Vivanti as another blow lands, clipping my arm and catching my ear.

I curl into a ball.

Oh, how did I get onto the floor?

There's blood in my mouth.

With my arms covering my face, the horrid band is at eye level. When I jolt from the next kick, some bone inside me crunches. I stop trying to ward my mind and instead spit the blood in my mouth onto the null band— blood is powerful—and mentally throw everything I have at it: my combined powers, the charms' weird and wonderful mix of chants, along with all the intention and the utter belief in my getting this bloody thing off my wrist.

I whimper as another kick gets a sore spot.

I see something happening to the band... hundreds of tiny, transcribed runes, all in small, neat rows, flash up.

The second row cracks, and then the third, then odd, discoloured spots start appearing on the surface. The null band blackens, crumbles, and falls to the floor as dust.

What the f... How did that happen?

I did it. I did the impossible!

In too much pain to be frightened and angry enough to fight, I grab the elf's boot and twist. He trips over my leg rather than because of any skill on my part, and when he crumples to the floor, I roll on top of him. My sides and weak abs burn as I throw my hands down and, like a kid in a playground, slap the shit out of him. I grab a handful of his silky blond hair, the intricate plaits making it easier to pull, and kick my legs, all the while letting out an ungodly scream.

He's not smiling now.

He flips me, and his heavy bulk pins me to the floor while his knees force my legs apart. The elf's arm comes up for another punch.

I wince.

Then a massive boot sails over my shoulder, and the elf is booted in the face. Even though it hurts, I can't help laughing. It's Vivanti's turn to be sent flying. Like something from a movie, he must zoom a good eight feet until he hits the wall headfirst and slides down, out for the count.

I roll onto my side, cough up some blood-laced phlegm, and through bleary eyes smile at Tru and Corbin. "Hey," I rasp.

"What was all the screaming and...?" Tru paws the air

and mimes pulling hair. "Remind me not to fight you, you crazy, unpredictable girl. You are nuts." She points a finger at my face, and her eyes sparkle with amusement.

"I don't know how to fight."

"Yeah, I get that. I can tell." She grins and again slaps at the air with a roll of her eyes. "Crap on a cracker. Pepper, that was hilarious."

"I'm glad I amused you."

Corbin crouches in front of me, his brows furrowing with genuine concern. He palms the back of my head, and his eyes flick over my face.

"We need to get you self-defence training. Really, Pepper, that was terrible," Tru continues.

"Thanks." The thought of learning to fight makes my entire body cringe. That sounds like way too much work. She has a point, though. I'm used to magic being a defence with my instinctive run-and-hide moves. I can't expect myself to suddenly go from running to being the all-magical Rambo.

You didn't do either, so you're equally shit.

Very true. I snort at my inner voice. *Ow, my ribs.* I could have disappeared into the other tunnel. When I got the band off, I could have made myself invisible. I could have done a whole host of things instead of just standing there and letting him punch me in the face.

It's obvious now I can't do two things at once. That's not how I'm made. But I'll get better with practice. I think.

"Tilly?" I ask.

"She is home safe," Corbin answers.

My shoulders sag with relief. "Thanks for the boot," I whisper. I try to smile even with the throbbing face. "And thank you both for coming."

"You're welcome. Here." He shows me a silver Heal Me Now potion. "Is this okay?"

Wow, and that right there is a miracle: the tiger asks for my permission.

"Yes please." He spills the potion onto my neck, and I instantly feel better as it gets to work, healing me. "Thank you. That feels amazing. There are six of them."

Tru lets out an impressed whistle.

"One of them is trapped in the wall." I flop my hand in the general direction. "Four are sunk in the floor of the toilets, one in the ladies, and the last three elves are in the gents."

"Ooh, I've got to see what you did to them," Tru says with glee as she heads to the men's toilet with a bouncy stride. Over her shoulder, she calls back, "Six elves. I take it back, Pepper. You did great." She gives me a cheesy smile. "You might have lost a few cool points with that finish, but girl, you did really great. If you want, I'll help you personally with your fight training." She disappears inside. There's a flash of a new light spell, and I hear her laugh.

"Don't tell her the stone magic did all the work; I want to bask as a cool girl for a few more minutes," I mumble out of the side of my mouth.

"I don't want you—"

I turn back to him, and Corbin swallows. He reaches over and picks grotty bits of ceiling paint out of my hair.

His eyes are haunted and sad. "I don't like the thought of you having to learn to fight, but I never want to see you on the floor with a bruised face and a cut lip ever again." He sweeps his thumb across my healed bottom lip in a caress, and the sweet moment is ruined when his eyes flash with anger. "If you wait right here and perhaps look away, I'm going to kill that damn elf."

Vivanti hears the threat, and in the next breath, he's up, stumbling to his feet. Swaying, he pulls out another one of those spell balls. This one is a deadly red.

Ah, no. "Corbin, he's got a nasty red spell!" That spell is going to blow us all up. Near the toilets, I hear Tru groan.

"Elf!" Corbin bellows.

"I'm going to kill you all!" Vivanti cocks his arm to prepare to toss the spell.

The floor behind him visibly shifts, and I see a tuft of purple hair on the top of a head and a massive, big mouth. Serrated teeth fill the creature's maw and the... *worm*. I blink. I'd recognise that tuft of purple hair anywhere. That's the little worm I lost only a few days ago.

It has grown!

The worm rises like a snake, dives, and swallows the elf whole. His screams are cut off when there is a crunch and then, a few seconds later, a pop of the spell. Then nothing. The worm lets out a burp and what I can only describe as a happy purr and disappears into the floor, and as if it's liquid, the concrete falls back into place as if it was never disturbed.

Corbin snatches me up off the floor to hold me princess-style. I don't know what picking me up will do. But I enjoy being in his arms.

"What on earth was that?" Tru whispers.

"A. Guard. Worm," I reply, an edge of panic in my voice. That sounds about right.

"Just now, there was some... um..." Tru swallows; she looks a little pale. "...crunching." She wrinkles her nose and points into the bathroom. "Before it ate the blond elf, I think it ate your other prisoners."

"Oh," I whisper.

"Will your guard worm be doing that all the time? Eating people? Do you think it's coming back for dessert?" Corbin protectively hugs me to his chest and stares at the concrete. I'm sure he is ready to leap away with me at a moment's notice. That's kind of sweet. Unless... unless he's going to use me as bait and throw me at the worm while he runs away. That's less sweet.

The snail communication spell warms on my wrist, and a soft female voice whispers in my head. *Ello. I'm sorry I didn't get to you fast enough. Are you okay?*

Am I okay? My eyes widen when I realise the worm is talking to me. *I'm fine*, I mentally whisper back. *I appreciate your help.* That's okay, right? To thank her for eating the elf and saving our lives. He was horrible, and that spell would have taken out the subway and us with it.

You are so welcome, and you saved me first. Gave me a home away from that jerk. It was a pleasure to eat him. Tell the unicorn and tiger that I'm a death worm. I only have to eat a few times a year. But if they have any bodies to dispose of, I will not say no. I'll happily get rid of any evidence. I've already eaten the five other elves; the one in the wall was fun. I wanted to let you know that as the reaper and my friend, you have nothing to fear from me.

Okay, well, thank you. The worm's thoughts disappear from my mind, and the charm goes cold. I guess we can discuss not eating my friends another time.

I relay the conversation, and Tru mumbles, "I might know a few people who would make great worm food."

"Can you put me down please?"

Corbin gently lowers me, and I feel his intent gaze. "You have an impressive new ward encasing the tunnels. How did the elves get in?" Corbin whispers the last few words into my hair. I stiffen and tilt my chin, blinking up at him.

I really like this man, but I don't trust him to have my back or to know my secrets. "Oh, well, I…" I clamp my lips closed.

Oh heck. Please don't see that I'm lying. I'm a little lost for words. What do I say? I can't very well tell him I let them in.

CHAPTER
THIRTY

WHEN I DON'T SAY anything, Corbin continues, "Your stone magic trapped the elves and let us in without your input as soon as we came close. It looks like things are better with the communication?" He says all this with a soft growl.

He's fishing.

The last time he saw me, I was struggling to even get into the subway, and then hours later, I am trapping elves in the floor. He can't know I've no longer got the runes. I need to lie like I never have before, and I have to stop tugging at my sleeve and giving the game away.

Come on, Pepper, you can do this.

I know it's not ideal getting smacked around by the

elf, but in hindsight—if I ignore the ache in my still-healing bones—it's the best thing that could have happened, especially with Corbin turning up when he did.

I look like a victim.

A victim with no magical powers—no one magical would have taken a beating like that—and I'm not even going to think about the null band. I did the impossible and destroyed it. Who can do that? That kind of power will instantly get me killed. Now I'm glad I wasn't throwing magic around or invisible. That would have been a nightmare to talk my way out of. Corbin needs to think I'm still covered in runes, with my magic locked down nice and tight, just as his boss wants.

I'm a terrible liar and won't be able to keep up the ruse of not having access to my magic. I'm not sneaky enough, and I'll make a mistake. They need to go. I cough and clear my throat. Time to lay the guilt on nice and thick.

"With the runes, I haven't got access to any magic, and I think they are so strong they're even stopping me from using the charms. When I do, it hurts so bad it gives me huge headaches. The ward keeps fluctuating, and it feels like glass is stabbing me in the eyes when I try to fix it. When the elves came, it gave me a horrible nosebleed. The residual stone magic keeps doing random things." I throw my hands in the air with frustration. It all sounds plausible, truth mixed with lies. "I couldn't, you know…" I shrug and drop my arms to my sides.

I see the bloom of shame in his dark blue eyes. *That's it. Yes, that's it.*

"You need to work on getting those runes off her, Corbin," says Tru. "If you don't do it, I will—or I can call Forrest, and nobody wants that. I'm sure she'll get them off in a jiffy, but not before she burns down a quarter of Faerie."

The tiger winces. "I'll fix it."

Okay, now I'm feeling guilty. I give Tru a grateful smile and do my best to change the subject. "I'm glad you could get in and rescue me. I wouldn't have lasted much longer if you hadn't. Let's hope, with my poor connection to the stone magic, I can get you both out and it doesn't eat you." I grin sheepishly.

It is not quite what I wanted, but suddenly they both look keen to leave. Fancy that.

"Don't worry, guys. Even without my magic, these tunnels are still mine; it's my domain, my home. Up there"—I point to the ceiling and the street above—"I have zero control, and I'm easy pickings. I'm scared out of my mind all the time. But here I've spent ten years soaking my magic into the stone. Anything with even a spec of stone dust is mine. Well, it used to be."

I allow myself a self-deprecating laugh; it's not difficult to remember how awful it is to be powerless.

I give the tiger sad eyes. "It was only my lack of experience and not having control of the magic that was my downfall this time. Next time, I'll do better."

"Let's hope there won't be a next time." The tiger

leans down and kisses me on the tip of the nose. "I'm sorry, Pepper. I'll fix this. I was wrong. Not having your magic made you vulnerable, and I could have got you killed."

"That's what your boss wants, right?" I avoid looking at him. "It's okay. You can go. I will be fine. I have some cleaning to do."

"Do you need any help? Oh here." Tru pulls out a potion and shoves it into my hand. "It's an extra-strong Clean Me Now spell. It's the type we use for crime scenes."

"Are you sure? That's very kind."

"No bother. Hey, do you need a ward?" She digs back into her pocket. "You said the one you've got is acting up?"

I can't in good conscience accept a ward when the one I have works perfectly well. I really shouldn't have taken the cleaning spell. "It's fine. It is very difficult to get down here. The elves came through the tunnels, and they only got here with a tracking spell. As long as there are no other elves with access to my blood or hair, I'll be fine."

I walk them to my exit spot—as there's no longer an elf leader hunting me, there should be no issue if they leave that way. I'll still be using random paths in and out. The slaver elf might be dead, but I still have a tiger and the other elf problem and an issue with Death.

"You can't stay here with that worm," Corbin says behind me. "Come with me. Please give me a chance to keep you safe."

Safe?

I swallow and avoid his eyes. "Why ever not? She's my worm, a guard worm. I will be perfectly safe."

"Guard worm," Tru huffs as she stares at the wall, doing her best to give us some privacy.

Corbin takes hold of my hand. "Can I at least replace your phone? If you're not coming with me, you need a communication method, and I can't keep coming down here." His handsome face flashes with disgust as he scans the subway.

I shake my head. If he gives me a phone, there's no way anything I do or say will remain private. He'll know every message and every call. "I will get a phone this week."

He narrows his eyes.

"Tomorrow. I'll get a phone tomorrow." I frown down at the floor and scuff the concrete with my boot. All this lying is taking it out of me. My stomach is bubbling. "Thank you both for your help; it must have been a long night. It was lovely meeting you, Tru. Good-bye." I tug my hand from his and wave.

The tiger leans in and gives me a kiss on the cheek.

I close my eyes at the feel of his lips. I don't ask the magic to do anything and to be cautious; I lock it down tight into my core so it can't interfere with my final last piece of acting. Instead, I continue to stare at the floor, awkwardly shuffle, and make a face like I urgently need to use the bathroom.

Corbin and Tru exchange glances.

"It will just be one second…" I hold up a finger. "Could you… erm, let them out?" I beg the concrete in a weird-sounding whisper. Hmm. My acting skills are subpar, and I feel like an idiot.

The magic at my feet stirs in confusion, but it sluggishly moves, and I observe the stone cautiously do its thing and shove them up to the promenade.

I stand there for a moment, allowing my power to unravel, my breaths loud in my ears. There's a massive lump in my throat. My body still feels like it has been used as a punching bag—healed, but the memory of the trauma still clings to me.

I move, and my boots echo around the subway. I stop in the centre and direct the stone magic to remove the broken doors and the sad, broken cone. The potion vial Tru gave me is warm in my hand. It makes no sense to use it as I know I can't stay. No one can get down here to appreciate a clean floor anyway. I slide the spell into my pocket and hobble towards the redbrick tunnel and my room.

I may have overdone the entire stone thing, and when he has time to get over his guilt, he'll see that things don't add up. Then he'll be back, growling. Even if the tiger is suspicious, he won't expect me to have all the runes off in such a short space of time.

He'll be back, but I won't be here.

I need to leave. I can find another tunnel. It might not be as lovely as my redbrick one, but I will find another home and perhaps some more friends.

I'm gutted. I do like him, really like him. We could have been a thing. My first thing. A soft, disappointed sigh leaves me. Time to pack. I can be on a train within a few hours. The train station is the last one on the line, so whichever one I choose, I won't even need to pick a destination. I'll do it randomly. Just jump on the next train about to leave the platform, and it will take me far away from here.

As I move through the wall, I place my hand against the tunnel. The red brick is rough and oh so familiar under my palm. With heartfelt emotion, my magic pushes out my next words to the surrounding tunnels, the concrete, the stone on the promenade and the tarmac on the road outside. "I love you. Thank you for keeping me sheltered and safe." I wipe away a stray tear. "Thank you for always being there. It's not goodbye forever. It's just goodbye for now."

If anyone heard my words, they'd think me crazy. Yet I feel blessed to have this stone magic. It's different, odd and quirky, just like me.

I'm sorry to have to walk away.

It feels like I'm walking away from myself.

Things have changed. I can't fight Madán and Corbin just to keep my magic and sense of self, and I shouldn't have to justify my existence to powerful creatures.

I rest my forehead on the bricks. "Forgive Corbin, I have. He has a difficult job to do. If he comes looking for me or if he needs any help, please help him if you can."

For the last time, I pour as much power as I can spare into the stone, hoping it will sustain the magic I've created here.

Until the day I can come home.

CHAPTER
THIRTY-ONE

I SHUFFLE TOWARDS MY ROOM. I might even try London. The city is vast, with so many magical signatures no one will track me down. Not even the hellhound. I turn the corner and see a wolf stretched out on the floor.

I freeze.

"What the hell, Eurus! What are you doing here? You hand me over to the elves and then dare to come back here and sleep!" Did he think Vivanti had carted me off, so now it's okay to pop in and take over my home?

The bloody rude wolf! My nostrils flare, and then all my righteous anger is gone. He can have everything. It's no longer mine.

My bottom lip wobbles. I move around the big furry

beast to my shelves and pull out the folded fae bag. Might as well use it. I stand sideways to keep one eye on the beithíoch and give my cans of pineapple a sad look. There is no way the heavy cans can come with me.

It appears I may have misunderstood the nuances of such exchanges that offering information to elves was a customary practice. After all, the tiger shifter, with his warrior-elf companion, engaged in such diplomatic inter-actions, and forgiveness was granted to all, says Eurus.

I make a *humph* sound.

I merely confirmed the details of your location; they had a tracking spell. The decision to open the door, child, was an endeavour you undertook with much enthusiasm. The wards, once impenetrable, succumbed to your own actions, and you crafted a convenient breach of your cher-ished tunnel. The responsibility for welcoming the unsavoury characters rests solely upon your shoulders. You let them in.

I scowl and stuff in my clothes. "I know," I grumble. Once I've finished with my clothing, I start on the elf blanket. I attempt to roll it but promptly give up after only a few seconds. It gets the same shoving treatment as my clothes.

"I'm glad you are okay." The words are reluctantly pulled out of me. I *am* glad, and if it's the last time I'll speak to him, I might as well be nice. What does it matter really? I can't begrudge him for saving himself.

Wait a minute; something doesn't add up. "How did you speak to the elves?" Hands on hips, I glare.

I am a beithíoch. Eurus puffs up his furry chest.

"That doesn't explain it." I narrow my eyes and tap my foot.

As if he is taking pity on me, he explains, *I'm telepathic. This splendid vocabulary didn't just manifest from chatting with myself. I acquired the art of telepathy a thousand years past.*

"If you're telepathic and can speak to everyone, what does the charm do?"

I am telepathic while you, unfortunately, are not. The charm is designed to facilitate communication, the transmission of your thoughts directly into my mind. However, you insist on vocalising your words, rendering its purpose obsolete.

Ah, like when speaking to the worm. I spoke directly into her head, and that makes sense. But what about the hotel... "If that is the case, why didn't you talk to me at the hotel? Why did we go through the rigmarole of getting the charms before you'd speak to me?"

I had no desire to engage in communication with you; my sole objective was to extricate you from the influence of the tiger and the warrior elf. Your charm bracelet stood as a crucial component in ensuring your survival.

"Oh."

So he didn't speak to me until after we'd got the bracelet back. Good to know. My tongue pokes at a sharp tusk. All this time, Eurus seemed genuine enough while he manipulated me. You know what? I hate everybody. I turn to finish packing.

Where are you going?

"I'm leaving. The Lord of Winter is an issue, and his hellhound will cause even more problems for me, so I'm out."

You are leaving? Even so, Death will assuredly find you.

"Oh, I know." I know he'll find me. I peek at my arm, and there is no trace of the runes, nothing but Death's mark. "The Death rune is getting darker," I tell him as I roll down my sleeve.

Yes, Death has the ability to locate you more easily now you have achieved the status of a full reaper. Congratulations, child.

My hand freezes on the medical kit with the book of runes, and I turn my head to look straight at him. "I'm a full what? I thought I was a half-transitioned reaper. What's changed?" *Oh no. What did I do now?* I will not run around screaming in horror. I won't. I place the box in the bag.

The beithíoch sniffs. *You have finally harnessed the depths of your powers. Not a simple feat, really—a matter of embracing the magic woven into your essence. A task not unlike those undertaken by the heroes of ancient tales, where the impossible is made possible. Your encounter with the elven adversaries, those slavers, proved to be the catalyst that coaxed you out of your self-imposed cocoon. I had a hunch that a nudge in the right direction was all you needed.*

Eurus's wolfy expression is smug if his toothy grin is

any indication, as if I followed his dastardly plan to the letter.

I told Death all you needed was a bit of encouragement, and his intervention was unnecessary. He wanted to step in to help you and explain a few things, but I said let things play out, and lo and behold, events unfolded just as anticipated. I came to watch over you, a vigilant eye on your journey. My purpose was to ensure that matters didn't spiral out of control. You, child, not only weathered every trial fate hurled your way but also flourished in the process. You've become a testament to resilience, truly worthy of the revered title of a reaper.

It saddens me that your mate did not share in your triumph. Alas, he let misguided duty overshadow the path he knew to be right. A regrettable choice.

I don't know how to pick all he just said apart. I think my brain has melted. He's working with Death, and this was all some elaborate test I passed.

I won't even go there with the mate thing. I can't have a mate. If I had a mate, he'd be a troll, not a tiger shifter, and shifters don't have fated mates, and even if they did, and it's a big secret, surely their mates are not cross species.

Nope, I'm done. I pack my washbag. "What does Death want?"

To meet you, naturally. Come now, young one, gather your belongings. It's time we departed from this dreadful place.

I chuckle. He wants me to leave with him, and I'm

considering his proposal. Did I leave all my common sense on the floor of the subway when the elf leader attempted to bash my head in?

I fill the rest of the bag with the things I need and stuff I can't part with. Not that I have much. I've never been bothered about things.

"What about the worm?"

The worm? Ah, Dora.

Dora the worm. I rub my face. "Yes, will she be okay?"

Rest assured, she will fare well. Now let us proceed.

I grab the bag and my new coat, popping a couple of cans of pineapple into the pockets. I don't have it in me to leave them all.

You are prepared?

I nod.

Eurus places his paw on my leg, and we disappear.

CHAPTER
THIRTY-TWO

Eurus's power clears, and the world comes back together piece by piece until we are standing in an oblong room. The magic inside me pulses, gathering all the information it can. This structure consists of Cornish granite and Portland stone. The walls sing of an important job, of water, people, vehicles, and ships. I listen harder; it's difficult as this isn't my stone.

And I lock the thought down nice and tight, as it only leads to sadness. I've moved on before and will do it again without bemoaning why me.

We are in London, Eurus tells me. His furry coat brushes against my leg, nudging me to the left. *Death is waiting for you.*

I swallow. Without asking, I drop the heavy bag as it's

making my shoulder and back ache. I lay my coat on top to free my hands. I wring them. Suddenly I am frightened, but I'm here now. It is better for me to come to him rather than for Death to hunt me down.

I force my feet to move where the beithíoch directs me—no need to put this off any more than I have. We walk through a door, up a set of curving stairs, into a narrow hallway and a lovely library.

The scent of well-worn books and polished wood greets me. Rows of freestanding mahogany bookshelves are bathed in natural light from tall, arched windows on all sides of the room.

The wolf disappears, and I'm all alone.

I ignore the beautiful books. My vision is blurry; panic makes me hot and out of breath. Itchy. I'm way too nervous to make out the words on their spines. I wander across the room to a tall arched window, and with sweaty hands resting on a dark grey sill, I lean forward to gaze at the breathtaking panoramic views of London.

The River Thames is spread before me, and its brown waters reflect the changing hues of the sky. This building sits *in* the river. I can see the Tower of London, St Paul's Cathedral, and The Shard to the west, and I think that's Canary Wharf to the east. Now I know what the stone was trying to tell me; it all makes sense.

We are on a bridge.

And the bridge sings.

Goosebumps rise as I think of the tons of steel surrounding me on both sides. The stone is just a cladding, and steel is the building framework. This place isn't good for my health. As I gaze out the window, I scratch the back of my neck.

"Here, Pepper, I had this made for you. It will help with the metal." A charm drops, and I whip my hand out to catch it. As soon as the hammer settles its rocking motion on my palm, I instantly feel better; no chanting is required, the horrid itchiness is gone, and I can take a full breath.

"Thank you," I say, feeling my words come back from the glass as a warm breath. I'm struggling to turn my head to greet him—this man who is Death.

I drop my eyes and offer the charm to my bracelet, and the little hammer jumps into the space the cat charm left. I then gather my courage and lift my eyes to see an old man.

It's rare to meet someone who looks so old; humans grow old, but not like this. This man, this being, looks like he'll break in half with a stiff breeze.

Death.

He is an ancient-looking creature. Balding, and what hair left on his head is a fluffy white. The strands are almost floating. I glance at his hands. No sign of a scythe. I expected a billowing robe, not soft-looking brown trousers and a light green Argyle jumper.

"It's a pleasure to meet you, Pepper."

I expected him to sound like Eurus, posh and a challenge to understand, but he doesn't. He sounds more modern, which makes his ancient appearance odd.

Death's eyes, though, are ageless pools of wisdom that peer out from his weathered face. He looks like a retired professor, a human. And that is the scariest thing of all.

"It's nice to meet you too," I croak over the lie.

Death smiles at me, his eyes kind, and holds out a hand for me to shake. His knuckles are swollen, and his skin feels rough and paper thin around my hand.

"I believe I have some explaining to do." Two comfortable reading chairs appear from out of nowhere, and I stop myself from jumping by locking my knees. "Please won't you sit down?"

"Thank you." I sit.

"We are at my residence in the North Tower of Tower Bridge."

I know little about London and the city's bridges, but if I remember right, it's both a bascule bridge—that splits and opens in the middle like a drawbridge, and each piece of the bridge rises to allow the passage of tall ships down the River Thames—and a suspension bridge.

"It's a beautiful bridge."

"It is, thank you. It was designed to complement the Tower of London." He moves to the other chair and throws himself down like a teenager. Huh. I think his wizard-old-man look is a disguise. "I am Death. Do you know what you are?"

"It has been explained to me that I'm the reaper."

Death nods. "Indeed, you are."

I need to know—and it might be impolite to move Death's planned introductory conversation along, but if

I don't, I will climb out of my skin. I need to know what he wants. "What do you want me to do?"

Please, please don't say kill people.

"Do?" A deeper wrinkle forms between Death's bushy white brows.

"Yes. As the reaper, what is my job?" My heart is pounding so fast it feels like it's going to fly out of my chest and land on the floor in a bloody mess. "Why have you asked me here?"

"You've noticed the souls, the balls of light? Yes?"

"Yes."

"Great." He gives me a warm, wrinkly smile. "And you've noticed they seem to sink into your skin, or as soon as they touch you, they disappear."

"Yes."

"Well, Pepper"—he points a crooked finger at me—"for now that's your job. You are one of two portals. A portal for all the realm's souls to move on to their next life." He flops back in the chair. "Recycling isn't a new concept. I've been an advocate from the beginning since all the realms began. You're doing your job by merely existing. I know it's not very glamorous, adventurous, or exciting, but it's an important job you do."

"That's all I do? Just hang about and wait for souls to just"—I make a *puff* and flick my fingers at my chest.

He shrugs. "Pretty much. Until you die a natural death, and then I get to retire." Death props his legs on the coffee table. "You'll take over my role as Death and find a reaper soul of your very own in a few hundred thousand years or so, and that reaper will take over for you."

"What the heck do you mean I'm going to live for a few hundred thousand years or so?"

Death shrugs. "More, you are truly immortal."

Oh. I'll unpack this later when I'm on my own. I can't freak out in front of Death, not when I'm doing so well. The tightness in my throat is burning. "What happened to the other one, the other reaper before me?"

"Ah, well, the last reaper was me. There have only ever been two born portals, and that's us. Let's be honest: Death walks in the door, and everyone freaks out." He waves his hands. "The reaper is less of a heart-attack-inducing creature, Death's minion. I made the entire reaper thing up to keep the warrior elves under my thumb, but you know magic and fate have a fantastic sense of humour and ridiculous way of making imagined things real. Here you are."

Okay. We are both soul-recycling portals, but that isn't all he does, right? There must be more to this. "If you don't mind me asking, what do *you* do?"

"Ah, well, it's all very fascinating. I deal with wicked souls and get them where they need to go. You might think we destroy evil, but good and evil must be balanced." He holds his hand up and tips it like scales. "You can't have one without the other. When it's your turn, you will do things your way. Your magic will manifest with what you need, what the realms need. Some things I could have done millennia ago are lost in time.

Wars, great evil, incredible feats of survival—you will experience the realms as they fall and rise again.

"What you went through with your clan... I'm sorry, Pepper. The magic that makes creatures forget our existence went into overdrive on your blood relations. Fate's parameters for the spell didn't change to account for your youth." He winces and scratches the wispy hairs at the back of his head. "The ways of fate and its insistence on creatures learning life lessons can be hard on a soul. Perhaps one day you might come to believe it was necessary, or perhaps not. It's wearisome on any creature to see so much change. Perhaps that is why fate made your early years so hard. You had to be capable of surviving; no one, not even I, could interfere. Not that I knew." He frowns, and those bushy eyebrows of his dance.

"What about love? Family, friends."

Death waves his hand. "You can have love; if you choose a mate, they will be by your side forever if that's what you both want. But even with the most loyal of friends, you will fade from their minds after a few weeks or months of not seeing them."

Like Jessica at the dry cleaners and other acquaintances I know. If I don't see somebody regularly, they forget about me. Things finally make sense.

Gosh, that's horrible.

"And Pepper, you will fade from everyone's mind; your deeds might be remembered, but not you unless you give them the power to see through the cowl."

"A power that Madán and his line of aes sídhe warriors have."

"Yes. I gave them that power. What we are is an amazing gift and a terrible burden, and it can put the people we love at significant risk. How you live your life is up to you. You can continue to be the messenger; you can open any portal to any realm. You can work in a shop, travel the realms, or sit at home and read amazing books. Fate will test you along the way. That is an unfortunate given. This is just the start of your journey."

I absorb all his words. It's a lot to take in. I have so many answers and so many more questions. I don't understand his appearance, and I might as well ask while he's here answering my questions. "You don't look like that, do you? You aren't an old man."

"Of course I don't. We live in a world where age is overlooked, experience and wrinkles are frowned upon, so many creatures are immortal and keep their good looks. They stay vibrant, and with the vibrancy of their youth, the powerful are dangerous and swiftly eliminated. What appears before you is a disguise to pad their feeble minds. If people look at me and see an ancient man, most can't help but acquaint that with a doddering fool. When age and wisdom were important, I appeared as a child. Being overlooked by the arrogance of creatures is something I will always take advantage of."

"So you're trying to trick me?"

"No, Pepper, I'm not trying to trick you. Fate guides the changes, and it's been so long since I changed my appearance that I've forgotten what I used to look like, and I'm lazy. It's easier to stay as I am, and it doesn't bother me as I am not a vain man. I don't stare into a mirror in horror. My health and strength are the same as my youth. I might not look it, but I'm in my prime. Come. Let me show you to your room, and then perhaps we can have a spot of breakfast."

"Will I have to stay here?"

"What? No. You are not a prisoner, Pepper, and you aren't a child. You can stay wherever you want. Your role as a reaper is instinctive, and you already have everything you will need." He touches his chest. "Inside you."

CHAPTER
THIRTY-THREE

IT'S BEEN A FEW DAYS, and everything feels a bit strange; who knew Death would be kind? I sure didn't. I'm cautious around him, but he hasn't done anything yet to freak me out.

The guilt of not going to see Tilly is eating me up. I sent an email of apology and then deactivated all my accounts. Soon it won't matter. I've been walking around London, mouth open like a proper tourist. It's so strange seeing places in person when you've seen them on television, and the history of the buildings and beauty blows my mind.

I miss my tunnels, and I miss *him*.

I'm unsure if I was too harsh or cold in walking away the way I did, and then there is Eurus offhandedly mentioning we could be mates. The beithíoch's flippant words are constantly with me along with Death's. *You will fade from everyone's mind.*

Soon the tiger will forget about me if he hasn't already. Crap, that is seriously messed up. It's bloody traumatising.

Corbin is going to be the one who got away, and he will never know.

Then I get angry with myself. What does it matter? The tiger is all duty and honour. He'd fight for his Council and the Lord of Winter, yet he wouldn't for me. Who wants to be with someone who won't fight for them, who's not in their corner nor their biggest supporter?

Just like I am with him?

Yep, and I'm a hypocrite. I'm just as bad—worse. I never gave him a chance to fix anything. I ran away, explaining nothing. I didn't trust him enough—with good reason, but I can't moan about him not taking on the mighty Winter Court while screaming my name. Corbin is powerful, but he isn't stupid.

What a mess, and I'm being ridiculous 'cause we haven't even kissed. A kiss on the forehead, nose, and cheek, whoop-de-doo. I'm such a stud.

I sidestep a group of office workers and push the thoughts of Corbin away. I don't want to live in London. It's too busy, and I don't need to be invisible to remain unseen here. This beautiful city isn't for me. I need to move on. Death owns so much property; he has offered me the use of various residences and access to funds that make my head spin. I can move anywhere, even to realms I've never heard of.

Yet I have this big thing I need to do. It's been niggling in the back of my mind, and I know it's a risk that can get me hurt, but it's been giving me nightmares. I need to know if Vivanti's slaves have been freed or if they've gone from him to another owner. It isn't in me to let this go. Now I've had some time to think and some sleep, I'm ready. I'm going to Faerie to track them down, and if I need to get them out, I will.

I have a responsibility. I was them, even if it was only for a painful few hours.

I've yet to figure out what I will do with any bad guys I find or their victims. But I know I'll need to handle things like I dealt with the first few elves. I frown— before they got eaten by Dora the worm, that is. Using the advantages of my magical strengths first instead of getting into another punching bag situation because of a bizarre and dangerous need to do a hero speech with the bad guy.

Who does that? *Me. I did that.*

Getting kicked and punched in the face, then almost carted off with the slaver elf for the second time. I shake my head. The lesson of stealthy surprise—if I go hunting —has now been hammered into my brain along with a painful reminder of what not to do.

I've so much to learn, but I won't know a thing hiding behind Death's robes. I don't care if creatures don't know it's me or no one knows what I'm doing. It is better they don't.

I was the messenger for a long time and never felt the need to brag or let the realms know. The same rules apply: head down, keep invisible, use my magic, save some creatures, and learn more about myself as I go. Live. Live my life. And this is the best way to keep myself busy and safe from the Lord of Winter's reach.

Madán. I wrinkle my nose. Out of everyone, he'll remember me. Great. How unfair is that?

Death is sure that now that I'm a full reaper, Madán will leave me well enough alone. But *I'm* not too sure. I saw his eyes. His fear controls him, and what Corbin said was right. I've seen it with my own eyes. Frightened powerful creatures with massive egos are dangerous to your health. I don't think he'll stop.

The River Thames laps below as I turn left and make my way onto the pedestrian side of the bridge deck leading to the North Tower. I see a few bright-coloured kayaks taking advantage of the calm waters on this cold but sunny day. There's a splash, and a green fin disappears below the brown water, a mermaid's tail. I grin. The water is brackish—a mixture of fresh- and saltwater that the mermaids seem to like.

A niggly pain shoots from my hand, and I glance down at the straining shopping bag. It is so heavy it's making the skin on my fingers a dark green. I swap the bag to my other hand and rub the sore digits against my leg. I might have put too many cans in the bag. I found the pineapple, the beautiful black-label kind Corbin bought me, and of course buying them makes me miss him more.

What a fool I am. At least I'm aware of my own foibles.

I lift my eyes back to the path and see Madán with a smug, unhinged grin. His large pale blue eyes sparkle, and his dark hair is pulled back in a tight, intricate plait close to his skull. His black warrior runes track down his neck and disappear beneath the collar of his shirt. He's dressed to fight, with a few iron knives strapped to his legs and a sword on his back.

I groan and shake my head. *Damn you, fate.* I've really got to watch what I'm thinking as creatures tend to pop up out of the stonework.

My heart jumps, and butterflies bounce and dance in my stomach as I notice Corbin behind him. The tiger leans against the ornate blue-and-white railings, his back to the river. It's a misleadingly relaxed pose; his fists are bunched against his sides.

He looks like he's had zero sleep these past few days. The tiger also looks straight through me, as he can't see me while I'm cloaked, but by his observation of Madán and his tense expression, he knows I'm here.

An invisible enemy.

Will he remember me? Will his beautiful dark blue eyes be hard or, worse, glazed like my mother's? *Oh boy, that hurts.* I don't have the strength to go through that again.

Come on, Pepper. You can deal with it later when you are alone and not dealing with a warrior elf. Later you can fall apart.

A warrior elf who has an iron sword.

Have they come to kill me?

Fantastic. Well, they've chosen an excellent place to confront me. I can't use my stone magic here as I've got zero magical finesse with this location, and over the water on a steel bridge... my chances are not great. Not unless I want to go for the concrete supports and kill hundreds of people and destroy a nineteenth-century bridge.

I could knock Madán out with a good swing of my pineapple-heavy bag.

Gah. I brush a hand down my face. I have so much to do and plan that I do not have time for this confrontation.

"There you are, Pepper. You removed my runes, I see." His voice is oily.

I tilt my head to the side as I contemplate lying and telling him Death removed them. But I removed them, and he needs to see me as a creature in my own right and not the scared little girl that I was only a few short days ago. I can save myself with the powerful magic at my fingertips. Even on a bridge, I'm not defenceless. I am a reaper and a troll.

I'm also not his enemy but can be if he makes me. I'm done tiptoeing around silly creatures. *It might be best though to avoid any heroic speeches.*

"Yes, I removed them. I removed them the same day

your pet hellhound put them onto my skin." Guilt eats at me as soon as the words are out of my mouth. It's wrong to call Corbin a pet. It's also a lie; it wasn't really the same day. But it was close enough.

A muscle ticks in the elf's jaw.

"Madán, what do you want?" My voice holds no malice. I feel so tired of all this.

His chest puffs up, and his eyes flash with anger. "I am the Lord of Winter. You will address me as such."

My lips twitch, and I bow my head with amused respect. "Then you may call me Reaper. If we're throwing around the titles."

Corbin tenses when halfway through my little speech I drop my cloak, popping out of nowhere; even when the hellhound knows I'm here, it must be a bit of a shock.

Madán scowls. "I'm a fae lord. I have people, thousands of creatures at my command, and I'm beloved in my court. I earned my title."

Now then, is he saying I haven't? I shrug, and the plastic bag of pineapple in my hand rustles. Whatever. Okay, let's play this game. "I take the realm's souls to their afterlife. I'm eternal and one of two portals to another plane of existence you will never comprehend. Decillions of souls will make their last journey with me. Including you, Lord of Winter."

"Is that a threat?" Madán snarls.

I roll my eyes. "No. I'm stating a fact, everyone dies." Okay, well, it seems I must get down to business. "I've been given permission." I say the following words in a soft, rehearsed tone. "We have granted you a precious gift, one you've misused by wielding the power of sight against a creature you swore to protect and forcefully blocking magic for your selfish purposes. Madán, Lord of the Winter Court, you are a vow breaker, and I have been granted permission to reclaim that gift."

There, I've said the words. Now comes the freaky bit. I somehow have to touch him. This is going to be fun.

"What are you blathering on about? I have had no gift from you."

I shrug. It's like talking to an iron girder.

"Kill her," he commands Corbin.

"Really, you're not going to do this yourself? And you have such a nice pointy sword." I dare to point at said sword.

Both the hellhound and I look at the elf.

The tiger's bulging arms cross his chest, and he raises a single eyebrow. An impossible low warning growl comes rumbling from his chest, and as he meets my gaze, his eyes roll with fire.

Oh, that's not good.

I latch on to my magic, readying myself. But hope stops me. I've just been moaning about not giving Corbin a chance. So against my best judgement, I don't recloak and run away screaming—which when confronted with a tiger shifter who can set himself on fire would be the most sensible thing.

I wait.

CHAPTER
THIRTY-FOUR

Congratulations, Pepper, the guy you have been pining for is going to kill you. My chin quakes. *Please don't let me be wrong. Please. Please. Please.*

Corbin moves.

The tiger springs towards me, and his hand snatches the back of Madán's collar and yanks. The surprise attack makes me gasp and throws the elf off balance. Madán chokes as the tiger drags him ten feet out of sight of the main walkway and onto the curved concrete viewing area that juts into the River Thames and is the tower's base.

I hurry to follow. The few people hanging around scatter. Creatures and humans know better than to stick around for a fight. It also helps motivate them when the tiger roars out a forceful, "Move out of the way!"

One-handed, Corbin rips his coat off and kicks it aside. When the last few people are clear, controlling the environment further, the tiger throws down a temporary ward. The spell blooms to life, covering the entire area so no one can hear or interfere.

Then he lets Madán go.

I press myself against the stone facade of the North Tower, set down my bag of pineapple, and with my hand over my mouth, I watch the Lord of Winter go ballistic.

The air crackles with tension as the elf lunges forward, expertly swinging his sword at my tiger's neck. Corbin easily sidesteps, and two gleaming long knives —around the length of my forearm—appear in his hands.

On the sword's return swing, the blades clang as Corbin meets the elf weapon with lethal grace.

"You dare to strike against me. I am your lord!"

"You are not my lord." To hammer his point home, Corbin twists his arm, and Madán gets a blow to his face from the tiger's elbow. "I told you, buddy, I don't work for you." His knives blur as he counters the sword's next swing.

Corbin is fast.

And without his coat hiding his outline, I can study the confident way he moves. Broad shoulders and a narrow waist give him that triangular shape, and muscular legs carry a man who doesn't know how to hesitate—no wasted gestures. His movement is predatory and aggressive against the agile but smaller elf. I wince each time Madán strikes as his weapon has a more extended reach than Corbin's blades.

"I work for the general and the Hunters Guild. He ordered me to keep you alive as he owes you. That favour will not cover this." Corbin grunts when Madán kicks him in the stomach. "The general will be appalled when I tell him you ordered me to kill a defenceless, innocent girl. You have gone too far this time. Pepper has done nothing to you, and I will not allow you to hurt her."

"You've made a mistake, hellhound. Death has also made a mistake in choosing a lesser fae as a reaper, a troll." Madán lets out a strained laugh as the blades once again clash. "I'd rather the reaper be a human or a half-blood than a weak, nasty troll. Do you know how embarrassing that is?"

Wow. What a dick.

"You can smell her fear, right? Just as I can see it in her eyes. Trolls can't do real magic. In battle, they are used only as cannon fodder. Your precious Pepper is even weaker than her useless brethren. She is pathetic. Going against me on her behalf is a huge mistake."

The sword and the knives connect, and with a swift, calculated manoeuvre, Corbin does something fancy with his blades. One moment they're crossed, and then he twists his hands. The movement is so fast I can't track it. The tiger expertly disarms the elf, sending the iron sword clattering to the ground.

Madán chuckles as he stands defiantly against Corbin, oddly calm about losing his sword. His hand hovers over his knife, his eyes narrow, and a peculiar expression crosses his face—the black runes on Madán's neck pulse.

Oh heck. I forgot about his magic!

The air shivers with growing fae energy and the scent of green grass and flowers. I know he's chanting an incantation in his mind. I can feel the power swirling inside him, a prelude to an impending deadly spell.

With an assured motion, Madán raises his hand, index finger poised to etch a rune into the unseen canvas of the air.

Uh-oh.

He smiles as a twisting ball of magic ignites from the finished rune and barrels towards me.

Corbin moves, blocking the oncoming spell with his bulk.

My fear turns to seething anger. *How dare he!* Madán will not hurt my tiger. A strange new coldness burns in my chest, forcing its way down my arms and into my hands. My vision flickers into second sight, and instead of green, the magic pooling into my palms is black.

I dodge to the side and extend my hands, calling upon the powers from another plane of existence. The magic blasts out of me with a resounding *boom,* and a torrent of black power smashes out of me in what feels like a never-ending wave.

The warrior elf freezes.

Corbin freezes.

And the entire world stops.

It pauses.

For a moment, my rapid breaths are the only sound. *Come on, Pepper, you can freak out about this later.* My boots clomp as I stroll around the tiger. The deadly rune magic is inches from Corbin's chest, and my tiger's handsome face is frozen in an angry snarl of determination to protect me.

Reaching out, I carefully pluck the spell out of the air and away from him. Letting fate guide me, I pick the elements of the spell apart until they harmlessly disperse.

I turn my attention to Madán. His soul flickers within my reach, and if I want, I can pluck it apart like I did that spell. Kill him. His fate dances in the palm of my tiny green hand.

It all comes back to fate.

Madán was right when he said Death can see the threads of fate, of life. Death can see them and so can I.

I see them linking him to others and the realms. I'm surprised to see he has been a good man who has lost his way over the past few years. Being the Lord of Winter is a heavy burden on his shoulders.

I trace the hate for me back to when he was young; trolls hurt him, and the memory of it still hurts him. It's a horrid, twisted thing he has clung to, and it leaves a mark on his soul.

I don't remove the memories, but letting fate guide me, I heal the emotional scars and then watch what the changes do to the threads. Another tweak, and I leave him better than I found him.

Now I need to fix the other mistake.

The voice that comes out of my mouth isn't mine. Each word I speak echoes with thousands of voices. *Creepy.* "You are a vow breaker, Madán of the winter lands. Death's gift you've been given is now revoked."

With my thumb, I boop him on the tip of his nose. "Boop," I ominously whisper.

My single touch causes the black marks on his neck to shiver. The aes sídhe runes flash, and I feel Death's magic crawl out and slip inside me. The aes sídhe warrior marks are still powerful, but Madán and his warriors will no longer see us while we are cloaked, and like everyone else, they will forget we ever existed. Fate and their own minds will fill in any blanks.

Death and the Reaper will become more fairy tale than real.

Fate urges me to check again, and all the threads of fate look good. Well, all but one. Driven by instinct, I return Death's magic to a beautiful golden thread and allow Forrest to keep the gift.

I smile. Perfect.

I turn my attention back to Madán. "How did you find me?" I mumble. The answer comes, and I easily find the glowing green magic ball in Madán's left coat pocket. The spell hums, it tickles my fingertips, and the sensation travels almost past my wrist. It's potent magic and reacting to me. A tracking spell that holds my essence. Without overthinking, I dissolve it.

Scowling, I rub my itchy palm and wrist against my

thigh. They made it with something unique to me; blood would be difficult to obtain, but hair… I didn't leave any personal traces behind unless… I was unconscious in Corbin's presence, and it would take but a moment to get a hair sample.

Could he be so devious? No. I don't believe that.

I dig a little into Madán's past and again find the answer I seek. It was from the hotel in Ireland. Corbin left the hotel quickly, chasing after me, and the hair was found later without his knowledge.

When he pulled his jacket off me, I remember losing some strands and never disposing of them properly. My fault. Also, my hair is long and sheds like a fenodyree— the hairiest of fairies.

There is a movement to my left, and Death drifts towards me. He is dressed in a thick black cowl with a tatted hem that dusts the floor as he walks. The cloak is so dark its blackness tries to steal the surrounding light.

The same fabric is around me. My cowl is a dichotomy of both heavy and light.

Death tilts his head to look at the strands of Madán's fate weaved in my hand like wool. "You allow fate to work through you. I told you that you have what it takes. You are doing a wonderful job. Well done, Reaper. Madán will be a happier man without the knowledge of our existence."

I let the threads go.

The charm on my wrist heats, protecting me as I then pick up the Lord of Winter's fancy iron sword and awkwardly slide it back into its sheath. There, I've left nothing remiss. *I hope.*

"Why Forrest?"

"It feels right."

He puts a hand on my shoulder and gives me a fatherly squeeze, and then his gaze brushes over a frozen Corbin. "He is a good choice for you. If you'd like to, you can invite him to dinner." He smiles. Then his tone changes and the next words become a command that rattles me to the very bones: "Now, Reaper, let this realm go."

CHAPTER
THIRTY-FIVE

I NOD, close my eyes, and along with the remaining aes sídhe magic, tug the swirling black power back inside me. It's so cold it burns. It's like how I imagine pulling a deep-sea fishing net with your hands, an almost impossible task. I release all the magic back to where it came from, but I retain a light hold on Madán, keeping him frozen until I can explain to Corbin what has happened.

Death and my cowl disappear as time begins once again.

To counteract the now non-existent spell hurtling at his chest, the tiger's entire body ignites. The fire rolls from orange to blue, getting hotter. I shuffle out of the way and stand in front of him so he doesn't undo all my hard work by killing the elf.

I hold my hands up and continue to whisper, "It's okay."

It's okay? Yeah, right. My nose and lips are still buzzing from the residual magic I used. What the heck was all that about? How can I have that kind of power?

We make eye contact, and after he assesses the situation, the impressive flames snuff out. He takes a shallow breath. I hold on to his wrist, pushing his hand so he lowers one of the blades still in his grip. The tiger's fire magic hasn't burned a single hair, weapons, or clothing.

"It's okay," I tell him again.

Corbin drops his chin to look at me.

I wave, and his brow furrows. "It's okay." I nervously smile and scratch the back of my head. "The spell Madán conjured is gone. I froze him"—I froze the world and plucked on the threads of fate, but who will believe that? It's genuinely unbelievable—"and removed the fate-given gift so the aes sídhe will no longer be able to see Death or me while we are cloaked, and Madán and his warriors will not remember us at all. No one will." My lower lip wobbles.

No one.

I stomp across the concrete and scoop his jacket off the ground; I vigorously shake it, fold it over my arm, and hug myself.

"Is it okay if I unfreeze him?" I keep my back turned.

Corbin grunts.

Great, we're back to the grunting. "I'll just do my thing, cloak myself, and you can both be on your way."

My voice cracks on the last word. I unfreeze the elf, cloak myself, and move to stand beside the tiger. I hold his jacket and tremble. I'm in shock. I feel shaky and cold, but Corbin is safe, and he put himself between me and a nasty spell.

He fought for me. And now he's going to leave.

It takes Madán a few more seconds to fully unfreeze. He wobbles and rubs his face in one long blink while he takes in his surroundings. "I apologise, Corbin. What were you saying?" He shivers and stares at the ground. "So strange, it felt like someone had walked over my grave."

With a flick of the tiger's hands, his knives disappear. The movement goes unnoticed by the still-disorientated elf, so I risk passing him his jacket, and he slips it back on.

"We were discussing my leave of absence. I've cleared it with the general, and I wanted to arrange it with you. I have something essential to sort out." He can't see me, but he reaches and takes my hand.

Oh. My heart does a strange little pitter-patter flip.

"The matter is urgent."

"No problem, that is fine. If you speak to him before I do, please inform the general that I'm beyond grateful for his assistance, but I will not require a replacement, and you will not need to return to my service when you return to duty. I hope that doesn't leave you in a bind, Corbin. I appreciate your help, but I no longer need an extra guard. The Winter Court can handle things from here." His entire demeanour is relaxed and friendly, which transforms him. His sharp, angular features usually speak of the cruelty he is capable of, but not now. Now he's nice.

Not taking his eyes off the elf, Corbin bows his head. "Of course."

"I hope everything is all right. You have the expression of a man with the weight of the realms on your shoulders." Madán gives him a sympathetic smile.

Corbin tenses. "It's my girl, *Pepper*." He says my name as if he's testing an unexploded spell. He watches Madán for any hint of an adverse reaction. Body tight, ready to spring into action.

The elf's smile doesn't change. There's not even a flicker of recognition. "I hope you get things sorted."

"I hope so too."

"I need to convince *Pepper* of my intentions. She thinks I'll forget about her, but from the first moment we met, I fell for her."

Fell into the subway is more like it.

"She will be the *Death* of me," Corbin continues, squeezing my hand. I know not to take his words at face value. His oversharing with the elf is purely a recognition test.

"I'm sure you will convince her. Tell you what, it seems my meeting has been cancelled. I will message Mac to bring the car around. Why don't you finish now and get a head start?"

"Thank you, Madán. That would be very helpful."

The elf takes out his phone, and with a friendly pat

on the tiger's shoulder, Corbin drops the ward and Madán leaves. "Mac, change of plans, bring the car around. I'm done for the day..." His voice fades as he walks away.

I drop my cloak, and Corbin growls low in his throat. Not letting my captured hand go, he boxes me against the wall and from sight with his bulk. "Tell me again how you turned the raving elf back into a relaxed and agreeable creature," he murmurs in my ear.

I don't know how to explain what happened so I fire back with, "What were you thinking throwing yourself in front of that spell?"

"I reacted. My fire magic can burn most spells, and it's in my nature to protect, and nothing is more important to me than protecting you."

"Oh."

"I haven't known you long—it's barely a week—but I can guess what you are thinking. You expect me to leave and forget about you, that the magic will make me forget. If you can do that"—he points to where Madán has gone —"with your magic, stop a spell, freeze the creatures around you, dig about in his mind to completely fix his outlook on life, and remove all traces of your existence..." He raises his eyebrows. "I hope you'll use your magic so I will not forget you."

He leans in close, and his nose brushes against mine. "Give me a chance to prove I'm a good man. A good mate. I can't forget about you, Pepper. I won't. I will move heaven and earth to get to know you better. We can live in your tunnels, and I'll buy you a new cone."

I laugh at his sincere expression, and my hand cups his face.

"Just give us a chance. Give me a chance. I can't forget you, Pepper. There's a nagging voice inside me that will not allow me to let go, and if I must handcuff myself to you so I don't forget one single thing about you, I will. I've made mistakes, I've hurt you, but I'm willing to earn your forgiveness. Please tell me if there is a chance."

"Okay. I've seen the threads of fate; I can make it so you don't forget me—well, unless you want to. We can try to see where this leads."

"Well, you like my face, so it would be a shame for you not to see it around, and as you said in the café, your feelings will likely go away as they go against all your common sense." He grins, and it lights up his eyes, and then his smiling mouth hovers over mine, giving me ample chance to move away. "You know, with the null band, the kidnapping, the runes, and the stalking."

My lips brush his as I smile like a loon, and my fingers stroke the rough, bristly stubble on his handsome face. "I'm going to Faerie to check on the welfare of the dead elf's slaves. Would you like to come along?"

"It's a date. I'd love to. Okay, little thief, I'm going to kiss you now."

Dear Reader,

Thank you for taking a chance on my book! Wow, I did it again. I hope you enjoyed it. If you did, and if you have time, I would be *very* grateful if you could write a review.

Every review makes a *huge* difference to an author—especially me as a brand-new shiny one—and your review might help other readers discover my book. I would appreciate it so much, and it might help me keep writing.

Thanks a million!

Oh, and there is a chance that I might even choose your review to feature in my marketing campaign. Could you imagine? So exciting!

> Love,
> Brogan x

P.S. DON'T FORGET! Sign up on my VIP email list! You will get early access to all sorts of goodies, including: signed copies, private giveaways, advance notice of future projects and free stuff! The link is on my website at **www.broganthomas.com** your email will be kept 100% private, and you can unsubscribe at any time, with zero spam.

ACKNOWLEDGEMENTS

I want to express my heartfelt appreciation and say an extra special thank you to Machell Parga for our incredible Kickstarter collaboration, which involved building a character. It was an absolute honour to work with you, Machell, and I am indebted to you for helping and inspiring me to bring Eurus to life. I hope you love him as much as I do.

Thank you for being a part of this journey.

To everyone who contributed to *Cursed Fae*, your support and encouragement have meant the world to me. Thank you.

Love Brogan x

ABOUT
THE AUTHOR

Brogan lives in Ireland with her husband and their eleven furry children: five furry minions of darkness (aka the cats), four hellhounds (the dogs), and two traditional unicorns (fat, hairy Irish cobs).

In 2019 she decided to embrace her craziness by writing about the imaginary people that live in her head. Her first love is her husband, followed by her number-one favourite furry child Bob the cob, then reading. When not reading or writing, she can be found knee-deep in horse poo and fur while blissfully ignoring all adult responsibilities.

facebook.com/BroganThomasBooks

instagram.com/broganthomasbooks

goodreads.com/Brogan_Thomas

bookbub.com/authors/brogan-thomas

youtube.com/@broganthomasbooks

ALSO BY
BROGAN THOMAS

Creatures of the Otherworld series

Cursed Wolf

Cursed Demon

Cursed Vampire

Cursed Witch

Cursed Fae

Cursed Dragon

Rebel of the Otherworld series

Rebel Unicorn

Rebel Vampire

`

www.ingramcontent.com/pod-product-compliance
Ingram Content Group UK Ltd.
Pitfield, Milton Keynes, MK11 3LW, UK
UKHW041513150825
7418UKWH00029B/152